A TASTE OF YOUR OWN MAGIC

AGENTS OF A.S.S.E.T.

KATIE SALIDAS

A Taste of Your Own Magic
AGENTS OF A.S.S.E.T. Book 2
Copyright © 2018 by Katie Salidas

PRINT ISBN 978-1-7321014-4-9

Print ISBN 978-1-7321014-3-2

Cover Art by
https://www.wegotyoucoveredbookdesign.com
Editing by Sharazade
Published by:
Rising Sign Books

For more information about my books email:
katiesalidas@gmail.com
Autographed Editions of all Katie Salidas books may be purchased at
www.KatieSalidas.com

Books by Katie Salidas

Chronicles of the Uprising
Dissension
Complication
Revolution
Transition
Retribution
Annihilation

Little Werewolf
Pretty Little Werewolf
Curious Little Werewolf
Fearless Little Werewolf

Immortalis
Carpe Noctem
Hunters & Prey
Pandora's Box
Soustone
Dark Salvation

Olde Town Pack
Moonlight
Mated
Being Alpha

Be sure to stop by KatieSalidas.com and sign up to the Paranormal
Posse Newsletter.
All new subscribers will be sent a FREE ebook.

Autographed Editions of all Katie Salidas books may be purchased
at
www.KatieSalidas.com

The world is full of magical creatures and artifacts. That's
where the A.S.S.E.T. agency comes in:
Anonymous Supernatural Security and Elimination Taskforce.

The front line, maintaining the balance of power, ensuring humans remain safely oblivious to the dangerous
magic around them.

Acknowledgments

This book was a product of tough love, and I want to thank the team of readers who really put me through my paces.

Anne Loshuk, Jacob Devlin, & J.E. Taylor!

Thank you for going over multiple drafts, giving me all of your honest feedback, and really paying attention to the small details. You're honesty and critical eye have shaped this story into something special.

Beyond the critical, thank you as well for the enthusiasm you've had for this book series. You guys jumped on this project the moment I announced it and devoured each section faster than I could produce them. The late night chats, encouragement, & feedback was just the encouragement I needed to keep this project moving, even when I felt it was all for naught.

And last but not least, thank you to my readers!
You are the reason I keep writing!

ONE

Game night was supposed to be fun. Unfortunately, no one sitting around the small table in her kitchen had gotten that memo. Rage simmered below the congenial smiles, passing like an infectious disease with the rotation of the dice. Barely nine o'clock, and all the temper tantrums and interruptions had worn Sage's nerves as thin as the cards she held in her hand.

Dice clattered against wood.

Mournful howls followed.

Another defeat.

Outside her tiny kitchen window, silence beckoned; still and calm. Not even a breeze dared disturb the sleeping trees. A picture perfect summer evening, just beyond her reach; peace that sharply contrasted with the raised voices and empty threats flying around the room where Sage sat waiting for her turn to enter the fray.

"You're stunned for two rounds, Matt," Josh called from behind his Game Master's divider. "Or wait. Hold on a moment. Do you remember the number on the red die?"

It shouldn't take a degree in calculus to figure out if a player failed an attempted attack, but this wasn't their normal dungeon crawl.

Julie had already scooped up the dice to take her turn, a blessing in disguise that prevented any further argument over what number the die had landed on.

"Forget it. I'm stunned. Let's just keep going." Matt's tone carried a raw edge that failed to mask the annoyance he'd been desperate to hide. He was more than partially to blame for subjecting them all to this hellish fantasy land. His boyfriend Josh had command of their fate as Game Master. Matt could have taken one for the team and said no when Josh demanded they all play his new game. But love makes people do stupid things.

Coward. Sage groaned and sank lower in her chair, wishing she possessed the magic to melt into a puddle under the table and slither away. If only. Magic or not, her turn to roll the dice would come soon enough. Death might be her only way out.

Julie took her turn, whooping and cheering as she successfully snuck past the Black Mage.

The dice landed like a judge's gavel in front of Sage. If she played her cards right, she might be pardoned. She took her deck in hand, spotting a winning combination, and a smile etched its way across her face. Luck, at least for the moment, had chosen to be on her side.

"It's hero time!" She laid her playable cards on the table before taking her roll. "Does the Black Mage have any last words?"

"You can't use those!" Josh pounced with the speed of a cat before the dice hit wood.

She ground her teeth audibly while Josh scrutinized her cards.

"You need Divine Aura to protect you against the Mage's attack." He shoved the cards back toward her.

"I have magic immunity in my abilities." Her temper on a hair trigger, Sage teetered on the edge of a self-destructive rage quit that might end game night forever. If he would just let her use the cards she'd chosen…. But no, another damn interruption. Another look at the rule book. At this rate they'd all die of natural causes before reaching the main boss.

"No one has immunity to magic." The moment the words left his lips, Josh ducked behind the flimsy shield of his Game Masters folder. It wouldn't protect him from the angry mob staring at the top of his head. Sage might have been his latest target, but she was far from his first. All the others around the table were shooting murderous glares his way. Nearly every turn had necessitated the same pause to check rules. The Game Master controlled the fates of everyone around the table, but clearly Josh hadn't bothered to study before subjecting them to this indie dungeon crawler; a game that hadn't passed the crowdfunding phase of production.

"Magical immunity is an innate ability," Sage argued, slamming her remaining cards down on the table. "I don't need to use Divine Aura if my character already has a natural defense."

"Who has magical immunity?" Matt cut in sharply, targeting Sage with his anger. "Where does it say that on your character sheet?" His words were more accusing than inquisitive, and as soon as Sage realized what he'd implied, embarrassment replaced the rage she'd been ready to unleash. Confusing fantasy and reality, she'd nearly let her secret slip.

Among all those she counted on as friends, Matt alone knew that Sage was part of a magical lineage as old as time itself. The Terras had once been members of the three magical races, but when the Great Mother chose them to be her soldiers – and guardians of magical law – their active powers had been exchanged for innate magical immunity.

Short of the gods themselves coming to strike her down, Sage felt certain she would never need to fear a Shadowrunner's deadly mist or an arc of conjured lightning from an Ethereal Pixie. Fae, Otherkin, Fair Folk—whatever name they chose to go by–none could harm her with their power. But, just like in the rule-books of the games she played, there must always be balance.

Sage's gift negated any magic she might hope to conjure for either good or evil. Characters can never be too powerful.

Had she been raised to know all of this, keeping the secret wouldn't be an issue. But Sage had only recently learned about her special lineage: an inheritance passed down with the death of her mother.

All at once, magic bled like an open wound into every aspect of her life, and with the veil lifted, she saw the truth of what lurked in the shadows and peeked behind the masks magical creatures wore. A crash course that left Sage's head spinning as she questioned everything she'd ever known.

She opened her mouth to reply to Matt, but no words came. What explanation could she give him or the others now glaring at her? Interruption number…whatever. Her fault.

Josh lifted his head behind the shield of his GM folder, impatience etching deep lines across his forehead.

Awkward silence hung like a fog in the air. Her mind had gone blank.

"I… uh…" Sage had no explanation for her near slip as she gave up the pretense of searching her character sheet. "I guess I didn't add that. Whoops."

Julie pushed back from the table. Her chair scraped across the floor like nails on a chalkboard drawing attention away from Sage. "Since we're on a break – again – anyone want a beer?" Julie helped herself to one from the fridge.

Matt's annoyance deflated into exhaustion. Sage could see it in his eyes – the desperate pleading for the game to either start going somewhere or just end completely. "Cheating isn't going to get us through this raid." He held a red die in his hand. "Divine Aura. Throw down the spell and roll for it."

Sage pulled the card from her stack and laid it on the hand-drawn map next to her character token. She rolled the twenty-sided die and closed her eyes, praying for a ten or better.

"Two," Josh called from behind his GM folder.

"Dammit!" Sage yelled.

"Your shield spell failed." Josh pulled up a page as he rolled his own blue die. "And I rolled eleven, so it looks like… you're dead."

"Had to go up against the Black Mage, didn't you?" Julie scoffed, as she returned to her seat, beer in hand.

"You know me… charge in, guns blazing." Sage secretly prayed her mistake had taken her out of the game completely. "How long do I have to wait for a resurrection spell?"

Josh shuffled pages behind his shield. All she could see of him was the top of his head and those long auburn locks Matt adored. "First the team has to defend or safely flee from the Black Mage you just pissed off. And if they do, it will be another turn while they wait for mana regeneration. You're out for now."

Sage threw her cards into the pile in the center of the table. She'd have to draw new cards if her character was ever revived. "Sorry," she half-heartedly replied.

"Relax, guys." Matt tapped the red dice on the table calling the group to order. "Head in the game – let's see if we can't get through this one."

Sage walked away from the table and grabbed a beer out of habit. Since inheriting her mother's neutrality, she'd found alcohol no longer worked its magic to dull her senses, but it did provide a socially acceptable reason for her to leave the table.

The game ended before she finished her drink.

"Great time, guys." Julie looked more relieved than annoyed as she grabbed a few bottles on her way to the door. "Keep the beer flowing, and I'll see you next week."

Josh kissed Matt goodbye but didn't bother to acknowledge Sage as he packed up to leave. He could be angry with her if he wanted. The way she saw it, she'd done them all a favor, sacrificing herself for the greater good of all their sanity. They would never play that game again.

Sage picked up empty bottles and cleared out the bowls of popcorn and pretzels that had been strewn about the living room.

"Where was your head tonight?" Matt asked, as he began loading the dishwasher.

"Knew this was coming," Sage groaned.

"Damn straight. We could have beat that Mage had you not gone all Leroy Jenkins with your magical immunity. All we had to do was sneak past him."

"Sorry!" She closed the lid on the trash. "It's just a game."

"And your magical immunity?" Matt replied, with a passive aggressive slam of his mug down at the sink.

"I don't have the patience for a fight." Sage sighed. "Are we still talking about the game?"

Matt turned on her, his anger abating with each second as he stared. "You ready to tell me the big secret you've been holding onto?"

"I'm not sure what you mean." She shrugged.

"The ASSET agency." Matt threw the words at her like an insult.

"I don't want to go there." Sage's hand found the tree-shaped pendant around her neck as if drawn to it by the mere mention of the agency.

"I know it's eating you up inside." Matt had the dad voice down pat, making Sage want to fight back with teenage angst. "You can't bottle this up. Tell me what's going on."

"Being what I am…" Sage struggled to get the words out. A knot formed in her throat. It was bad enough she'd told Matt about being a Terra. He'd taken that as well as could be expected. But she'd kept the job offer quiet knowing that it tip the scales of what could handle.

Sage had only barely digested the massive helpings of magical mumbo-jumbo she'd been force-fed over the last week. One last little morsel stuck in her throat, refusing to go down. This was her life now. If she accepted Ava's offer to become an agent with ASSET as her lineage dictated, that meant the drama she'd just endured with the death of her mother would become business as usual. If she didn't take the job, magic would still be there, and she'd be left as a silent witness to all the devastating effects of its misuse without any resources to stop it. "My people…"

"You're already at the 'my people' stage? This must be serious." He set down the soap and wiped his hands on a dishrag. "Spill it."

"Stop it. Don't make fun. I'm trying to find the best way to say this."

"Out with it. When have we ever kept secrets?"

"My condition… isn't just about seeing beyond the veil of magic. It comes with a job offer. How's that?"

A muscle at the corner of Matt's lip twitched. "Didn't you tell Mark you could never work for the company that killed your mom?"

"That was then. Before I understood the reasons. And Mark doesn't run the Vegas office."

"What exactly does that mean?"

"My people…" Sage glared at Matt, daring him to taunt her again. When he didn't, she continued. "We're made for this type of work because we aren't affected by normal magic."

"Sounds like you've decided to accept the job." Matt's shoulders slumped.

"I should. I know it. But…I don't…" She groaned. "This is a really serious decision."

"You need someone to push you or you'll sit here and waffle about it forever. Normally I would, but…" Matt sighed. "They killed your mom."

Sage clutched at her necklace. "Not exactly. I mean. Working there. Yes, it's dangerous."

"You said it, not me," Matt agreed.

"But, it is what I was made for. And I should honor my mother's sacrifice."

"By taking on dangerous missions that could get you killed?"

"I could get hit by a bus walking to the pub."

"Only you'd probably walk away from that." He pointed a finger at her like an accusation. "I, however, would be dead."

"Exactly. I'm kind of bullet-proof." She looked up, meeting his eyes, desperate for encouragement. Deep down she knew what she had to do, but without the nod from her best friend, she just couldn't make the leap.

Matt's nostrils flared with each breath. His eyes revealed the struggle behind his silence. Then, finally, he replied, "You're built for this life. With all that innate magical immunity…"

He really knew how to rub salt into the wound. Sage hung her head in shame. "Sorry. I forgot."

"You nearly let that one slip." Matt surprised her with laughter. "Remind me never to let you be my secret keeper. Loose lips sink ships."

"I got nothing." Sage tried to fight the smile blooming across her face. Damn him, and his super cute boyfriend, too. All the good ones were gay or taken. In this case, both. Double whammy!

"Look. I want you to be safe. And I want you to do what you were meant to do. I'm not going to say I like you working there. But…" He clenched his fists at his side and released a heavy sigh. "I think if you continue training with Devon, you'll be able to handle whatever ASSET throws at you."

She hadn't been back to Devon's gym since the day she'd been forced to kill Rina, nor had she planned to. But Matt had a point. She did need more training, and Devon was the best of the best in the city.

"They don't by any chance offer office position, do they?" Matt waggled an eyebrow.

She cringed, hissing as if the words had burned her. Working for ASSET Director Ava Williams as an assistant was ten times more deadly than fieldwork. "I'd take on a whole coven of vampires again if it meant avoiding clerical work under Queen High Bitch herself."

"Maybe that's what it will take to get you to make a decision. Do or do not. There is no—"

"Okay!" Sage stopped him before he went full Yoda. "I've made up my mind. I'm going down there tomorrow."

"Be warned – if you join, you will have to tell Josh." He'd helped her to make this decision, but by the sound of his reply, wasn't too happy with her for it. "I can't keep secrets from my man, especially when you come home looking like you've been beaten within an inch of your life."

"Jeez. I haven't committed to it yet. I just said I'd go down there to talk. This deal is getting worse with each passing moment"

"Pray I do not alter it further." Matt's Vader was much stronger than his Yoda.

Sage wanted to laugh at his impression, but a sigh came out instead. "That's what I'm afraid of. For now, just tell him I'm working for a private investigations firm that takes on special cases."

"Only if you promise me one thing." Matt's tone turned serious again.

"Anything."

He arched an eyebrow sharply at her. "I'll hold you to it."

"I guess I'd better know what else I'm signing up for."

"Don't let your work follow you home. This apartment needs to be our place of normalcy."

Sage crossed herself and held up a Girl Scout salute. "I solemnly swear…"

"I mean it."

"I'll do my best," she answered truthfully. "I don't want work invading our happy home either."

TWO

Every time she thought of signing on the dotted line and becoming a full-fledged agent at ASSET, Sage's mind replayed that horrible moment she'd come face to face with the dismembered head of her mother.

Matt couldn't truly understand the dangers the came with working for ASSET, or he would never have helped her make the decision. With or without innate magical neutrality, being an agent meant facing all the dangers of the magical world, including losing one's self.

What had happened to her mom could just as easily be her fate. If ever an agent went dark, it was the duty of the others at ASSET to end their suffering. Grey had done his job without hesitation. Miranda couldn't have been saved, no matter how much Sage wished for it. And though the memory still haunted her, she no longer blamed Grey. Dealing the deadly blow that ended her mother's suffering had been mercy. But that sobering memory would forever remind her of the truth: working for the Anonymous Supernatural Security and Elimination Task-force was dangerous business.

Immortality…is a lie. But as the years pass by with little effect, those who buy into that lie lose their fear of death. It becomes a joke. And the punchline is: only the gods live forever. Everyone else has an expiration date. Some reach theirs faster. And others, like her mom, are helped along by the careers they choose.

Sage took in the night air as she walked around her apartment complex. For all the reasons she'd come up with to avoid ASSET, none compared to the sense of duty she felt.

She reached for her necklace, a silver pendant shaped like the Tree of Life, the symbol of her people. She bore the same mark on her left wrist, originally thinking it a birthmark; little had she known it was a sign of her destiny. To be a Terra was an honor. And like the branches of the great tree, their family lines stretched out in hundreds of directions, covering the world, protecting it from dangerous magic.

Sage's inheritance, the necklace her mother had given her, contained a single seed from the fruit of the Tree of Life – one of the most powerful magical artifacts in the known world.

It was only because of her innate magical neutrality that she could even wear the damn thing. Anyone with magical blood would be sucked dry of their essence if they touched it. A weapon of magical destruction in all but a true Terra's hands. War had nearly broken out when the seed had gone missing. Protecting it had cost her mother's life and now that Sage had become the guardian and secret keeper, no one could know that she had it, not even Matt.

A burden she felt far too young to have to bear, and at the same time, Sage knew she had to rise to the challenge. She was a Terra.

Time to stop being a baby. This is your destiny. Embrace it! Her mother's voice echoed in the back of her mind. Equal parts accusing and caring, that tone never failed to break Sage's stubbornness. Moms could throw guilt better than an Olympian with a javelin. Whether it had truly been Miranda speaking to her from beyond the grave or just the manifestation of her subconscious knowing how to push her buttons, the decision was no longer up for debate.

"You look like you could use a drink," an unfamiliar male voice called out to her.

As many times as she'd been snuck up on by vampires, she should have been used to surprises, but deep as she had been in thought, Sage had failed to pay attention to the shadows. She frantically turned around to locate the voice's owner.

A dark figure lurked under the stairs leading to a second-story apartment. His face half concealed all she could make out were a pair of silver eyes, glowing like a beacon. Enchanting, as if possessing their own light, his eyes instantly gave away his magical nature.

"I've never seen such a pout before. Someone run over your favorite pet or something?" The man flicked at the cigarette in his hand, emitting a miniature explosion of hot ash that faded before it hit the ground.

"Long night. I'm fine." Her oh-shit-there's-a-dude-lurking-in-the-shadows-in-the-middle-of-the-night senses were tingling. She casually reached her hand down to the knife she kept folded in her pocket. Just in case.

"Didn't mean to surprise you." He stepped out from under the stairs into the porchlight of the lower level apartment. Holding his hands out in plain sight, as if to show her he wasn't a creeper, he made all the right motions to appear non-threatening. "We're having a party upstairs. Kind of a housewarming. Haven't met too many of my new neighbors."

His gesture wasn't lost on her, though she kept her hand firmly grasping the knife. Under the path lighting, he appeared to be about her age. If she had to guess, maybe early twenties, but the shaggy beginnings of a beard masked his features enough to make accuracy impossible.

"How do you know I'm a neighbor?" Sage asked, with a little more attitude than she'd intended. *Definitely not a local. New to the apartment complex.* She held on to the Cliff's Notes of the conversation so far to recall later.

"Lucky guess. I mean, most people here have to have a key after hours, right?"

His smile didn't look forced. No twitching muscles or clenched jaw.

"Right. Smart." Sage hated small talk; her mind was too busy with the mystery of his magical type to move the conversation forward. She inspected him slowly, starting at his face. His teeth were normal, though not well taken care of. After her first failed encounter with vampire Zack, Sage remembered to always check for the teeth. This guy checked out – definitely not a vampire. But the silver eyes clearly placed him in the magical creature category. "You can never be too sure about people you meet after hours."

"Sorry. That was a bit forward of me. Let's start over." He flicked away his cigarette and extended his hand as he walked over. "My name's Luke."

She couldn't detect a specific accent to give him away, but his attitude had the casual easygoing feel of someone from the south, though the chin patch of a beard attached to a thin moustache gave him a distinctly Hollywood trendiness that suggested otherwise.

No ring on the finger. Not married, but he did say 'we're having a party." Probably not single. So there could be more people like him in the apartment.

Dark as night, his hair fell around his head in long layers, creating a stunning contrast with his silver eyes. She'd seen that color before. It took her brain a few moments to run through all the faces she'd seen recently. Then it struck her – Devon had a similar color.

But this Luke… his eyes reflected the light like a demonic cat. Definitely magical.

Ogre? No. Devon's muscles had muscles, and this guy looked more like a skinny hipster in comparison. Troll? No. She'd see through their glamour. Though both of his ears were pierced and enlarged with hoops big enough to see through, they were still normal ears. And even in the light, she could see his skin wasn't green.

Sage realized she'd been standing silent too long to avoid awkwardness. "Sage." She finally managed to coordinate her voice and thoughts.

Being a teensy bit more knowledgeable of the magical world would have come in handy at that point. Should she take the hand or not? So far, most of the creatures she'd met had been okay, but there were few that she wouldn't want to touch any part of her, magical immunity or not. But short of being rude, Sage decided to reach out and meet Luke's outstretched hand.

His eyes instantly sank below her neckline. Knowing where they were headed, Sage held her breath for the reaction. Her mark was proudly on display, like a neon sign for those with magic. Everyone knew what a Terra was.

And as expected, the recognition was there in his eyes as his hand met hers. She let her eyes drop as well, taking a peek at his arms for marking that might clue her into his type.

He had an impressive sleeve of tribal flame tattoos reaching from his wrist all the way to his elbow. But where her birthmark was static, his tattoos were alive. In constant motion, they burned silently, the flames gently licking at his elbows. She fought the urge to pull back in shock and reveal her ignorance. Marks like his had to be as notorious in the magical community as her own.

He gave her hand a quick business-like pump and let go. "Nice to know ASSET is in the neighborhood. Always makes you feel safe."

She took the opportunity to play off his admitted newness to the area. "When did you move in?"

"Today, actually." Luke had the type of smile that appeared without effort, like resting bitch face in reverse. She wondered if he had to work at pouting or looking angry.

Shadowrunner? Couldn't be. He'd remained fully formed the entire time she'd watched him. She'd figure him out eventually, without asking.

His tattoos demanded admiration. Sage could hardly stop herself from looking at them. *Gorgeous!* She searched for something else to say to move the conversation along and came up short. "Just popped right in, I imagine."

"More like commanded to move here by my ma…er…mate." He chuckled nervously. "But I couldn't have wished for an easier move." His words sounded as if they carried a double meaning, but the joke flew right over her head.

She was right about one thing: he wasn't single. Damn. He was cute, whatever he was. Sage grinned stupidly, not sure if she should laugh at his attempted joke. Silence never failed to create awkwardness.

Luke waggled his fingers like a magician. "You know, because I'm a djinn."

"Right." She nodded casually, hoping to hide her ignorance. He might as well as called himself a Martian. *Djinn* conjured up about the same image in her mind. She'd make damn sure to look him up when she made it back to her apartment, though. "Well, welcome to the neighborhood."

"You sure you don't want to come in and have a beer or something? We've got pizza too."

The offer sounded sincere enough, no denying that, but embarrassment trumped spending more time with the guy who caused it.

"Raincheck?" Sage masked her unease with a neutral tone. "Got an early day at the office tomorrow."

"Right. You guys are always busy." His expression faded. "Keep protecting and serving."

"You know it." Sage snapped her fingers and pointed at Luke as if firing a pair of six-shooters at him. Instantly, she regretted the move. *Embarrassment, party of one, your table is ready.* All she needed were the *pew pew* sounds to really drive home her social awkwardness. Might as well put a bag over her face to complete the look.

Luke laughed, but she couldn't tell if it had been directed at her or with her. Gods, she needed to get home and quick before she fell too far down the rabbit hole of awkwardness.

"See you around."

"Yes you will," Luke replied.

His words caught her off guard, but by the time she'd realized how strange they were, she'd already made it to her door. Had he been flirting with her, or was he up to something? Luke had the advantage. He'd pegged her as a Terra the moment he met her, but she had no clue what a djinn was or what they were capable of. What could it mean to have one in such close proximity?

THREE

After a night of uneasy and way too little sleep, Sage dragged herself into the blazing sunlight.

Decision day.

She knew what lay ahead but that didn't make the steps any easier as she headed toward the parking lot to meet her ride.

"Don't you have a car?" Grey tossed a helmet at her.

Way too early in the morning with far too little caffeine to jump start her brain, Sage lacked the wit to reply to Grey's brusque greeting. He'd been kind enough to drive her into the office, so it was probably best her tongue remained tied.

ASSET's headquarters were miles away in the heart of downtown. Sage had no choice but to test her semi-immortality by riding on Grey's motorcycle; either that or spend hours riding the bus and making transfers to get there.

"Cars cost money," she mumbled, as she fought to get the helmet on over her head. So much for doing her hair this morning. All that effort to present herself had gone to waste.

"Obviously." Grey seemed to be amused by her uncoordinated effort. She didn't need to see his face, hidden behind the visor of his helmet, to know he was beaming.

"So…" She let the words hang in the air. He had a snarky reply coming. She'd die of shock if he didn't. That was their language, her and Grey. When they weren't sniping at each other, they had nothing to say.

"You're going to need more than a bus pass to work at ASSET."

"Then they're going to have to pay me well. Or provide a company car." She hadn't really sussed out the minutiae. With her old job, she'd just ridden a single bus in and out. ASSET would have her going on excursions all over the city.

"Listen to you already demanding things. It's as if you feel you're a shoe-in for the job."

There it was – the snark she'd been waiting for. Until she'd had a cup – possibly two – of coffee she wouldn't have the processing power needed to take him on. But when she did, words would clash, and they could duel properly. *May the best tongue win!*

Sage mounted the bike. She already had the job; all she had to do was face Ava and accept it, though the thought made her seriously consider going back to the accounting firm. Her old boss might have been a troll – warts and all – but Ava was a ball buster in a category all her own. If only she could return to Phoenix and work for Mark. He'd be such an awesome boss. But everything in Phoenix would remind her of her mother. Time would heal those wounds, no doubt, and maybe someday she'd return. But not now.

Grey sped out of the parking lot, and Sage instantly regretted asking him for a ride. She'd never get used to the feeling of being so close to death with nothing to protect her but a helmet. He weaved in and out of traffic, narrowly missing rearview mirrors as he squeezed between cars.

The tighter she held on, the faster he seemed to go, as if her fear fueled him. She could just imagine the shit-eating grin hidden behind his helmet as he sped narrowly between a line of cars.

Sage reminded herself over and over, whispering it like a mantra, *I'm immortal, I'm immortal, I'm not going to die.*

The rational part of her mind did little to override pure terror. She clung to Grey tightly, not caring if she pierced his leather jacket or his skin with her nails. When he finally pulled into the ASSET parking garage and whipped the bike into a small parking spot, she leaped off ready to kiss the ground.

"You won't die on my bike, but don't count on your immortality to keep you safe from what's beyond those doors." More taunting. More snickering laughter. It was as if his primary goal in life was to get her to smack him. And as he exchanged his helmet for that stupid fedora he always wore, she nearly did. The only thing stopping her was the knowledge that if she did, he would win this round. He'd walk away the champion button pusher, able to get under her skin. No. She had to remain calm. Fight the urge to beat him physically. The mental game was where the true champions battled.

"Let's get this over with." Sage took the lead, keeping her head held high as she headed to the elevators. Outwardly she hoped to give off the impression of casual courage – an empty façade, but armor enough against anyone who might question her intentions. Fake it till it's real. She'd made her mind up. This was happening. But that didn't negate the apprehension of actually committing herself for what might be eternity.

Slow, controlled breaths helped as she rode the elevator to the top floor. When the doors parted, another wave of panic nearly drowned her. Rina had been a fixture during her short time with ASSET. She'd manned the reception desk and worked as assistant to Ava.

She'd died in Sage's arms. Of all the things she'd worried about, Sage had given little thought to how she'd feel seeing that reception desk again. But there it was, the first thing in view from the elevator. In Rina's place sat a new girl. Just as young, just as fresh-faced as Rina had been, though missing the awesome blue hair.

"You sure you're ready for this?" Grey pushed her forward and took the lead toward Ava's door before Sage had the chance to say hello to the new assistant. She did at least give a cursory glance to make sure the mark of the Terra was there on her left wrist – a real mark this time, not a tattoo. She wasn't about to let herself be fooled again.

Grey disappeared into Ava's office.

Sage gave herself one last minute to center herself— and stop her knees from trembling— before she followed across the threshold.

Clacking away at her keyboard, the head of Las Vegas ASSET office, Ava Williams had her nose buried so deeply into the screen it looked as if she were trying to push it through a portal.

"Finally made a decision?" Ava asked. Her Grand High Poobahness didn't bother to look up from her screen.

After their last meeting, and knowing how important she was to the organization, Sage expected at least some form of acknowledgement. A smile. A secret nod. Code word, perhaps? Something to show they had a connection that went beyond the typical subordinate and boss relationship. But then Ava never treated anyone with respect. Showing Sage any form of deference might draw unwanted attention.

Sage nodded and replied, "Yeah," with a strained sigh.

"Good. I'll expect you sworn in and suited up before the end of the day. See Devon for your training schedule, and since you worked so well with Mr. Maddox on your last mission, I'm making him your partner."

"Wait. What?" Grey choked on his words.

"Mr. Maddox, when I want your input, I'll ask for it. You were all too eager, not a week ago, to partner with Ms. Cynwrig when you plotted your little trap. I think it only fitting my two biggest troublemakers are easy to track down."

Sage snickered to herself. Working with Grey wasn't ideal, but seeing how much it bothered him made it worth it. Despite his annoying personality, he was as knowledgeable as they came and more than capable with a machete. They might not like each other, but she had no doubt he'd have her back when needed.

To his credit, though he ground his teeth loud enough for the whole office to hear, Grey kept his mouth shut.

Ava hadn't earned the reputation of Queen High Bitch for nothing.

"Before I sign on the dotted line," Sage said, staring down at the back of Ava's monitor, pausing just long enough to see if the director would look her in the face, "I want assurances that I will not be held prisoner here."

Ava slammed the laptop closed, and Sage instantly regretted her choice of words. The icy glare of her new boss sent Sage a few paces back, ready to make a hasty retreat. "Let's get one thing straight, Miss Cynwrig. My job here is not to replace your mommy. And don't you ever presume to talk to me as if I'm one of your girlfriends, either. I don't care about your feelings. What you *want* is inconsequential. My job is to ensure that the well-oiled machine of ASSET runs smoothly, with minimal deaths among my agents."

Sage gulped audibly, earning a look of pure satisfaction from Ava as she continued the lecture.

"When we first brought you in, assigning you barracks here was to facilitate you protection. You're as green as they come. You have no training, which makes you a liability. Of all the new agents here, you should have more respect for the sacrifices of our people and the work that we do." The words struck harder than any blow she might have dealt by hand; salt in the wound in the wake of Miranda's death.

One day Sage would learn to keep her big mouth shut. She wouldn't soon forget the speed at which Ava had put her in place.

"However, if you feel that our protection is an infringement on your freedom and rights, I pray death does not find you or that human roommate of yours. If it does, so be it!"

All the snark had left Sage. Even if she could think of a reply, she knew better than to tempt fate. Ava's office was a museum of ancient weaponry, easy to grab and deadly in practiced hands. Her mouth hung open stupidly as she watched Ava lift the laptop screen again and resume working.

"When you've finished with Devon, I'll administer your oath personally."

Sage gulped again, imagining a knighting, only with Ava holding the large axe that sat in the corner of her office, threatening to remove her head if she ever talked back like that again.

Grey tugged at her arm. "Time to go, newbie."

"One last thing," Ava called to them. "I have the perfect assignment for our headstrong little recruit here. You two will be starting immediately."

FOUR

Devon, at least, looked pleased to see her. The moment those silvery eyes caught sight of Sage, his whole face lit up.

"How are you holding up, kid?" He welcomed her into the training room with a hug that nearly crushed her ribs.

This was the kind of greeting she'd hoped for – warm and inviting, another reason to solidify her enlistment to the agency. The five minutes she'd spent with Ava had her seriously questioning the sanity of her decision. Devon more than made up for it with his joy in seeing her.

When she managed to escape his python-like grip and catch her breath, Sage tried to find the words, but came up short. Polite society always expected to hear *fine* or *good* in response to questions like that. A no-bullshit kind of guy like Devon appreciated a real answer.

She opened her mouth to tell him she was coping, but the words felt hollow.

He spared her having to answer with an excited, "Hey. I got something for you."

Grey cleared his throat. He'd stopped at the training room door, rather than joining the little reunion. "I'm going to check in on the assignment board." He held his arms stiffly, crossing them as he set his jaw; his body language practically shouted his displeasure. Being assigned her partner clearly hadn't sat well with him. Not that it mattered. Going against Ava's wishes came at one's own peril.

"Don't let this one out of your sight." Grey turned to head back down the hall. "I'll be back."

"Aww, do you have to?" Sage teased. Not exactly her ideal partnership, but better the enemy you know than some stranger. The prospect of their ongoing trolling match kept a smile on her face.

"We're partners now, newbie. You're going to be seeing so much of me." Grey surprised her, poking his head back into the room for one final taunt. "Hey, maybe I can crash on your couch too. We could be roommates."

For all his grumbling moments earlier, he had certainly laid it on thick with that last comment. Maybe he wasn't as angry as she had thought. Or he'd realized it gave him more time to play. And just like that, the game had moved to the next level. Grey's laughter echoed down the hallway as if to say, "Your move!"

Oh, yes. Game on!

Devon's expression begged Sage to give an explanation.

"He caught me laughing when Ava assigned him as my partner. Now he wants to punish me," she answered.

"You two make such a cute couple."

"Eww. Don't. Just. No!" The stupid hat Grey always wore was enough to disqualify him as a potential date. Looking like a tool was just surface-level douchebaggery, not even taking into account his abrasive personality. How could Devon even tease her about something so…. She cringed at the thought.

"Match made in heaven." Devon chuckled on his way to the bank of lockers mounted to the wall. He opened one and pulled out a white box. "You'll invite me to the wedding, right?"

Clearly having a thick skin was a prerequisite for the job. Even Devon couldn't resist a chance to push her buttons. A smile tugged at the corner of her lips. This was just the kind of thing families did with each other. Another player in the trolling game; though Devon was far more intimidating than Grey. He wouldn't hesitate to drop her on her ass…for the sake of training. *Challenge accepted.*

"Why am I agreeing to work with you jerks again?"

Devon crossed the room and presented the box to her. "Because you know this is where you belong."

Suspicious of what lay inside, she hesitated before opening it. For all she knew, the box could have some kind of spring-loaded weapon. *Hopefully not.* Holding her breath, she lifted the lid. Eyes half shut, she squinted to see inside the box.

"You okay?" Devon looked at her like she'd lost her mind.

"Just making sure you didn't booby-trap it."

That drew a genuine belly laugh. "Just open it."

"You can't fault me for being cautious." She shrugged, hoping to play off her hesitation as just messing around. Inside the box lay a folded length of crushed purple velvet.

"You've earned your place among us." Devon beamed with pride. "Go on. Take it!"

"What is it?" Confusion stunned Sage, leaving her unable to move before figuring out the mystery. Devon had always told her not to let her guard down. It could still be a trap. The material was too thin to be a blanket; a table cloth, maybe? But that would be an odd gift.

Devon's silvery eyes glittered mischievously. He was enjoying this way too much. "I said I'd make you a cape when you earned it, Captain Trainwreck."

He remembered! Excitement bloomed across her face so fast it scorched her cheeks.

When she'd demanded a cape, it had been a joke. The fact he'd followed through gave her all kinds of feelings she wasn't ready to process. It meant she had truly proven herself in his eyes. If he believed in her, then she was truly ready to be an agent.

Sage whipped the cloak from the box and twirled around with it before clasping it around her neck. Such a thoughtful and heart-felt gift. The words caught in her throat as she attempted to say, "Thank you!"

"You earned it back there with Rina. Quick thinking with that knife saved your life. I'm proud to see you put training into practice."

The mention of Rina hit Sage like a bucket of cold water. Death wasn't a thing she could celebrate. Rina had been a misguided girl who'd let herself believe revenge was a noble cause. She'd needed therapy, not a knife between her ribs.

"Hey now." Devon took hold of her chin, forcing her to look into his eyes. "Don't go getting all sad-faced. You did what you had to do. And she won't be the last, I'm afraid." His tone darkened. Devon's honesty always came with a blunt edge. Sage appreciated that. But it didn't soften the blow.

"It's part of the job, I know." Sage let her eyes fall to the deep purple of the cape, admiring the way it caught the light as she moved. It would be the perfect addition to her game night wardrobe, too. Matt and Josh would love it.

"Defending yourself in life or death circumstances? Definitely. But only when necessary. I promise, Sage, there is more to being an agent. You'll see. But my job is to prepare you for those dangerous times, so you don't end up like Rina." His hand left her chin, coming to rest on her shoulder. He gave her a reassuring squeeze. "Just don't wear the cape when you're on duty. Velvet is a pain to clean."

At least he gave it to her straight, the good and the bad.

"Now, speaking of duty… You've still got a lot of learning to do. You fought off a girl your size no problem, but most creatures you'll come up against are going to be more like that vampire who took a bite out of you."

Her wounds had healed, but the skin still felt tight around the scars. Her hand lifted on its own, finding what remained of the teeth marks in her neck. She had been no match for that vampire, and their kind were only the tip of the magical iceberg. Which reminded Sage – her new neighbor. He'd called himself something magical. "Hey, speaking of that, let me ask you a question."

"Shoot." Devon angled his head inquisitively.

"What's a djinn?"

For the first time since she'd known Devon, fear, or something very close to it, reflected back in his steely eyes. "Not someone you should be dealing with just yet. Let's stick to out-of-shape desk jockeys for now. You can wait a bit before hitting the bigtime baddies." He winked and threw a fake punch toward her jaw.

She dodged easily, and fell into a fighting stance. "I'm a superhero now, remember?" Even when she didn't have training scheduled, there was always a chance he'd try to teach her a lesson. "I can handle anything!"

"Oh, that's right. How silly of me." Devon's eyes narrowed. "Faster than a failed autocorrect text." He ducked down to sweep her legs.

She moved out of the way just in time. It took all she had not to laugh at his playful taunts. Devon could be pretty witty off the cuff when he wanted, but she wasn't about to let him throw her off guard. Keeping her eyes on target, she readied herself for his next move.

"More powerful than an internet meme!" His fist went flying again.

Sage deflected. The impact sent her stumbling backwards. Devon launched into another attack before she could regain her balance.

He sliced high; she blocked.

He kicked round; she dodged.

They danced the dance of war, neither of them pulling their punches.

"Able to kick massive booty with a single shot of espresso." Sage executed a beautiful takedown that sent her confidence soaring.

"Nicely done, Captain Trainwreck. But don't get cocky, kid. Your skills are improving," he chuckled, "And before you get out there and face the big baddies on the streets, you have to do it right. Swear in and sign on the dotted line. Have the backing of the Agency with you."

"Why does that sound like a trap?" She reached her hand out to help Devon up.

He glared at her, all but calling her a drama queen with his eyes. "No one is twisting your arm."

"But you're happy to break it," she replied.

He shrugged. "You'll heal."

"This place better have good health insurance. Sounds like I'll need it."

"You're a Terra." Devon crossed his arms as if that were all that needed to be said.

The scared skin at her neck said otherwise, but there was no use arguing that point. "So what's my new training schedule looking like?"

"I'm going to put you on a daily regimen. When you're not training with me, I want you in the weight room, working those muscle groups. You need to get some strength into those string beans you call arms."

"Whatever. As long as I get to wear the cape!" Sage took the edges in her hand and flapped like a bird before wrapping herself up like a bat.

Grey cleared his throat. She'd been so caught up with Devon she hadn't even heard his footsteps in the hallway. How long had he been standing there listening to their conversation?

"What the hell is this idiocy?" Grey sounded like he was on the verge of laughter.

Sage twirled, fanning out the edges of the cape as she rounded to face him. "A superhero has to accessorize!"

Caught somewhere between a scowl and a laugh, Grey's face hadn't committed to either look, leaving him with an expression that ruined any serious words he might have spoken next. Before he could summon his voice, Sage lifted her head and strolled proudly across the room.

"If I'm going to pledge my allegiance to the order, they need to know who they're getting as an agent." She sauntered into the hallway.

"And so begins the glorious career of Captain Trainwreck." Devon's laughter echoed behind her.

"Great songs will be sung of my adventures. Mark my words." Tears burned in her eyes as she fought to keep a straight face. With her head held high, she marched onward to victory.

"Sage…" Grey called out.

Mr. Wet Blanket had to have the last word. She turned on her heel and shot him a look that could rival even Ava's icy glare. "Don't spoil this for me. I'm having a moment!"

"Okay." He doubled over, hyperventilating as he gasped for air between snorts of laughter. "But can you have your moment over there?" He pointed as he fought to catch his breath. "Ava's office is the other way."

Dammit!

Grey was right, of course, but no way in hell was she giving up the high ground. She wheeled around and cat-walked down the opposite side of the hallway, channeling her inner diva, adding a wicked flap of her cape as she passed Grey. Overconfidence was better than letting him feel he'd taken the wind from her sails.

He clapped slowly, sarcasm echoing in each elongated slap of his palms. "Are you planning to take any of this seriously?"

She wasn't about to answer that baited question. Joking aside, this was the hardest thing she'd ever thought to do – signing over her partially immortal life in service to ASSET.

FIVE

Sage stepped into Ava's office, cape still hanging like a security blanket around her neck, determined to say her vows. The moment had come, and for all her joking and silly antics, she couldn't deny the weight of the decision that lay before her. She took a good hard look at her wrist. The mark of her people: Terras.

Where once she'd found the lines in their haphazard pattern hideous, they now clearly resembled the Tree of Life. Surrounding its branches, freckles in the shape of leaves created a canopy. The base of the trunk turned into roots that twisted and wound down and around, creating a semi-circle below.

The sound of Ava clearing her throat suggested Sage had stood studying her mark for far too long. She looked up sheepishly. Her appearance was already impish enough, to earn a place on Ava's shit list. She might be new, but no one was special when it came to the Grand High Poobah of the Las Vegas office.

"I need a few words with Ms. Cynwrig before we begin." Ava dismissed Grey at the door, waving him off as if he were an annoying fly.

Being alone with Ava in a room filled with weapons felt like a really bad idea.

Eyes of turquoise scrutinized Sage from the other side of the desk. Hard and cold as the stone they were named after, Ava's eyes reflected no emotion as she stared across the mahogany expanse. Sage tugged uncomfortably at her neck, loosening the cape. Admittedly it was over the top, and in the company of Devon or Grey, it had been a statement of her true nature. Standing in front of Ava, however, Sage felt more than a bit childish, but had resolved to wear it while she awaited her boss's next order.

Oppressive silence made the moment all that much more unnerving. Sage dropped her gaze submissively and as she looked down, found a subtle but very important change in the room. The normal fixture of Ava's laptop, which usually sat dead center of the large desk, had been replaced with a book as thick as a cinderblock.

"Do you know what this is?" Ava asked.

Runes were etched into the ancient-looking leather binding, symbols Sage had seen only once before, on her boss's wrist. She'd never dared ask Ava how old she was, but if the book were any indication of her time in service, then it was clear they'd both hung around for the better part of a century. Maybe even more.

A leather strap, that might as well have been a belt for as long as it was, held the book closed.

"Book of records?" Sage mumbled. Devon had given her a few history and mythology books, but none near as massive. Even the books she'd seen Quarn release from his personal library had not appeared as ancient as this intimidating tome. It had to be special. "Family lines of all the Terras, maybe?"

"More or less." Ava smiled approvingly, and that little gesture filled Sage with an unusual sense of pride. "This is the book you will swear your oath on."

"Like a Bible?"

"If you need to use that word to equate to the importance of what you are undertaking, sure. It is a recording of family lineages as we know them. This one in particular has been chosen for you. It speaks of the mother and her sacrifice and the original family bloodlines. It reminds us of the Tree of Life, and our connection to it." Ava's fingers tip-toed across the binding. "Our people were the answer to a problem. We all began among the warring masses. The blood of Ethereal, Elemental, and Shade all flow through your veins."

A chill ran down Sage's spine. She understood the significance. Visions had come to her in a dream when her mother had gone dark, and she'd seen the carnage of the first great magical war.

"The Mother stripped us of our magic but not our roots." Ava's voice grew louder, commanding Sage's full attention. "What she gave in return was the ability to protect the very magic that corrupted our ancestors. Its influence is still felt to this very day. And that is why ASSET is here."

"I'm ready—"

"For what?" Ava cut her off before she could finish the sentence. "Do you know what it is you are agreeing to?"

That had been the question plaguing Sage's mind since she'd learned about ASSET. Some in the magical world looked to the agency as a police force. Others felt they were rulers, demanding obedience out of fear of retribution. Some hated Terras outright, whether or not they worked for ASSET. None of that truly answered the question, and Sage found herself unable to do the same aloud.

"Our sole purpose is to protect magic from being corrupted, as the Mother once charged us to do." Ava's eyes fell to the chain around Sage's neck. Buried under her shirt, the pendant lay against Sage's chest, its deadly power kept safe, out of sight, but not forgotten. "You and I share a secret that need never be spoken aloud. You are already a guardian of magic. You have seen the corruption that is capable from even the most innocent among us. To accept a position here at ASSET is to pledge to do just that, not only in secret, but in all things for as long as there is breath in your lungs."

Ava locked eyes with Sage once more, like a predator scenting its prey, ready to strike the killer blow. "You've proven to me you are capable. You have seen what we do, and why. Are you ready to say your vow and take your place with us?"

This was it. Time to put up or shut up. She'd already made her decision, but for some reason confirming it here and now made Sage's heart pound so hard she felt it might punch a hole through her chest. She gulped down a knot in her throat, hoping it would help the anxiety, but it only served to mute her voice. She mouthed the word *yes*, but rather than hear it in her own voice, the only the sound that escaped was a dry rasp of air.

"Grey, you may return," Ava called out, startling Sage with the sudden volume of her voice.

Her partner had to have been waiting at the door. The moment his name was called, the knob on Ava's door turned, and he entered the room.

"I'm here to bear witness," he said mechanically, as if he'd uttered the words more times than he'd like to admit. Scripted and oozing with prospect of ceremony, it gave Sage a small thrill of excitement. Might as well make a show of it. She was, after all, signing her life away.

Grey held an old-fashioned quill and pot of ink, further adding to the excitement of a real swearing in. She hoped to see more people file into the room wearing robes and chanting. Sage glanced around, waiting to see who or what else might come in, but after moments of silence save for the papers being shuffled around, her excitement faded.

"The Mother has blessed you with the mark. You are one of her special children called to guard the ancient magic that runs through your veins." Ava dryly read from the pages in front of her. "Honor, duty, so on and so forth…. Read the manuals." She set each paper down as she skimmed over its details. "On the job training, necessary equipment, and financial management are provided by the agency. Next of kin will be notified and recruited upon your death. Are you ready to take your place within the Anonymous Supernatural Security and Elimination Taskforce?"

Sage nodded.

"I need you to acknowledge verbally, Miss Cynwrig."

"Yes," Sage replied.

Ava looked to Grey. "Witness?"

"I have heard her acknowledgement." He signed off as a witness, followed by Ava. Once they were done scrawling their names, the papers were stacked and laid out on the book.

"Good." Ava slid the book over. "You will read and sign here."

She'd hoped for a bit more ceremony, given the importance of what she was doing. Had this been part of her weekly game night, Matt would have had candles all around the room, ambient music playing, and maybe even a few sticks of incense. Instead she got Sir Grump-a-Lot and the Wicked Witch of the West giving her a high-pressured sales pitch.

At least she had the cloak. Devon had come through like a champ with that one. Immature as it might seem to Ava or even

Grey, it was a symbol of her accomplishment, and more pomp and circumstance than she was getting now. Sage wrapped herself in it as Grey nudged the ancient writing implement toward her.

Sage looked down at the words on the page.

The Mother has given her blood. She has bestowed on me this great gift, and in return I will protect that blood from being spilled. I will uphold the laws of magic over the laws of men. I will not judge between the races of magic. I will punish only those who break the Mother's laws. I will keep the magical world secret from men to the best of my ability.

I, and those who follow in my bloodline, shall follow these orders, from now until the end of time.

"My roommate knows about me. Is that going to be a problem?" Sage asked, hesitating to sign anything that prevented her from speaking openly to Matt. He was more than just a mere human; he was her rock. Putting a gag order on her when it came to him was simply impossible. She couldn't keep anything secret from him for long.

"I wish you hadn't said anything to him, but within reason, some humans must know about us," Ava replied impatiently. Her eyes already jumping to the laptop that lay closed on the credenza behind the desk. "Sign here." She pointed to a spot at the bottom of the page. "And initial all of the statements, please."

Sage pulled out the quill and dipped it into the ink. She signed her name, expecting to see some kind of magic happening on the page, and then realized that since she was Terra, there would be no magic attached to her hand. It was simply ink. And because she had never used a quill before, her signature bled heavily into the page, rendering it nearly unreadable. The same thing happened with her initials, but it didn't seem to matter to Ava or Grey.

"Very good." Ava grabbed the contract and snapped the book shut. She rounded the desk and returned to her seat. The still-drying ink continued to spread out on the page as she thrust it unceremoniously into a file and tossed it into her in-box.

"That's it?" Sage asked. As much as she'd struggled with the decision to sign on with ASSET, the act felt extremely anticlimactic.

"Were you expecting a party?" Ava's tone sharpened. She stowed the book in a lower drawer of her desk and immediately retrieved her laptop.

"Kind of, if I'm being completely honest."

Ava reached into her desk and pulled out a small plastic bottle. Before Sage could see what was inside, Ava opened it and poured the contents into her hand. She threw a shower of purple glitter at Sage and said, "Poof. You're an agent."

Had Ava's expression shown even the tiniest bit of amusement, Sage would have laughed at the gesture, but it was clearly done in spite, so Sage kept quiet as she blinked away the specks that hit her face.

"Now if we're done with the formalities, take off that stupid cloak. You and Mr. Maddox need to have a chat with the Mentalist on the Strip. There's been a report of two assistants not surviving his magic tricks."

SIX

The Las Vegas Strip might only be a few short miles in the hospitality corridor of the city, but once across its boundaries, visitors are magically transported into a land of adult fantasies, a world completely unto its own – gauchely decadent, promising tantalizing riches to those willing to tempt fate. Anything one's heart desires can be had for a price, even items not listed on the public menu.

What happens in Vegas…. Everyone knows how it works. All sins are forgiven, or at least forgotten, with enough alcohol. Mutually assured destruction keeps those with better memories from letting slip the truth of the mischief they were party to.

Sage's magical immunity couldn't protect her as Grey drove his bike straight down the center of Las Vegas Boulevard. Like a cartoon come to life, the Strip was alive and animated with colors that couldn't possibly belong to the real world. Try as she might, there was no denying the twinges of excitement as she looked up to the neon glow and dazzling lights.

Video screens three stories high flashed advertisements for high-end restaurants, boutiques, and spa treatments – luxuries she had never been able to afford. With the right player's card and a little time spent at the slots, she might be able to earn points. Deviousness wrapped in simplicity. It was no wonder most people didn't bother to resist the allure. Anyone could be a winner and have it all.

All one had to do was play…

Vegas in a nutshell: Temptations aplenty orchestrated to keep patrons trapped in a few square miles of the city, creating willing prisoners with the promise of leaving richer than they arrived. If that didn't do the trick, there were always other distractions to throw money at: scantily clad women, thunderous men from down under, Broadway-style shows, endless buffets, and all manner of shopping. Truly an adult playground built on one thing: disposable money.

Living in Las Vegas at least for Sage meant staying far away from the Strip. Temptation was easier to deal with when it was completely avoided. Being short on money and having even less luck meant nothing could be thrown away on games of chance.

Grey drove his bike up to the third floor of the mega-resort's parking garage and then led Sage straight into the heart of fantasyland.

Clicks, *pings*, and the rhythmic *ding ding ding*s of slot machines provided ambient noise as they arrived on the gaming floor. Hardly her first time inside of a casino, Sage knew what to expect, but in the moment she struggled to ignore the deceptive noises suggesting people were winning jackpots.

It's all a trick. She shook herself and tried to refocus on Grey, who stood reading the signs above, searching for the right path.

Everywhere she looked, there were electronic machines screaming for attention. Harkening back to her childhood days spent at the arcade. They beckoned with HD graphics and playable games beyond just lining up cherries.

"Snap out of it." Grey nudged her forward. "You act like you've never been in here before."

"Not this casino, no," she replied, her eyes roaming toward tables in the center of the gaming floor. The gentle clack of chips being stacked and moved around the felt added another layer of distraction.

"If you've seen one, you've seen them all." Grey alone seemed immune to the sirens calls all around him.

Who needed magic when you could wield temptation so easily? Everything was carefully choreographed and packaged to trick the senses: the colors; the placement of the variety of games; the ease of access to alcohol; the lack of natural light or clocks on the wall to let players know how long they've been there. The house always wins for a reason. They knew the game better than anyone else.

Grey power walked across the gaming floor, a man on a mission. Sage followed closely as he weaved in through machines and found a secret door along the wall. "Employee hallway," he said, as he opened and held it for her. "Keep your head up. Act like you belong here."

Sneaking behind enemy lines. A devious smirk kinked her lips. Grey had suddenly taken on a different look. Replace that stupid fedora with a fez and slap a bowtie on him and he could easily become the Doctor. This newfound devil-may-care attitude while entering restricted areas was exactly the kind of antics Eleven would get up to.

Sage whispered "Geronimo" as she stepped into the brightly lit employee hallway.

"What?"

"Allons-y?" She giggled at her own private joke. Zack would have totally gotten the reference, the only good thing about their vampire informant. Grey, on the other hand, stood clueless for a moment before shaking his head and moving on.

"Did we just enter the Twilight Zone or something?" Sage wondered aloud.

A stark contrast to the adult playground she'd just left, this area had an institutionalized blandness that numbed all excitement. White walls as far as the eye could see had been dulled into a sandy crème from years of wear. The only twinkling light came from fluorescent bulbs nearing the end of their life. A labyrinth of hallways ran through, under, and behind every one of the public areas to the casino floor and hotel. Signage consisted of arrows with acronyms, though a few she understood. The one labeled EDR led to a hallway wafting with the fresh smell of coffee, something she desperately wanted.

"Less talky, more walky." Grey moved as if he'd been there before, decisively heading up one hallway and down the next.

Sage followed as closely as she could without looking too much like a lost little child. If she did get lost, who knew when she might finally emerge? Down one flight of stairs and into a new but no less drab hallway, Grey led them toward a door labeled *Small Theater*. A nameplate below the sign read *Magnificent Marrin the Mentalist*.

Grey adjusted his fedora and cracked his knuckles. Definitely not the Doctor, Eleven or otherwise. *Fedoras are not cool.* His sudden posturing made him look like an angry hipster. Thank goodness he didn't have a goatee or skinny jeans. Partner or not, she'd have to draw the line there.

"You going to bust some heads in there, tough guy?" she asked, as Grey knocked on the door.

His jaw tightened as he struggled to ignore her and listen for sounds. The hallway was quiet enough to hear a pin drop. Footsteps from employees in other areas of the building echoed in the distance, but nothing else could be heard from where they stood.

"Maybe he's not here yet?" Sage suggested.

Grey grunted as a reply, all the while keeping his eyes on the door as if trying to see through it.

"So what's the deal with this guy?" Sage asked.

"Do you ever shut up?"

His tone more than the question threw her off guard. They'd been ribbing each other since day one, but his sharpness now suggested something else. Sage bit back the angry comment she would have thrown at him. They were on the job and supposed to be acting professional – the opposite of what she'd been doing. What would Mr. Marrin Magnificent, or anyone else, think if they saw ASSET agents bickering?

She put on her game face and gave Grey a curt nod to show she understood.

"Listen and learn," Grey whispered, his eyes still fixed on the closed door.

When his second knock went unanswered, he tried the knob.

Unlocked. What were the odds?

Grey nodded for her to follow and put a finger to his lips, as if she needed another reminder.

Marrin might be Magnificent on stage but – if the disastrous state of his room revealed anything – behind closed doors he was a complete train wreck.

Papers covered every inch of his desk. Some had taken the plunge toward an overstuffed garbage can, only to end up adding to another equally large pile on the ground. Trash appeared to morph into clothing as the landfill reached a dresser where clothes were escaping from overstuffed drawers. A few costumes clung to hangers on a small rack, but one stiff breeze would send them to the ground.

"Has he been robbed?" Sage's first thought spilled out despite Grey's warning to be quiet.

Grey walked to the desk and sifted through the piles of paper, old bills by the looks of them. "Inside a casino? Doubt it."

Sage recognized the red stamp of Final Notice on more than one. "Someone's in trouble," she whispered.

"Gambling problem would be my guess," Grey replied. He turned toward the dressing table. Bottles of rum and vodka peeked out from a curtain of feather boas draped around the mirror. "And drinking. Neither of which are magical, so I don't care."

"Motive not magic," Sage suggested.

A toilet flushed in an adjacent room.

Grey crossed his arms and turned toward the restroom door.

Known drunk; money problems; theatrical type. Sage expected to see a shaggy, pot-bellied, and stinking washed-up old magician, the kind who'd employ the scantiliest of clad assistants to cover his own appearances for shows. Her jaw nearly dropped when Magnificent Marrin came through the door. Clearly the name had more to do with looks than magic. She could see through glamour, so his looks were the real deal. He might as well have stepped off the pages of a men's magazine. Perfect strands of golden hair, not a lock out of place, framed a strong masculine face with a chiseled jaw, cleft chin, and glittering emerald eyes. He had the kind of perfection that could only come from magic.

Some people have all the luck.

"ASSET, I presume?" Marrin flashed Sage a smile that nearly blinded her with its brilliance.

"You clean up well," Grey replied with a scowl.

"It's my job." Marrin waved his hand with a flourish to highlight his immaculate suit. "Unfortunately maid service is not among my skills. I do apologize for the state of my office."

"Saw one too many of them in half?" Grey's deadpan delivery failed to convey whether he was joking.

"This one doesn't mince words, does he?" Marrin met Sage's eyes with a flirtatious wink.

She shook her head and kept her mouth closed for the moment. Still processing the sight of him contrasting the state of his office.

"Bit of a low blow coming from an ASSET agent. I thought you guys were supposed to help solve cases, not insult victims." Marrin's smile had to have been plastered on. It never faltered for a moment while he spoke. His words had been directed at Grey, but those sparkling emerald eyes remained locked on Sage. The effect might have been disarming to others, but the more he stared, the less enamored she felt.

"Sorry, never saw your show," Grey replied, sounding anything but apologetic.

"But you know of me, certainly." Marrin finally turned his attention to Grey. "I'm the Magnificent Mentalist. I can read your thoughts, predict the future, and temporarily remove your inhibitions."

"You're a siren. Yeah, I've read your file," Grey answered, unamused. "What I want to know is what you think happened to your missing staff."

The brilliance of Marrin's grin dimmed. "If I knew what happened, I wouldn't have called you."

"Humor us and take a guess." Grey crossed his arms.

"They just failed to show up for work." Marrin shrugged. "Calls, text, voicemail…all go unanswered."

"Paychecks?" Grey asked.

Marrin's eyes narrowed to crinkled slits, and the muscle in his jaw started to twitch. "Are you insinuating something?"

There was a sinister side to that man; that was a bet Sage could make. His whole persona was a caricature. She'd never met a siren before, but it didn't take a Terra to spot a sleaze ball.

Grey's eyes darted to the desk and back. "Just asking questions."

"Paychecks have always been cut on time." Marrin slithered between the piles of debt and Grey's accusing glare. "My personal finances do not mix with business."

"In my experience, that is never the case." Grey kept his tone light, but Sage could see he'd already written this off as a simple case of no call, no show.

"Money will be a problem if I have no staff to help me with my shows. That's why I called you here. Not to be insulted."

"Again, I'm just asking questions. We need to get a full picture on how the operation runs to establish a reason for their departure." Grey's tone remained flat.

"My girls had no reason to leave. Today is payday, and they still haven't come to pick up their checks. No call; no show. They're not at home either. They're gone. Poof." He snapped his fingers. "Like magic."

His pun had clearly been intended, but he lacked any solid evidence to back it up. "How do you know this?" Sage asked.

"Their cars are still in the employee parking garage," Marrin answered, swiping up a memo written on the hotel's stationary. "I've been put on notice to have them moved or they'll be towed. Been parked without moving for going on a week now."

"And your employees are all human or…?" Sage asked.

"Gemini twins!" Marrin replied cheerfully.

"So they weren't hired by the hotel's HR department?" Grey asked, sounding a little more interested.

"No. My contract with the hotel pays me for shows. Whom I hire is my own business," Marrin replied.

"And the people you hired?" Grey asked. "They are…"

"From the Sortilege agency. All registered, I assure you." Marrin replied again, sounding a little put off by having to answer such accusing questions.

"Any disagreements between you and your staff? Harassment? Salary?" Grey asked.

Marrin's eyes flitted down to the past due notices piled high on his desk. "As I already said, my people are always paid first. And better than any other showgirls on the Strip, I'll wager."

"Please. No bets." Grey nearly broke into a laugh but caught himself. "And who else gets paid? Are there any debts you haven't settled? Enemies you've made who might like to sabotage your show?"

Marrin loosened his collar. "None who would cause this kind of trouble. I take care of those issues when they crop up."

"How, exactly?" Sage finally found a question she wanted to ask. Despite being too good-looking, he wasn't overly muscular. She doubted he would hold up in a fight against a few thugs.

"Let's just say I use my charms to ensure those I owe money to either forgive or extend my credit." He finished with a wink.

"Siren," Grey whispered, like a curse.

If Marrin's powers worked to alter the mental state of those around him, that could make a man many enemies. Sage wondered if his people had been run off by someone or had bolted to avoid his powers altogether. She hoped Grey might have better ideas.

"I'm going to need a list of those whom you say have forgiven you," Grey said.

"I assure you, no one who might have issue with me would ever take that anger out on my staff," Marrin replied, a little less cocky than he'd been. "It's bad form to hurt the innocent. They'd break my legs before ever hurting my staff."

"But running off your staff does essentially break your legs," Sage whispered to herself. Anyone could put two and two together there. But that didn't explain why their cars were still in the parking lot. One missing piece, screaming *foul play*, just didn't fit. "How will you manage your show in the meantime?"

"My dear, I'm still a mentalist, with or without all the eye candy. I'll just have to add a little extra charm until I can secure another assistant. Care to stay for a show? You could be my volunteer."

It was a damn good thing his powers had no effect on her. The eyes alone were enchanting, and combined with confidence and a quick wit, she could see him working his powers well enough to entertain. But what was a magician or mentalist without a pretty assistant?

"Make me a list of your debtors, and we'll be on our way." Grey might not have looked it, but he had the dangerous tone down pat. "And the staffing agency contracts, too."

"If it will help." Marrin threw himself into his desk chair and started scrawling out names on the back of a past due bill.

Grey snatched the paper when Marrin finished. "If you hear anything, let us know. We'll be in touch."

SEVEN

Having missed lunch, both of them were eager to grab a quick meal before heading back to ASSET. Grey pulled his bike into the parking lot of a bar boasting the best burgers in the city.

"Some siren he is." Grey chuckled to himself as he pulled off his helmet. "He lost a pair of gemini in the space of a week."

"Gemini twins?" Sage asked, not entirely sure what that meant. She had so much to learn about the magical realm.

Grey's eyes twinkled at the mention of them. "They have their talents." His lip kinked up crookedly – it might have been a smile, but it didn't look right on his face. "Let's just say they are perfectly suited to being a magician's assistants."

More than enough of a clue to their nature, Sage didn't feel the need to delve further into their special talents. But she wondered if Marrin, sleazy as he was, had not been the target. Perhaps the twins were in some trouble of their own, and it was only coincidence that they worked for a man whose middle name was debt.

"What would make two people just disappear without a trace?" Sage mumbled to herself. She didn't think Marrin's sleazy siren abilities had scared them off. "I'd be interested to see if others are missing that we haven't learned of yet." She pulled off the helmet and tied her hair into a messy bun.

"You're already jumping to conspiracy theories? Slow your roll there, rookie. It's only your first assignment. Ava isn't going to give you something that complicated yet." He looked far too amused for her liking. As Grey swapped the bike helmet for that stupid fedora, she had to force herself to resist the urge to knock it off his head.

"Really? Because my last unofficial assignment was such a walk in the park."

"Trial by fire is not always a bad thing. But I doubt this is that serious. We live in one of the most transient cities in America." He shrugged and turned toward the front door of the bar. "I hope the burgers here are as good as they say."

Sage's stomach growled at the mention of food. The smell of cooking beef hung heavy in the early evening air. "They don't have to be good. I'm starving." She followed Grey to the door.

"We'll pull up the Geminis' files when we get back. But don't get your hopes up. The twins aren't very important people. We may not have much to work from." His bedside manner left a lot to be desired. Grey could have at least sounded somewhat bothered by two women vanishing. It didn't need to be ranked in importance by how powerful they were.

"They're missing. That's pretty important."

"Yes, bleeding heart, all people are important. But as far as our filing system goes, if they don't have a criminal record, we might not have more than names and addresses to work from."

"But you have other resources, don't you?" Sage looked up, noticing the sun had already set. Somehow the day had passed them by without her realizing it. Night had taken on a whole new meaning since learning of the supernatural realm. The weight of unseen eyes fell on her back. Sage increased her pace as she followed Grey into the bar. "What about that staffing agency?"

"You're learning, young one," Grey teased. "We'll make an appointment there soon. Right now *why* they disappeared is a bit more interesting to me. And sometimes that information can't be found in a database. If there are any others who've gone missing recently, it could give us a connection."

"I don't like this," Sage protested. Grey didn't have a network of informants, he had one. And she never knew how to read that specific one. Equal parts smooth-talking charmer and viper ready to strike, Zack had a reputation that gave people a false sense of security. Toothless, for a vampire, he'd bleed your wallet dry before your neck. A cunning façade, but she'd seen his true nature and how deadly he could be if he wanted.

"Are you going to complain every time we take on a mission that requires a little street savoir faire?" Grey turned just before reaching the door, his turquoise eyes daring her to admit defeat.

"Are we always going to have to involve the vampires?" she countered, defiantly meeting his gaze. Like it or not, she had to go along with Grey's plan. He was her partner.

"They have a finger on the pulse of what's going on." Grey held the door open for her. "We use our resources."

"They use us just as much." Everything came with a price of some kind. And the vampire he had in mind freely admitted that his services required payment.

"Are you afraid of the big, bad vampire?" Grey taunted.

If she answered truthfully, he'd never let her hear the end of it. Vampires were the one creature whose cursed magic could affect a Terra. "Whatever. Let's just get this over with."

Grey walked toward an open booth. "Is this public enough for you to feel safe?"

Sage gave the small room a once-over, counting the patrons on one hand. "Hardly."

"You're just a ray of sunshine tonight." Grey slid into the booth.

"Not bright enough to harm me," Zack appeared so suddenly it was as if he had materialized into existence. But Sage knew better. She'd be willing to bet he'd been lying in wait for them to show up, just to enjoy the shock on her face when he made his entrance.

He scooted, uninvited, onto the bench next to Sage.

Instinctively she moved over, pressing herself against the wall. Now she was trapped between the table and a vampire. *Why couldn't he have sat with Grey instead?* Words she couldn't give voice to. Both men appeared to be amused by her annoyance. If fear truly had a smell, no doubt the both guys had picked up on her own personal brand of eau de scared-to-hell.

"Evening, killer." Zack chuckled at his joke. "No one ever forgets that first taste of blood. You don't have to be a vampire to savor it, you know." He winked and turned to Grey. "You remember your first, right?"

"We're here on business tonight," Grey replied.

"Always business with you lot. Don't you ever just want to chat?" Zack's feigned sadness did not elicit a response from Grey. When he turned on Sage with those icy blue eyes, she remembered his duel nature. She'd seen the viper in him, quick to strike with teeth like needles. But there was a person behind the monster, one she'd had more than a few fun conversations with. It didn't change her feelings toward his kind or remove the apprehension she felt in his presence, but there was no reason to fear him at the moment.

"What are we going to chat about, then?" Sage volleyed the words back to Zack.

"Well, nothing now, if you're going to take that attitude about it," Zack responded, with all the snark of a teenage girl.

Sage found it hard to hide her amusement.

"Don't play into his ego." Grey pretended to look over the menu, but Sage knew food had been nothing more than a tease. This meeting had been planned.

"At least she has the sense to act as if I'm a real person, not some information console." Zack played the drama queen to near perfection. "Insert coin and out pops a fortune cookie with the answers."

"If only it was that easy." Grey looked up from his menu with a devious glint in his eyes. "Where do I swipe my credit card?"

"That Grey." Zack turned back toward Sage with a wink. "He likes to…fuss."

The way to her heart was always through nerd-speak, and Zack was more than fluent in that language. His careful usage spoke volumes, easing her apprehension at being around him.

"Fuss…" She let the word hang in the air for a second, struggling to remember the line. "Fuss. I think he likes to scream at us." She giggled.

"He really doesn't mean us any harm," Zack replied instantly.

"But he is seriously lacking on…" Sage snorted before she could finish her sentence. "Charm."

Grey didn't appear to recognize the movie they were quoting, which made the moment all that much more satisfying.

"You have a gift for rhyme." Zack waggled his eyebrow.

"Some of the time." Sage stuck her tongue out at him.

"I think we're starting to make Grey nervous." Zack waved his hand in the air as if to say he was done. "Besides, I'm much more interested in hearing how you, Sage, are doing."

"Don't," she warned, not wanting to revisit the memory.

"Joking aside, I am truly concerned. An innocent like yourself has to be feeling something after that whole mess at Devon's."

"I'd prefer to not discuss that," Sage replied, more sternly this time, hoping he'd get the message and return to quoting *Princess Bride*.

"As you wish," Zack winked.

Funny how three little words could have such an impact on her mood. Grey didn't understand, of course, but Sage allowed the smile to return to her lips.

"If you truly wish to be a friend and not simply some information vending machine, as you so oddly put it, then let's talk about what's happening on the streets," Sage countered.

Zack turned to Grey. "Nicely played. You see what she did there? You could learn from her. Sweet talk me with movie quotes, and once she's reeled me in…"

"Do I look like the sweet-talking kind?" Grey stared across the table, delivering the words deadpan.

"And you wonder why I demand money from him." Zack shrugged. "The streets are vast. What specifically are you looking to learn?"

"Supernaturals disappearing without a trace ring any bells?" Grey asked, before Sage could open her mouth.

"Just can't get a day off from all the doom and gloom in this world, can we?" Zack scoffed.

"Comes with the job. Or so I'm learning," Sage picked up the menu from the edge of the table and began to look it over. Grey might have forgotten the promise of food, but her stomach would not allow it to be broken.

"Well… When you seek trouble…" Zack let his words hang in the air.

"Trouble seeks us." She sighed.

"I haven't heard of any contracts. Are we talking vanished as in wiped from the earth, or dead bodies popping up?" Zack asked, as casually as if he were asking if she was planning to order fries.

"No bodies… yet," Grey answered.

Talk of death and bodies silenced the growling of her stomach. Tempting as the smell of bacon and cooking beef was, the conversation at her table was seriously ruining it.

"What about talismans?" Zack asked curiously.

"That's oddly specific," Sage noted loudly, as she slammed her menu down.

Zack shook his head. "Just an observation. People, especially magical ones, don't just poof out of existence. Their magic goes somewhere. Like with you – when your mother died, her magical lineage passed to you."

"Blood magic passes to the next in line. These were not heritage bound," Grey said.

"Was anything left behind by the victims?" Zack asked.

"Their vehicles," Sage replied.

"I was talking about pieces of them."

"Like body parts?" Sage asked, grimacing, her appetite completely ruined by the thought of severed limbs.

"No. Physical representations of what they were. If magic was absorbed, something is left behind. If someone is killed, then there's a body. Have you found either?" Zack asked.

Sage thought back to the office. It had been a mess of costumes and bills, but she couldn't remember seeing any trophies or tchotchkes.

"What you're suggesting would take powerful magic. Few registered in this city wield that kind of power." Grey's expression darkened as if he already knew what he'd have to do next.

Sage was left clueless. She'd only scratched the surface of this new-to-her realm, and beyond the very basics of magical classes, she knew nothing of the range of abilities someone could possess. As much as she wanted to open her mouth and ask for clarification, she hesitated, knowing it would only earn her more mockery for being such a noob.

"Just an observation, and hopefully one that does not prove to be true," Zack said, with a note of caution.

"I think you're on to something." Grey nodded. His expression shifted between a pained look that said he was thinking and the wide eyes of an epiphany. "We need to head back into the office and check some records."

"Aww, but you've only just arrived. You can't leave me so soon. I thought we'd have dinner." Zack licked his lips for effect, causing a shiver to race down Sage's spine. If her appetite had not already been ruined, that would have surely killed it. With that one move, he'd negated all the good will his nerd-speak had earned.

"All work and no play." She nudged him to move out of her way so she could escape.

"Makes Grey a dull boy." Zack finished the sentence for her with a chuckle. "But what will it do to fresh-faced Sage?"

"You're teetering on the edge of super creepy right now. Stop while you're ahead!" she warned as she exited the booth.

"As you wish." Zack bowed with a flourish. "Have fun stormin' the castle."

"I'm guessing you've got an idea of what we're looking for now?" Sage asked, following behind her partner, happy to be free of Zack, though her stomach growled in protest.

"Ideas, yes. I'm not sure yet. But Zack was right about magic leaving a trace. If their magic was absorbed, there should be something left behind. Otherwise we're going to be looking for bodies."

"You still think it was someone targeting Marrin for debts?" Sage asked.

"No. They'd hurt him, not innocent assistants."

"So you think Zack is right, and someone is stealing magic?"

"That's what doesn't make sense. Why steal low-level magic?"

"Practice?" Sage said more to herself than an answer to Grey's question. Rather than admonish her for such a silly suggestion, his eyes grew even wider.

"Testing out new abilities. Or maybe someone new to the area who's testing out our defenses. Possibly."

"What kind of being has the ability to steal magic?" Sage asked.

But Grey didn't answer. He looked as if he were rolling that same question around in his own mind. He tossed her the helmet and mounted his bike. "C'mon. I'll take you home. It's too late tonight for the amount of research we're going to have to do."

EIGHT

Grey stopped the bike just outside of the night gate at Sage's apartment complex. "We start at eight tomorrow."

"You picking me up again?" she asked. The day had worn her thin, and sleep was calling.

"Let's not make this a habit." He nodded. "I'll message you when I head out." Grey sped away before she could get in another word. The transportation situation was going to become an issue soon, but it ranked low on her immediate needs for the moment. Sage dragged herself in through the night gate and headed toward her apartment.

"Hello, neighbor," Luke called out from his balcony.

Sage looked up and waved politely.

"Want to stop in for a beer?" he asked.

A hopeful edge to his tone threw her for a moment. Didn't he say he had a girlfriend? That was bad news right there if he did.

"No, thanks. Been a long day," she said, trying to keep her tone friendly. Whether he was well-intentioned or not, he was a djinn and their reputation demanded she take special care to keep him at an arm's length. No bringing business home.

"Raincheck, then?" Luke asked.

"Sure." Sage quickened her pace, making a beeline for her front door.

"Late night at the office?" Matt's tone had more concern than curiosity.

She checked the locks and peeked through the peephole, half wondering if she'd see Luke out there still, watching her front door. And as the thought struck her, so too did the realization she was making herself paranoid without reason. Just because someone is a being of magic did not make them evil. Then again, Devon had called them big baddies.

"You okay?" Matt's concern amplified, but he hadn't stood from his comfortable position on the couch. "Did you sign on the dotted line?"

"Yeah. I'm official now!" She feigned a cheer. "It's been a long day. And my head is killing me." The rich aroma of espresso roast tempted her with the promise of renewed energy. She set her bag down on the table and walked over to pour a cup. "Apparently both come with the territory."

Steaming cup in hand, she strolled into the living room. Josh and Matt had claimed every inch of the couch, stretching out across all three cushions, leaving only the busted old recliner for her to use.

"Please tell me they're paying you well," Josh said. Mr. Practical! It was a damn good thing, too, because between the three of them, someone needed to have a responsible head on their shoulders. Left to their own devices, she and Matt would have the apartment filled top to bottom with movies, collectables, and games.

Sage shrugged. "Well enough, I guess. But I'll have to buy a car soon. I've got lots of driving to do."

"Healthcare? Dental?" he continued his interrogation. She could have used his sleuthing skills earlier with Marrin the Magnificent; Josh might have gotten more information out of him.

Sage chuckled to herself at that thought as Josh droned on. "Matt told me how dangerous your new work is. Private investigations with an emphasis on the weird." He spoke with parental authority; clearly fishing for more information that had nothing to do with her vision care or 401K. Sage wondered just how much Matt had told him.

Josh and Matt were human, which fell under the 'do not tell' category of ASSET regulations. But more than that, they were partners, and Sage counted them as close as family. With Matt already knowing, how long would it be before Josh figured things out? Beyond that, how fair was it for her to ask Matt to keep something so important a secret from his own partner?

"ASSET takes care of its people. You don't have to wait up worrying for me." Sage sipped her coffee as an excuse to stop talking.

Matt's eyes darted back and forth between his boyfriend and Sage.

Don't. Just don't! Sage wished she could use the force and stop her roommate from nervously chewing his bottom lip off. She'd seen that look before. Matt was practically bursting to speak, but the effort it took him to bottle it up made him act like a toddler on a sugar high.

Worriers, the pair of them. Not that Sage could blame either of the guys. But knowing such a crazy secret wouldn't remove any of their concern.

"So, I was thinking… About game night." She shifted gears, hoping the boys would keep pace. "We need to get back to dragon raids. Why not try a new map? We need a change of pace."

"I'm not sure we should change maps yet." Josh turned his puppy-dog eyes on Matt. "We haven't beaten the last one we played."

"You're probably right," Matt agreed. "Sage needs to recalibrate her character sheet anyway. Miss Magical Immunity. That's just not fair."

"To whom?" She stuck her tongue out, refusing to be baited into that conversation again.

"To the rest of us who build our characters by the book." Josh narrowed his eyes, clearly still angry for her ruining the last game.

"What if the rulebook got it all wrong?" She looked away, squirming uncomfortably in her seat. *Damn it.* Even with the change in topic, she still couldn't escape talking about magical mumbo-jumbo for one night. "It is an unpublished game, after all. Why not act like real beta testers and provide notes on how to create better characters?"

"You can't twink a character just to win a game." Matt jumped in before Josh could.

"I wouldn't call what I did *winning!*" She'd turned away from him, but could feel his accusing eyes boring into her skull. "Magic neutrality is not a twink. It's an ability. I could still get my head chopped off by a damage dealer," she added stubbornly.

"You're not ruining game night with your newfound love of magical protection." Matt put his foot down hard.

"Yes, sir!" she replied, with a one-fingered salute. He was about to explode with the truth and she knew it.

"You two have some secret you're not sharing with me?" Josh's tone shifted from suspicion to confusion.

She had to perform damage control before tempers flared. Matt had said he would make her tell Josh, but so soon? Had he been spooked by something while she was at work? *Luke.* Their super-friendly djinn neighbor? Had he come over and said something he shouldn't have? Luke had recognized her mark immediately. What if he'd assumed... Sage realized both

Josh and Matt were staring at her, waiting for an answer that apparently she was expected to give.

Anticipation weighed thickly in the air during the awkward pause holding the room in silence.

"Well, we are madly in love." Sage forced herself to giggle as girlishly as she could for effect. "But that's no secret."

"And planning to run off to Tahiti." Matt picked up on her lead; always on top of his game. "But other than that, no." He gave Josh a little peck on the cheek.

Josh rolled his eyes. "If you're taking off, please use my member number so I can at least get the airline miles."

"How else am I going to get the first class upgrade?" Sage batted her eyes coquettishly.

"Really, though, what is going on between you two?" He might have kept his tone level, but the insistence was there. "You're acting weird, and that's saying something."

Despite Sage's efforts to derail the conversation, Josh's train of thought arrived right on schedule.

"Sage's new job bothers me. That's all." Matt replied flippantly. "You know she's basically family."

"You helped me make the decision to take the damn job," Sage fired back. "Don't get mad at me for listening to you."

"The one time you listen…" Matt scoffed.

"Don't pull that crap on me." She whipped an accusing finger at him. How dare he sit there with a chip on his shoulder when they'd come to an agreement the previous evening? "You could have put up a better defense before I accepted the offer."

"I said my piece. You already had your mind made up. And we all know how defiant you are, Sage. If I told you *no,* and put my foot down, you'd have just laughed and done it anyway."

"Are we all taking crazy pills here? Because what you just said makes no flippin' sense." If she had known this was what she'd be coming home to, she'd have opted to stay in housing at ASSET. After the day she'd had, Sage didn't have it in her to go toe-to-toe with both boys over her new job.

"Since Matt won't say, and it's clearly bothering him more than he wants to let on…What exactly do you do at work, Sage?" Josh speared her with a look that dared her to try to derail the conversation again. Matt might have been huffing and puffing, but his boyfriend's calm voice commanded so much more authority.

First official day as an agent, she hadn't been given time to digest the full meaning of this new way of life, and here she was being drilled by the dramatic duo.

"Let me ask you this." Sage threw out a softball question to gauge his open-mindedness. "Do you believe in magic?"

"You mean the shows on the Strip?" Josh replied. "I loved the guys who had the tigers. That was an awesome show back in the day."

"No. I mean like people who are born with gifts and abilities," Sage said.

"Are you going X-men on me now?" He chuckled, sounding more nervous than amused.

Matt picked at his nails. The effort it was taking him to not blurt out the truth had him chewing his perfect manicure down to the quick.

As annoyed as she was, part of her understood. Keeping secrets was hard enough; keeping the fact that your roommate was on the magical police force was damn near impossible.

"Less comic book, more fantasy." Sage hoped delivering the words with a lighter tone might make it easier.

"Like witches?" Josh asked. "We talking Salem trials here?"

"Sort of, sure. But with real abilities. And they don't need spells to make things happen. They can just do it," Sage confirmed.

"Like, *poof*, they make what they want appear?" Josh snapped his fingers.

"Right." Sage nodded and pointed a finger at the coffee table. "You think beer, and *bam*, there's a beer right in front of you."

"That would be awesome! It would save me so much on grocery bills." Josh snuggled back into the couch cushions and reached a hand out to stop Matt from chewing off his pinky nail. "You find people like that?"

"That's one way to put it," Matt mumbled.

"Okay, sure. Let's say I believe magic could be real," Josh replied. "Where do I sign up?"

"Don't jump into the deep end just yet," she cautioned. "Magic is real. And it can do cool things. But it can also do bad things too."

"You're being totally serious, aren't you?" The corner of Josh's lip twitched. His jaw tightened as if struggling to maintain the neutral expression he'd held up to that moment.

"Believe it." Matt nudged Josh with his elbow. "She's not lying."

They exchanged silent grimaces before Josh's attention fell back to Sage. "Fine. Magic is real, and both good and evil."

"Now, let's say that there were people out there who were innately neutral to magic, whether good or evil." She softened her tone, hoping to ease the sting of truth.

"You?" Josh jumped right to the point. "That's what you two were arguing about? Not the game?"

"I thought we were arguing over the game, but clearly Matt had more on his mind than he was willing to say." Sage held out her arm, showing off her birthmark, the Tree of Life. "This isn't just some deformity or birthmark. It's a special branding. All of the people who were born magically neutral have it. We're capable of withstanding pretty much all the magic that can be thrown at us, and because of that, we are called to be its protectors."

"Wait. Hold on one second here." Josh held his hand up like a schoolboy desperate to get attention. "So you're not magic, you just can't be hurt by it?"

He'd seen her birthmark many times in the past. Like everyone else, he'd asked about it, thinking it was a really bad tattoo, and dismissed it just as quickly. But as she held it up for him to see, revealing how much it had changed since her awakening, his eyes glistened with new appreciation. He leaned in for a closer look. His hand trembled as he reached out to touch the more defined lines of the Tree of Life. What had once looked like a haphazard tangle of broken veins had morphed into twisted Celtic-like knots very clearly shaped into a tree. His finger ever so lightly traced the outline from the roots all the way up the trunk to the leaves dotting the top of the canopy. "Okay, even I have to admit, your birthmark has changed a lot."

"It has. And that's part of why Matt is so upset." Sage sighed as she met her roommate's eyes. "See, when mom died, I inherited her gifts. The neutrality only activates when someone else in the family line with the mark dies."

"I'm so sorry, Sage." Josh knew how painful it was to talk about Miranda, and that wound was still so fresh.

"Yeah." Sage took a moment to get a handle on those emotions. "So, this whole job is kind of a family line thing. I was literally born for this."

"You were. There's no denying that." Matt dropped his eyes and sighed. "But I don't have to like it."

"And, if you haven't already guessed," she said, keeping her focus on Josh, "I'm not supposed to be telling people my secrets."

Josh leaned back against the couch. He nodded gently, not saying anything. His eyes shifted back and forth between Matt and Sage.

"Don't be too mad at Matt. He only just found out last week when you were away." Sage gulped down the knot in her throat. She understood his apprehension; appreciated it, even. But one mother hen was enough. Telling Josh ensured she'd never have a moment's peace. "He'd seen too much, and rather than lie about my partner or the battle scars, I told him the truth and swore him to secrecy."

"And you said nothing interesting happened." Josh glared at his boyfriend. "Battle scars?"

Sage's hand flew to her neck. The wounds had healed – thank goodness for super-fast healing – but faint silvery scars remained. "It's a full-contact type of job sometimes."

If Matt rolled his eyes any harder, they'd pop straight from his head. "Sometimes?"

"Do you see any wounds today?" Sage snapped at him.

"She heals insanely fast," Matt whispered in Josh's ear.

"Then what are you so worried about?" Josh asked.

"She's like a sister to me. Of course I worry."

"I was born for this." Sage felt like a broken record having to keep repeating it. "ASSET is the agency my mom worked for. All of the people with this mark work there to protect people and magic."

"It's not what I expected." Josh's voice stayed shockingly quiet.

"Would you rather we were running off into the sunset together?" Matt reached down, took Josh's hand, and gave it a little squeeze of solidarity. Neither of them looked happy having their eyes open to the strange reality they'd been blissfully ignorant to.

"I feel like this is a practical joke, but no one is smiling." Josh's jaw tightened; teeth clenching as if trying to keep his chin from dropping to the ground.

She couldn't blame him. "I said the same thing when Grey, my new partner, showed up on the front porch trying to get me to believe all this nonsense too." She snickered, remembering how angry Grey had gotten when she asked if she could fly. "Truth is weird. But no less truth," she added. "And now that you know, I have to swear you to secrecy. Like your boyfriend over here, you can't tell anyone about this. Okay?"

"Who would believe me?" Josh shook his head slowly.

"You'd be surprised," Sage answered.

"I kind of wish I hadn't asked now," Josh said.

"Now you know why I've been so bothered." Matt had to throw his two cents in.

"Here's the thing, boys." Sage couldn't believe she had to be the authority in this conversation. "This is who I am. This is what I do. And the best way you can support me is to trust that I'm capable of handling this."

"But yesterday you were on the fence." Matt sounded as if he were still trying to convince her not to take the job.

"Not about whether or not I could handle it. I know I can. I have Devon teaching me how to protect myself. I have Grey. He might be an ass, but he's a seasoned agent who has my back. I didn't doubt for a minute that I *could* do the job. What I waivered on was whether I wanted to."

"You could have said no." Matt pouted.

She hadn't expected him to go full diva on her over this. He'd seemed so level-headed about it the night before. If only he'd been honest, they could have worked though these fears together. But now it was too late. The die had been cast. "Sure. I could have." She reached up, her hand finding the necklace as if drawn to it like a magnet. "But I realized that what I want is

70

selfish. I owe it to my mother, and everyone else who bears this mark, to do my duty for the greater good."

"No more Avengers movies for you." Josh cracked the first smile she'd seen all evening.

"With great power comes–"

"Don't!" Matt interrupted,

"I could give you the whole it's my destiny speech. That's what everyone told me when I freaked out at my first troll sighting." She drew a finger around her birthmark. The truth was there plain as day. And as much as they needed to hear it, Sage too needed to say the words out loud. "My kind were born with a gift. My mom had it and used it to help protect those around her. How could I not do the same?"

"You met a troll?" Josh gasped.

Of all she had just said, that was what he'd heard? "Yeah, my old boss. Apparently they're expert number crunchers."

"That's all they crunch, right?" Matt asked.

"Yes." As far she knew, glamour was really their only magical trait. "Think about it, if trolls work with humans, do you really think they could get away with eating them?

"And that guy Grey?" Josh hadn't had the chance to meet him.

"He's like me. And he's one of the best agents at ASSET," she assured him.

"What about that other guy you mentioned before… Zack?" Matt asked.

"Guys, seriously. Relax. I work with some good people. I'm not in any more danger than I would be walking to the bus stop at night."

"You need a car." Matt huffed. "I don't like you, magical protection or not, wandering the streets at night."

Sage let go a relieved breath, seeing his return to normal levels of concern for her safety, though Josh still looked as if he wanted to devour his bottom lip.

"I need to pay off my student loans first," Sage countered, with the same argument she had given everyone else. "But if I ever need a ride, I'm calling you first, okay?"

"I don't really understand all of this." Josh motioned with his hand. "But for argument's sake, I'll believe you, Sage. Protect magic or whatever. It sounds like really interesting work. But, like Matt, I worry for your safety. You're family, blood or not."

"And I love you and Matt both for that. So, how about a compromise?"

"I'm listening," Josh said.

"If things are getting *real* at work, I'll let you know. I won't keep secrets from you."

"Okay. But—" Matt started to protest.

"But…you boys have to trust that I'm not some fragile little thing. I can handle my shit, and quit worrying all the time!" She demanded. "I'll tell you when it's time to worry."

Matt narrowed his eyes. His jaw set tight. But after a nudge from Josh, he muttered, "Fine."

"If a moment comes where I tell you that shit is getting real," she locked eyes with each of them in turn as she delivered the decree, "you must also promise to listen, and do exactly as I say."

Matt nodded.

"I can agree to your terms." Josh held his hand out. "As long as we have your word. No more secrets!"

"If you guys can stop being helicopter boyfriends, yes!" Sage shook Josh's hand. She'd tell them what she needed them to know, enough to keep them from feeling left out of the loop, but no way in hell was she telling them all the crazy that went on in her daily life now. She had enough on her plate with the djinn neighbor to check up on and the missing gemini twins she and Grey had been assigned to find.

NINE

"You seem to be settling in a little easier this week." Devon greeted her with a nod. Sweat poured down his bald head. He mopped his face with a towel draped around his neck. She might have just signed on for the day, but it was clear that he'd been up and at it for a while.

"No deaths so far this week." She set her bag down on a bench along the wall and took a quick sip of her water before heading to the mats for a lesson in getting her ass kicked.

"I guess that would make things a little easier to deal with." Devon tossed his towel aside and cracked his knuckles, one hand at a time, taunting her with each *pop*. "Well, that's about to change."

"Why ruin a good thing?" She took in a deep cleansing breath and mentally prepared for him to bring the pain.

"Don't think just because you got the cape, your lessons are over."

"How could I forget?"

"You showed good promise with the knife. So that's where we'll begin." He pulled out a knife from some sheath hidden behind his back. At first glance looked real, and huge. But after the moment of fear evaporated, she saw it bend and flex as Devon waved it teasingly in the air, Rubber, or something very much like it. Sage said a silent thanks to the gods. Had he opted to use real steel, she'd be leaving in a body bag. And that would just ruin her plans for the rest of the day.

"Attacking or defending?" she asked, secretly hoping she'd be the one holding it.

"Defense first. You still have a lot to learn when it comes to not being a victim." Devon pointed the fake knife at her neck.

She'd never live down her first failed fight with a vampire. If not Devon, then Grey would mock her every chance he got, reminding her that despite how badass she felt, she was still a noob. One day the student would surpass the master. She would just have to hone her Jedi-like instincts. Letting that thought fuel her, Sage set herself into a fighting stance, watching as Devon stalked up to her. "Let's do this!"

"No. Not like this. In an assault situation, no one is going to come straight at you waving a knife in the air."

"Sorry. Old habit." Sage stood and shook herself to loosen her muscles a little.

"Just like when Rina got the upper hand, you won't see the blade until it's almost too late. So you need to work on awareness."

Devon circled her, twirling the rubber knife in his hands as he left her field of vision. "Head up. Pay attention. Tell me what you see."

She followed him with her eyes as he came back around her from the other side, keeping her focus on him as he walked out of her line of sight with each rotation, then back in. Round and round he went in a numbingly slow pace that lulled her into a sense of ease. "Are you trying to hypnotize me?"

Devon grinned wickedly. "You're not paying attention."

She hated that look. It always came just before he put her on her ass. But it wasn't his hands that came around her torso, nor was the knife that came up against her neck the rubber one he'd been brandishing.

Sage struggled against an iron grip. "The hell!" she squealed as the sharp edge of a very real blade bit into her skin.

"Had you been paying attention, you would have noticed we weren't alone in here," Devon admonished her. "Out in the field, you can never let your guard down, not even for a moment. Just because you can see through glamour doesn't mean you cannot be deceived by the shadows."

Her back pressed against a wall of muscles. Whoever was holding her was tall. Male, she assumed, by the size of the arm around her chest. Clever. All Devon's circling had her slowly moving position so she no longer faced the wall of mirrors. Any hopes of getting a peek at her assailant was out of the question. Her mind ran a mile a minute as she struggled to deduce the identity of Devon's accomplice. Aquirming only made the knife bite harder into her skin.

"Slitting my throat in house is a horrible way to die," Sage whispered, more to herself than to the others in the room, but she knew they'd hear her anyway.

"How did you break Rina's hold?" Devon asked. "Remember the way you were able to use her strength against her."

Sage had been avoiding the memory of that day. She'd acted on pure instinct then. At least that had been what she had told herself. So much blood on her hands. And now Devon was forcing her to remember the moment.

"Life or death, Sage. Do something!" Devon barked, calling her back from the depths of her memories.

"I'm trying." She grunted. Rina had been equal in size. Sage had more of an advantage when it came to finding leverage then. And the poor girl had admitted she'd been given a desk job after failing to qualify for field work. Knowing Rina had not been much of a fighter had given Sage the confidence she needed to pull off such a risky maneuver, an advantage she did not have now.

Best guess, it had to be Grey holding the knife to her throat. And while he wouldn't kill her, he'd push her to the brink of her immortality to make a point, and then tease her endlessly for being a newbie. His strength and size gave him more than enough advantage. If she could only get her hand on the handle of the knife. Of course then she'd still have to find the leverage to push it away, and moved in the opposite direction.

"I can't." She felt the blade's sharp edge with every word she spoke.

"Then you fail," Devon spoke solemnly. "Better you die here than on the street."

"I'll make it quick and clean." Grey snickered

Of course it was him! He couldn't win. Her pride refused to accept that as an option. When you can't fight fair, you fight in any way that will let you win. She reached around behind her, groping for a soft spot. When she found her target, Sage gave his balls a *warning* squeeze. "Drop the knife."

Devon's hand shot up; covering his mouth as he spun around to conceal his laughter.

Grey pressed the blade harder against her neck. "You really want to do this?"

"You're not going to kill me. And I'm out of options." Sage squeezed again, digging her fingertips to make it count. "So, yeah."

Grey dropped the knife with a growl of frustration.

Devon regained his composure quickly, but when he met Sage's eyes there was no praise. "In a real fight, you'd be dead trying something stupid like that."

"Not true," she replied.

Devon's eyebrow lifted curiously. "Explain."

"I weighed my options and figured out the winning angle in *this* fight. I knew my life wasn't truly on the line. But I still had to get him to let go."

"That's cheating." Grey stepped away as he adjusted his pants. If looks could kill, she'd be cremated by the raw anger burning in his eyes.

"Interesting point. I like that you're thinking on your feet." Devon nodded. "However, in a real life situation you need skills as well as wits."

"Her wits will definitely get her killed," Grey scoffed. "And don't think you're getting off easy for pulling that shit with me."

"Don't be such a poor sport." She stuck out her tongue. "You'd have done the same with a knife at your throat."

"So you're saying it would be acceptable for me to tweak your boobs?" Grey squeezed the air with both hands.

"Do we have an HR department here?" Sage asked.

"Double standard there, love!" Devon snorted.

"Oh, no, I'm not crying harassment. I just wondered if that was Grey's next play." Sage winked at Grey.

"You two need to address your relationship quick. You're fire and he's ice. Damned if I don't hear sizzling every time you two come together."

"I think I'm going to be sick." She feigned puking.

"Don't flatter yourself." Grey rolled his eyes.

Sage blew a kiss at him. "Was it good for you too, baby?"

"Seriously. Quit acting like a couple of schoolyard kids," Devon barked at both of them. "You pull her hair, she kicks you in the nuts. Deal with your feelings so you have a clear head on missions."

"Speaking of…" Grey nodded at the door. "We need to get moving soon."

"Where to? I thought today was a research day." Sage hadn't logged into a computer terminal yet. Devon had stolen her away for training the moment she entered the building. "Did you figure out who or what we're looking for already?"

"The twins aren't even in our registry. They're too new to the city." Grey looked more defeated by that than by her grabbing hold of the family jewels. "We'll have to check out the employment agency they came from for their records. But that will have to wait. We've got another disappearance."

"Who's gone missing?" Devon asked. "Do I need to be worried?"

"You know how it is." Grey shook his head. "People go missing in this town all the time. Ava's just lobbing softballs at us to break the newbie in."

Sage walked over to the bench and grabbed a towel to mop up the sweat dripping down her neck. "There went all my enthusiasm." She patted herself dry and went to stuff the towel in her gym bag, noticing immediately how much blood had stained the white terrycloth. More than she'd expected to see. Grey had cut her deep. "This better heal faster than the vampire bite!" she grumbled. Any remorse she might have had for giving his nuts a hard massage vanished. Had she not been immortal, a wound like that could have killed her.

"Battle scars are badges of honor," Grey chuckled.

"I'll wear this with pride, then, having vanquished the great asshole of ASSET." She gave him a one-fingered salute.

"Want me to honor you again? Perhaps a little more to the left next time?" Grey returned the gesture with the same finger, drawing it across his neck.

"Careful now. Devon already thinks you like me. Leave him with a little mystery." She smirked. "Or he might take it upon himself to plan our wedding."

A little vein pulsed at Grey's temple. Tit for tat, they could do this all day now that she was beginning to get the hang of taunting him. It would certainly make working with him so much more fun.

"If you two are done flirting…" Devon sighed. With his hands on his hips, the ogre looked more diva than dangerous as he stood glaring at them. "Since we didn't get in a full training session today, it will be double tomorrow! And we'll work on proper breaks."

"Sir, yes, sir!" She saluted him and instantly regretted it. Snarking off to Grey was all in good fun. Devon would make her pay.

"Where to, partner?" She flipped her hair at Grey as she scooted past him out of the training room.

TEN

Grey kept the mystery of where they were headed a secret all the way up to the moment he pulled his bike into the dirt lot of the Wild Habitat animal sanctuary.

"I've been meaning to stop in here!" Sage pulled off her helmet and hopped off the bike eager to explore. Vegas didn't have a zoo to speak of. For a price tourists could view some of the animals used in various shows on the Strip. The Wild Habitat couldn't really call itself a zoo either – it paled in comparison to the kind of encounters one could have in a real animal sanctuary – but at least offered a chance to see a small variety of predators in an intimate setting. Best of all, it wasn't surrounded by twinkling lights or half-naked showgirls.

The sign in the dirt parking lot read *A Refuge for Retired Animals*. They listed lions, tigers, wolves, and even a giraffe among their residents. From the parking lot, large cages and chicken wire enclosures could be seen jutting up over the fence line.

Grey led the way toward a double-wide trailer that served as both ticket booth and access point to the fenced-off area beyond. "I shouldn't have to remind you, but...keep your mouth shut. Don't piss these guys off."

"If you're going to say it every time we go somewhere, why not just write it on your forehead and save us both time?"

"When you start acting like an agent, I'll start treating you like one." He turned his back on her and opened the door to the trailer.

Touché, she whispered to herself. She'd give him that one. They were on the job now, and heading in to meet another client. She'd save her snark for later. "Broad daylight and wild animals… I'm cool." Sage reached for her phone, ready to take pictures.

"Put that away." Grey held the door and waited for her to walk through into the ticket office reception area.

Quite a bit smaller than she'd expected, the room was no bigger than a closet, leaving little space for Sage to stand as Grey filed in behind her.

A lady with a short bob of golden hair sat behind a metal desk between the doors leading in and out of the trailer. "We're not open yet," she said pleasantly enough, though the look in her eyes was anything but. She busily counted the till drawer from an old-fashioned cash register that sat in the space where a computer would normally occupy on her desk.

Sage tried not to stare, but the moment she laid eyes on the ticket clerk, she sensed something otherworldly.

Amber eyes, predatory and fierce, like a lioness ready to pounce. The woman glared back at Sage as if daring her to make a scene, but her voice betrayed none of the danger. "Come back in an hour."

Grey rolled up his sleeve, showing the Tree of Life on his wrist, and just like that the danger evaporated from the woman's gaze.

Sage had hated her birthmark all throughout her life, thinking it a horrible deformity needing to be hidden. If she'd only known how powerful a symbol it was, she'd have flaunted it everywhere she went.

"ASSET? Why didn't you just say so?" With a toothy grin that reminded Sage of vampire fangs, the woman pointed Grey to the second door, granting access into the Wild Habitat. "Caleb is out cleaning the cages. You can't miss him."

Sage followed behind, making sure to show her mark as she passed, but the look she got wasn't nearly as friendly. The teeth were all there, but Sage wouldn't call what she saw a smile. A dare, perhaps, or maybe a challenge. Sage nearly broke into a run to catch up to Grey. He walked like a man on a mission, down the concrete path between giant fenced enclosures.

In the distance, lions roared. Sounds of chuffing and snorting gave Sage a little thrill. She'd never been able to get close to wild animals before, which made this mission an extra treat. The overpoweringly pungent scent of urine wafting to her nose she could do without, but it was still worth it for the chance to see real beasts up close.

Still following in Grey's wake, Sage peered into the cages as they passed, but despite hearing animals all around, she failed to see any hint of them.

"Am I missing something?" Sage wondered aloud. Grey had already made it pretty clear he wanted her to just follow along quietly, so she didn't really expect him to answer. It became pretty clear, though, why Ava had sent them. Something was definitely off. And she couldn't quite put a finger on what that was.

They wound their way through the first row of enclosures and as they reached the largest one at the end, Grey stopped suddenly, letting out a gasp. His hand flew up to muffle the sound, but she'd already heard the shock before he could cover his mouth.

She couldn't fault him for his sudden show of fear. The gate had been left wide open. Muddy paw prints the size of dinner plates tracked out of the gaping enclosure.

Grey bent to inspect the tracks.

Sage had wanted an up close and personal encounter with a large predator, and now it looked like she'd get that and more. If there was ever a time she wished she could use magic, this was it. Her thought returned to the conversation she'd had with the boys. Immunity wasn't everything. Just like in the game they played, she could get taken out by blunt force. How would she fare against a five-hundred-pound lion?

The hairs on the back of her neck stood on end. Something was watching her. The weight of eyes she'd yet to look into had locked onto her. She knew it, and before she could turn and see the beast with her own eyes, a loud snort accompanied a gust of air blew against her back.

She clamped a hand over her mouth to stop herself from shrieking.

It was *right there*. How the hell could it have snuck up behind her without her noticing?

Goosebumps prickled on her skin. Sage didn't need to look. It was there. A great big lion. The heat from its breath was practically drenching her in sweat.

"Grey," she whispered urgently, praying the beast wasn't hungry. Maybe if she stood really still, it would leave her alone.

He turned, his eyes nearly doubling in size with terror. That confirmed it. The beast really was behind her. "Don't move a muscle," he whispered.

Deep rumbling breaths vibrated the air behind her, more a growl than a purr. Definitely a predator ready to strike.

How fast she could run? Would she be able to get in and close that cage door behind her, before one of its massive claws made mincemeat of her?

Maybe, just maybe.

She could lock herself in safely, but that would leave Grey. Asshole as he was, he didn't deserve to be mauled by a lion. *Shit!*

"What's our play?" Sage whimpered the words at her partner.

"Stay very still. Don't move a muscle. Don't blink. Don't even breathe," he warned, taking a ginger step closer to her. He held a hand out for her, just out of reach. "Easy now. They can smell fear."

The beast chuffed, blasting Sage's back with moist hot air.

She choked down a scream threatening to burst from her throat. Every instinct she had demanded she run.

Grey's hand trembled. He took another tiny step toward her. "Keep control, Sage."

He wasn't planning on pushing her aside and taking on the lion himself, was he? Knight in tinfoil armor right there. She hoped he had his machetes on him. Though they wouldn't do him much good if they weren't out and ready to be used.

The beast's musty breath warmed her skin, leaving more goosebumps in its wake. Was it sniffing? Deciding if she would make a good breakfast? She prayed to any god that might listen to let her escape safely.

"Focus on me. Look at my eyes." Grey's turquoise eyes filled with tears. Mourning her death already, no doubt. He could barely maintain the eye contact he'd demanded of her.

"I can't. I have to run. We have to run. The cage." Her voice trembled nearly as much as Grey's arms.

His eyes flitted over to the open cage door and back to Sage in a fraction of a second. "Okay. On the count of three, make for the gate."

"One," Sage began.

"Two," Grey continued the count.

"Three!" She took off running as fast as her legs would carry her. Arms pumping, pushing herself to top speed, she made for the cage.

Once inside she reached for the door handle, ready to pull it closed, but Grey wasn't behind her. Breathing so hard she nearly choked on the air, she cried out for Grey before she could bring herself to look.

He didn't reply.

Silence sent her mind to all the dark places she didn't want it to go. Sage mustered all the courage she possessed and lifted her eyes.

ELEVEN

"You should have seen your face!" Grey clamped a hand over his mouth to mute his laughter. Next to him, where the lion should have been, was a man, naked as the day he was born, crouching on all fours.

Reality struck hard as a slap to the face. Of course the animals here were shifters. Had she turned around, she would have seen the lion for what he was. Grey, the bastard, had played her the whole damn time. No glamours could fool a Terra. But shifters were creatures of multiple forms. Even now, as she really looked at the naked man, she saw the shadow of his other form hanging around him like a ghostly aura.

"Laugh it up, jerk!" Sage popped him hard on the back of his head, knocking his stupid fedora into the dirt. "You're a dead man!"

The lion-shifter stood and shook out his wild mane of golden hair. "Be a good sport. It's not often any of us get to play with one of you Terras." He towered over Grey, standing at least seven feet tall.

"And you are?" Sage asked, with a calmer tone than she'd used on her partner.

"Name's Caleb." He extended a hand to shake. "Welcome to my Wild Sanctuary, home and way station to the shifter packs of Clark County."

Sage took his hand, finding it hard to avoid staring. He showed no signs of being embarrassed by his nakedness.

She however, had a hard time keeping her eyes up top where they should be.

"C'mon back to the office." Caleb waved them on toward a building at the end of the first row of cages.

"That was worth every bit of your ire." Grey dusted off his hat, still chuckling. "You have to admit, that was good. I thought you were going to shit yourself right there on the pavement."

"I'm not giving you that satisfaction." Sage vowed to pay him back in kind with something truly embarrassing. But as her anger abated, she added another point to his tally. He and Caleb *had* gotten her pretty good with that practical joke.

"We'd work a lot better together if you'd lighten up a little." Grey put his fedora back on, running his fingers around the brim to make sure it sat up straight.

"This from the Boy Scout?" she threw at him. "Who plays by all the rules?"

"When you know the rules, you get to bend them however you like." Grey overtook her and walked caught up to Caleb.

"If you'd show me rather than beat me over the head with the rules, we'd have an easier time," Sage called after him.

"It's much more fun to watch you squirm." Grey threw her a wink over his shoulder and tipped his hat.

"Jerk!"

Caleb held open the door to his office, though Sage would have preferred he act less chivalrously while naked. Try as she might, it was nearly impossible to avoid staring. He was definitely a lion. Her mind wandered. A great *big* lion. Probably the leader of his pride. Everything about him screamed alpha.

"Go easy on Grey boy here, he's not completely at fault." Caleb closed the door then walked around to his desk, and thankfully retrieved a pair of pants. "We like to have a bit of fun around here."

"What exactly do you do here?" She failed to keep her eyes level as she watched each of his legs disappear into a pair of dusty jeans. Only when he'd finally fastened them at his waist was she able to meet his molten amber eyes.

"People… Humans," he clarified, "like to see wild animals. And here in the desert, it's not exactly easy to keep them and care for them in the way they need. Our people, however, have a double nature, wild and tame. This sanctuary allows us to have the best of both worlds and earn a little money while we do it."

"So you shift and put yourself on display?" Sage asked, not sure if she should be impressed or sad by the way of life they had adopted to maintain their secrecy,

"Some of us even do tricks." Caleb winked, clearly at ease with his situation. "We have a little circus here every weekend for the kids. Lion taming is always a hit."

The thought of a great big lion sitting pretty for a hunk of steak brought a look of amusement to her face that couldn't be hidden. The circus came to town twice a year, and her mother had never failed to take her to watch the acts. Caleb had just cast the Greatest Show on Earth in a whole new light. What a smart way to live!

"So what happened?" Grey cleared his throat, shifting from amusement to strictly business. "Someone not show up for work?"

Caleb's expression soured. "Exactly."

"Wolf, lion, or something more exotic?" Sage asked, feeling that shiver of fear trickle down her spine.

"That's the weird thing," Caleb replied. "It was one of our caretakers. All our shifters are accounted for. But our resident brownie disappeared."

Sage mouthed the unfamiliar word to herself, trying to re-call if she had read about them during her research or maybe heard someone else mention them.

"Magical Maids," Grey whispered the answer.

"To top that, we received a code violation recently. Human inspectors from the city are coming to do a thorough evaluation of our facility." Caleb picked up an envelope off his desk and waved it in the air so they could see the city of Las Vegas seal. "Coincidence?" he growled with sudden frustration. "We don't require as much care as a legitimate zoo would, so now we have to up our game to appear on the up and up for the humans. And all without our best caretaker."

Grey held his hand out. "Mind if I look at that?"

Caleb released the letter and collapsed with a heavy sigh onto his desk chair.

"Did you piss the brownie off in some way? Did they just quit on you?" Sage asked. Her mind wandered to the Mentalist, whose assistants had suddenly dropped off the face of the earth as well. In both cases it created a potential to have their business shut down or at the very least put on hold.

"Nah!" Caleb shook his head causing his wild mane of golden hair to fan out around his face. "She was always paid handsomely. In fact, we'd just built her a new trailer to live in here at the sanctuary. If she wanted for anything, all she needed to do was ask. We take care of our people. Shifter or not, we're family. Hell, just last week she asked for some extra time off. She'd found herself a new boyfriend – some rich guy who spoiled her with jewelry."

"Do you know who this new boyfriend is?" Sage asked curiously.

"Naw." Caleb shook his head. "She never brought him around."

"Why did you say rich?" Sage asked. "That seems a very specific comment to make, especially if you hadn't met the boyfriend."

"Just a guess, really." Caleb gave a half shrug. His casual body language added truth to his words. The only time he'd shown signs of stress had been at the mention of city officials inspecting his home. "The new man gave her this gaudy necklace. She claimed it was a real ruby, though we all thought it was a fake. Either way, someone buying jewels like that in the first week has to have cash to burn."

"We'll need to take a look at her sleeping quarters. Maybe there's some info on the boyfriend we can use." Grey handed the inspection notice back to Caleb.

"Sure thing. You guys have full access. Go wherever you like." Caleb waved a hand around. "We're all shifters here. Jasper, the alpha wolf, should be returning from his morning pack run any minute. We'll be opening soon. Just try not to enter any animal enclosures in front of the humans."

"Would Jasper have maybe met the new boyfriend?" Sage asked hopefully. Two missing person cases and no leads so far.

"I doubt it." Caleb rubbed his chin thoughtfully. "Come to think of it. I never caught a whiff of him myself, so I don't think he came on the property. You think the boyfriend took her?"

"We have to look at all angles." Sage wasn't sure how many more angles there were to look at, though. She hoped Grey, with all his silence as he stared off into space, was deep in deductive thought.

"It's always the boyfriend or the husband, eh?" Caleb's eyebrow arched sharply.

"Did she have a car? When did you last see her?" Grey fired off a quick round of questions.

"Her car is still in the employee lot. Her trailer is spotless, as usual. We haven't seen anything suspicious on security footage," Caleb replied, without hesitation.

"We'll need a copy of your security records," Grey added.

"Whatever you need. We'd really like to get her back. She was part of the family here." Caleb's smile faded. He reached into the drawer of his desk and pulled out a file labeled *Beth*. "Here's her employment records, to start."

Grey took the file and began to thumb through the pages. "Have you or your packs made any enemies in the city recently?" he asked. "Stepped on any toes of the casino folks, maybe?"

"Nah. We don't stir up trouble. Those guys with the white tigers came to call once, but we made sure they knew we weren't trying to take their spotlight. We operate publicly as an animal sanctuary. The money we take in goes to the care and feeding of our... people, not some corporate sponsors."

"How long ago was that?" Grey pulled out his phone and snapped a few pictures of the file contents before returning it to Caleb.

"That was a long time ago. We keep to ourselves here, for our own safety. You can talk to Jasper and his wolves. He's in the main trailer round back. My pride is pretty much an off-the-grid group. But if I hear something, I'll let you know."

"And Beth... has she been in any trouble that you know of?" Sage asked, not really expecting the answer to be yes, but feeling the words needed to be spoken out loud.

"Doubt it. She hardly left the sanctuary. The only reason that she had, as far as I know, was that new boyfriend she'd been going on and on about." Caleb's response sounded more annoyed than his previous answers.

"You don't have a name or anything to go off of?" Sage asked. "It would help a lot to know who this mysterious guy was."

Caleb looked suddenly like a deer caught in the headlights. "Look. I loved Beth like family, but when it comes to relationship girly talk, I tune out. I probably should have listened better, but..." He shrugged as if that was answer enough.

Men! Sage scoffed to herself. *If they only opened their ears to listen every now and then.* "Okay, thanks."

"We'll let you get back to your work." Grey nudged Sage.

Caleb stood and moved to the door. "I'm just as curious as you. Beth kept everything sparkling. I have everyone scrambling to get this place ship shape before the inspection."

"Are the inspectors are tied to the magical community?" Sage asked.

"That would make life infinitely easier. But no, they're all humans. So we've got to play our part perfectly to stay in business. This is our home." His voice broke. Sage could forgive him for his previous joke. Under that level of stress, he probably needed something to lighten the mood. He extended his hand to shake as he opened the door. The smile returned to his face as Sage took his hand, but she'd already seen through the mask.

"We'll get to the bottom of this." She hoped her confident voice might perk him up, though there wasn't much to work with.

TWELVE

Grey led the search through the rows of animal enclosures. He moved from one to the other as if looking for specific clues, but didn't tell Sage what those were.

No wonder he'd been a loner when she met him. Partners were supposed to communicate, but all he'd done was tell her to be quiet and follow. This time was no different. As she wandered behind him through the lion and wolf pens, Sage felt more like a tourist than an investigator.

The animal pens were a far cry from five-star luxury accommodations: dirt, some rocks, the occasional barrel of stagnant water she hoped was not for drinking. They weren't the type of places one would stash away valuables or even hide a body. None of the pride were suspects, as of yet, and she doubted the pack that shared space with them would damage their reputation by harming their caretaker.

"This looks promising." Grey walked toward a tiny house set atop a trailer. "Just the kind of place a brownie would live in."

As if pulled straight out of a fairy tale, everything had been scaled down to childlike proportions. Inside it boasted a quaint kitchen, living room, bathroom, and bedroom loft. But, crafted for a little person, it had hardly enough space for Sage and Grey to occupy at the same time.

"I used to dream about having a back yard cottage just like this when I was a girl." Sage admired the detail work of the inlaid wood parquet floor. The kitchen had all the comforts of home. Sure, the oven was Easy-Bake-sized, and the stovetop had only one burner, but it was all so perfectly placed – with not a speck of dust to be found. That surprised her most of all. They lived in the desert; dust was a way of life. Sage ran a finger along multiple surfaces looking for traces, but her finger came back clean every time. "You said magical maids?"

"Brownies are the OCD neat freaks of our world. They live to clean." Grey crouched to avoid hitting his head on the ceiling.

"She's either put a spell on this house, or she hasn't been gone long. No dust anywhere."

"This doesn't make any sense," Grey whispered with frustration. He bent down and shuffled papers around on the small coffee table. Nothing appeared to jump out at him as his attention shifted rapidly to the closet and then up to the sleeping loft. Each place he looked seemed to be less interesting than the last. His growls of frustration, however, grew louder and longer as the minutes passed with nothing to show for their exploration. Sage peeked around the kitchen, opening cabinets and closets. Other than being immaculate, the house gave them little of anything to go on.

Caleb had mentioned Beth having a new boyfriend. Sage shifted her search, looking for notes or phone numbers and names – anything that might reveal that all important detail. But even the trashcan sat empty. No one could possibly live like that, or be that OCD about cleaning. It was as if Beth were a figment of their imagination and the house just for show.

"Another dead end." Grey sighed as if resigned to this defeat. "Let's go. There's nothing to see here."

The Animal Sanctuary had opened its doors to the public; enclosures that had been empty were now packed with multiple shifters. Sage had never seen such a spectacle. Being Terra, when she looked into the animal pens she saw the lions, and also their human shadow, like a ghost hanging around them. The effect had her constantly blinking and rubbing her eyes to be sure what she saw was real.

"Mommy – lion!" a little boy squealed.

Sage glanced over her shoulder as they passed, catching sight of the child dragging his mother toward the largest of the lion cages.

Being able to see through the glamour without trying added a new dimension to how Sage viewed the world, but she couldn't top that little boy's excitement. In his innocent eyes, those cats didn't need to be anything more than they were. By simply existing, they were magnificent.

"Bit too late to chat with the pride. I doubt any of them are guilty, but we may need to come back again later to conduct interviews." Grey walked slower than usual, as if not all together there – deep in thought perhaps, something that looked terribly painful for him. At any moment she expected steam to come billowing from his ears.

Still new to the magical world, Sage didn't have much to offer, and opening her mouth without something good to add to the conversation would only give Grey ammunition to use against her.

Zack had mentioned talismans, and she'd meant to do a bit of research on that. It had to be important – the vampire wasn't one to mention something if it wasn't. His information generally came at a price, but clues were freely given. What kind of items could be talismans? Caleb had talked about jewelry. What if it really was the boyfriend? What if the jewelry absorbed them straight into the gem? Sounded legitimate. After all, Sage herself was wearing a necklace containing a stone capable of sucking the magic out of someone. However, that would leave their body behind, and no one had found a body yet. Grey would surely point that out if she opened her mouth to offer that as an explanation. And that too came dangerously close to revealing her own secret jewelry. Rather than speak, she continued to follow quietly as they made their way toward the parking lot.

Grey stared at his phone as they walked. He'd taken notes during their interview with Caleb and Marrin, he'd photographed the Mentalists documents when they'd visited, and he'd confirmed names and class types of the assistants both had claimed were missing. If there was something tying them together, Grey hadn't said. Or maybe he hadn't figured it out.

Between Caleb and Marrin, she'd take the former any day. He seemed genuine and protective of his little home.

Marrin, on the other hand – that guy was too perfect. He had one of those smiles that was meant to disarm. And Grey had said he was a siren; perfect for a Mentalist working on the Strip. Terras were immune to that kind of manipulative magic, but a siren could easily implant thoughts and suggestions into the minds of humans. Kind of a buzz kill, now that she knew how it was done. But could his skills work on others of the magical community? She opened her mouth to ask, but Grey cut her off.

"This is a transient town, but even I am wondering why we have two missing persons cases in as many days, both without a single clue to indicate what might have happened. No body. No blood. No sightings. No suitcases. Nothing!"

"I feel like I'm going to regret asking this…" Sage hesitated, knowing it was a half-baked question. "Do some magical types prey on others?"

"Yes," Grey replied, without a hint of sarcasm. "But there's usually evidence of the kill."

"So they're not…"

"Dead?" Grey shook his head. "I doubt it. But without a body, we can't rule it out."

"So what happened to them?" The more questions Sage asked, the less she learned. Everything was a dead end in both cases.

"That's what we're supposed to figure out, but with no evidence, motive, or witnesses, we're left guessing."

"Could someone be collecting magic?" Sage wondered.

"That's a troubling thought."

"What would they be collecting it for? Can someone use stolen magic? Zack mentioned talismans."

Grey's eyes narrowed suspiciously. "Depending on who is collecting…yes."

"Okay… So, what creatures absorb and use magic?" Every conversation felt like dental surgery when it came to Grey. He was supposed to be her partner. It shouldn't have to be so damn hard to get him to talk.

"Most just feed on magic. To use it would…." Grey stopped short again and stared down at his phone as if it held the answer.

"Would what?" Sage demanded, getting more frustrated by the minute.

"I just had a terrible thought. I hope I'm wrong."

"Planning to share, or just keep me in suspense?" Sage growled almost as loudly as the lions back in the enclosure.

"Forbidden magic. A conduit of some kind. Not attached. Not affected."

"English, please."

"Genies. Tricksters. Their magic isn't attached to them. It belongs to a talisman that others control."

Sage remembered the new tenant in her apartment complex. "Like three wishes if you rub the lamp, right?"

"Bingo. But they're a dodgy sort. Not someone I'd want to cross paths with in the dead of night." Grey looked truly bothered by this new lead. Meanwhile, both times Sage had run into her djinn neighbor, it had been just that– late at night.

Either she was supremely lucky or there were different kinds of genies and djinn. She hoped it was the latter. "They can't be all bad, right?"

"I've never met one worth trusting."

"How many have you met?"

"Enough to know better."

Sage opened her mouth intending to mention her new neighbor, but Grey cut her off. "They're all magical contractors, of sorts. Due to their particular curse, they have to barter services. So, they'll make you think they can grant your wishes; however, those wishes ultimately only serve the genie's needs. And there's the caveat, too – all magic comes at a price."

"They charge for wishes?" Sage hoped it would be as simple as that.

"The genie is only able to use his magic when it is wished. The cost isn't to him." Grey shook his head. "The magical transaction is the wish that activates the magic. And oftentimes the price is a soul."

Words caught in Sage's throat before she could speak them. The guy she'd met, Luke, seemed so normal. Down to earth. Friendly, even. They had to be talking about two different kinds of creatures. Grey called it a *genie*, but Luke had clearly identified as a *djinn*. "Hold on. I'm confused. So the djinn owns the soul? Or they are owed some kind of magical debt with collateral?"

"The price is not paid to the genie; it's paid to the universe for use of the magic. But don't think that the genie isn't angling to get something out of their magic being used."

"So then people make a deal with them for a little magical assistance, and once the deal is over, they're left with no soul? Who would do that?" Sage turned around and took one last look at the Animal Sanctuary. Had Beth made a deal with a djinn? She'd have to have something to show for it. Sage doubted the brownie had bargained her life for that cute little cottage.

"Sometimes the promise of having it all is tempting enough to sell one's soul." Grey shrugged. "My advice? If you meet one, run. They're completely untrustworthy."

"You keep calling them genies. Are djinn and genies different?"

"Call them what you will. Either way, they're cursed."

"Wait. They weren't born like that?" she asked.

Grey looked as if he regretted mentioning these tricksters. Of course she'd be full of questions; and he'd have to be the one to answer them. "Djinn were once powerful fae. But they abused their power. Their magic was stripped and bound to a talisman. They're only able to use the power they once possessed at the request of another. Since they can't use it for their own purposes, they have to trick others into doing their bidding. They usually only go after humans."

"Right because they have no magic." Sage made a mental note to find a nice way to tell her roommate to avoid Luke at all cost. "So a djinn has lots of power, right? Could that power be used to wish someone out of existence?"

"They can't erase someone's existence, but they can kill."

"That's a scary thought."

"Which is why I hope I'm wrong." Grey offered her the helmet and mounted his bike.

Sage's thoughts again turned to the new neighbor. He'd openly claimed to be a djinn but had done everything in his power to present himself as a friendly person. Was it all a trick?

Could he be tied to the sudden disappearances? "Do we have a record of all djinn who live in town?"

"Reading my mind now?" Grey asked.

"If I only had that power." It would make getting information out of him so much easier.

"We can run a search when we get back to the office. Most people notify their clans when they change residences."

"But do they have to register?"

"You're starting to sound like an agent, newbie. I'd give you an attagirl, but it would go straight to your head."

"Just following the logic train to its destination." She made a mental note to search for Luke in the ASSET databases the next opportunity she had. Grey had painted the djinn as evil, but despite her newbieness, Sage hadn't gotten that vibe from Luke. Pushy, sure. Overly friendly, definitely. But nothing to get her spidey senses tingling. Maybe he was just that good of a trickster. Or maybe he really wasn't a bad guy. She couldn't throw him under the bus without reason. Not yet, at least.

Grey brought the motorcycle to life and sped out of the parking lot.

THIRTEEN

The Animal Sanctuary had been the highlight of her day. She'd spent the rest filing reports in triplicate, documenting everything they had seen so far. Since they were still uncertain if the missing gemini twins and the brownie were linked, each file had to be documented separately. Her hands ached from all the writing she wondered how she'd be able to hold on to Grey when he drove her home.

Magic might not work on her, but Sage counted it a miracle when they pulled into the parking lot just outside her apartment.

A car was definitely the next thing on her list once she'd put enough of a dent into her student loans to afford it. As far as walking-friendly cities went, Vegas didn't make the list. Busses might be accessible, if time weren't an issue. The city sprawled out for miles in each direction and had no light rail or subway system in place. Public transportation added hours to what would otherwise be a twenty-minute drive. How long would Grey chauffeur her? She didn't even know where he lived. Not that it mattered. It never took long for someone to find playing taxi driver a burden.

She stepped off the bike and handed her helmet to Grey. "You want to come in for a bit? We're having a game night!" Sage knew the answer, but asking the question elicited a much more satisfying response than his reply.

Grey cringed. "You live this crap. Why would you want to play at it on your off time?"

"Because in the game, I can actually use magic," she shot back, without a second's pause.

"Pretend," he corrected her.

"Better than nothing." She smirked as she turned to walk away. The office closed promptly at 6 pm, forcing her to use her key and enter through a small gate on the side of the building next to the pool house. She unlocked it and turned one last time to see Grey speeding off down the road.

Her mind raced with all the clues she'd picked up during their investigation. There were so many new things to research. If nothing else, she was getting a trial-by-fire education in all the variety of supernatural races, which no doubt had been Ava's plan when she'd assigned these missing persons cases. At least her exploits would prove for interesting reading.

Sage took the path around the busy pool, heading toward her apartment. Just past sunset, the night was young and full of promise. Game night was waiting – a chance to blow off steam and make up for her horrible performance in the last dungeon crawl.

"My favorite Terra in the whole wide world." Zack's voice crept from the shadows. She found him sitting on the stairwell leading to her upstairs neighbor. "Home so late?" He stood and walked toward her. The corner of his mouth lifted in a lopsided grin that revealed one of his sharp fangs. "They're working you too hard."

"They have a gate for a reason. No uninvited guests," Sage grumbled, so not in the mood to deal with his supernatural bullshit.

"That was the same thing your roommate said to me when I came calling." He pouted a little too dramatically to be taken seriously.

"Don't," she warned. Showing up on her doorstep uninvited – he had some nerve. They might be civil to each other in most cases, but this was her home, and he was a vampire.

Zack didn't seem to understand the line he'd crossed. His grin shifted into a playboy smile. He winked, drawing her attention to his icy blue eyes. "Aren't we friends?"

"Are we?" Anger afforded her immunity to those lady-killer look of his. Adrenalin sent her heart racing. A vampire – a few feet away from her front door. So close to *her* human friends. How long had he been there, waiting?

"I'm hurt. Deeply." His expression dimmed but didn't fade completely. "After all the time we've spent together. The adventures we've had."

"Melodramatic much?" She glared at him, debating whether or not to reach for her pocketknife.

"Touché." Zack cleared his throat. "Perhaps I did overplay my hand a teensy bit."

"Look, I don't have the energy for this. You've been waiting here ever since my roommate denied you access… why?" She wondered if the myth that vampires had to be invited in was actually true.

"I did scrounge up some dinner, but yes, my goal for the evening was you." Still refusing to accept defeat, Zack waggled his perfectly manicured eyebrows at her. "Definitely worth waiting for."

What the hell was that supposed to mean? His words teetered on the edge of serious flirting, too much for her liking. Zack was a vampire. Even if she did want to entertain the idea of dating, his kind were the most off limits of anyone in her book.

Besides that, how dare he think to hunt in her home? "My neighborhood is not your personal buffet!"

"You must really think lowly of me."

He could pull that bottom lip out far enough to wrap over his head; feigning a wounded ego wasn't going to earn him any points with her. "You said it," she replied.

"You implied it. But let me set the record straight, so there can be no more of this drama between us." He straightened up to his full height and met her eyes. "I wouldn't dare harm those you care for. I respect you too much." His faux sadness faded with an impish smirk. "I got takeout along the way."

"I don't want to know." She groaned, covering her ears in case he decided to slurp or make any further show of how he took his dinner. Of all the Terras in the world, he had to choose her to be his friend.

"Can you stop pretending you hate me already? This game of ours has gone on long enough." Zack reached out and pulled her hands down from her head. "I get it. I should have called first. Sorry."

"You should be! This is my home. My sanctuary from all the crazy."

"Oh, honey, you have yet to see true crazy." He chuckled, but when she didn't join his laughter, he stopped and cleared his throat. "I'm guessing, by your sour mood, your day at the office didn't go well?"

"It was fine. No. I just have a lot on my mind."

Zack slapped his cheeks in mock surprise. "Captain Obvious. I didn't know you were a woman."

"Do you ever take anything seriously?"

"Only when I have to. Serious is boring. But from the look in your eyes, that's today's secret word."

"Ding, ding, ding!" Sage answered back.

"Oooh, what do I win?"

"I need a sounding board."

"Well, that is a prize worth celebrating. You're coming to me and not Grey or master Yoda?" Zack looked as if he wanted to laugh but held back, leaving his lip twitching at the corner.

"You just wait until Devon hears you called him that."

"Well, traditionally ogres are green." Zack beamed at her, all of his teeth showing. "But my point still stands. You're seeking me out for the wealth of my ancient wisdom."

"Slow your roll there. You might be ancient, but I have serious doubts about the wisdom angle you're selling. And technically, you came to me." Sage pointed to her front door. "My house."

"You got me there." Mischief glinted in his eyes. "What if I promise to act really smart?"

"How about you cut the act?"

Zack stared at her like a lost little puppy.

"Okay, look." She hoped she wasn't going to regret this. "You want a shot at proving your ancient wisdom?"

"I'd die all over again just for the chance."

"You tell anyone I asked you for advice and you just might."

"Promises, promises."

Sage blew out a cleansing breath. "Being a newbie means constant ridicule for what I don't know."

"Got it." Zack nodded like a bobble-head. "You don't want me to laugh like a madman when you say something stupid."

"For starters, yes. Jerk!"

"But much less of one than your partner, right?" Zack asked.

"Half a percent. Maybe more." If she didn't know better, she might have thought he was jealous of Grey. But that would be ridiculous.

"This is how you ask for help?" Zack huffed like a disgruntled teenager. "Comparing me to the Grumpy Avenger?"

"If you're too busy, I understand." Sage turned as if to leave, but hesitated before taking that first step.

"Wait. For you, anything." He answered too quickly; too easily. Zack's help always came with some kind of price.

"Careful, now. I might take you seriously."

"And I might have to kill you." His teeth glinted under the porchlight.

Sage refused to be intimidated. "If you ever do, make it quick."

"You take the fun out of everything, you know that?" Zack feigned annoyance. "Whatever. Speak. I'll be your secret keeper."

"You mentioned talismans earlier. Was that a direct clue or just an observation?"

Zack gave a non-committal shrug. "Bit of both, I suppose."

"Trying to point me toward a djinn?" She went straight to the point.

"That's more than just newbie speculation there." All the humor left his eyes. "The djinn are advanced level criminals. Please tell me ASSET is not having you investigate them?"

"But you pointed us toward them, right? Magical talismans? Aren't those what bind a djinn's power?" she asked.

"Yes and no. If your boss thinks a djinn is responsible for the missing people, then you need to pass that assignment to someone higher up the chain. Please, Sage…"

Hearing her name added weight to his statement, as if he truly cared. Sage glanced quickly over her shoulder, toward the balcony of Luke's apartment. Lights were on. Was he in there?

She'd forgotten to tell Grey about him. Buried under a pile of paperwork, she'd let the day get away from her. She made a mental note: Tell him tomorrow.

"I have no control over what assignments I'm given." Sage turned back to face the vampire. "And no one has confirmed the suspect yet. It's all speculation."

"You have no proof then?"

"No."

Zack sighed impatiently. "What *do* you have?"

"Magical assistants of various groups are disappearing. And the people they work for are at risk of losing their businesses."

"That sounds more like a mob takedown than a djinn," Zack suggested. "Is there a connection to the people being shut down?"

"Not that we could see. Both I guess are tourist-type attractions run by people from the magical community. The wild sanctuary and a magician on the Strip."

"There are plenty of those in this town." Zack sat down on the steps. "Magicians, I mean. Easy work. Competition isn't much of an issue there." His expression tightened in that same way Grey's did when he thought about something a little too hard. Sage might have laughed if she weren't interested in what he might say next.

"Who benefits if they're shut down?" Zack asked.

His question hit the nail on the head. The dots might line up if she could figure out the beneficiary. Random acts of violence weren't uncommon in a big city like Vegas, but the supernatural community was more closely knit and had a smaller pool to draw from.

Her silence forced Zack to speak again. "While you figure that out, I believe it's time to pay for services rendered."

"What?" She hadn't agreed to pay him for anything.

"Everything comes at a price, dearie." Zack cackled like an evil little goblin, reminding her of Rumpelstiltskin.

"How about a swift kick in the pants?" She offered, narrowing her eyes and daring him to charge her more.

"It is game night, right?" Zack batted those icy blue eyes at her. "Let me join your group." She'd never noticed before, but he had some impressive lashes to match. Like he was born to be beautiful. It wasn't fair.

"Yeah, we're having a make-up game tonight. But why would you–?"

"Have you met me?" He nearly snorted as his amusement came bubbling out. "I'm as geeky as any vampire could be. Why would I not want to join game night?"

"It's a dungeon crawl–"

"Need a warrior?" He offered eagerly, before she could finish her sentence.

With that one question, Zack totally cast himself in a new light. And Sage realized she'd been subconsciously giving in to her own prejudices. How many times had she been told that what a person was did not make them evil? Individual actions qualified that distinction; a lesson she needed to pay closer attention to, especially where Luke, the self-proclaimed djinn, was concerned. She could pass judgment on him later, if she survived her night with Zack. He might be a vampire, but he'd been nerdier than she in the short time they'd known each other, which was an excellent test of this "Not every bad guy is evil" theory.

But would her roommate be able to overlook the fangs? Matt had already shown himself to be touchy on the whole magical world issue.

"Give me a chance. I promise good behavior. Scout's honor."

"Did they even have scouts when you were born?" Sage deflected snarkily.

"So does that mean you'll let me join your game night?"

She looked to her front door and sighed. "Let me check with the boys first. It's their house as much as mine." The sudden thought that he might not be allowed inside came back to haunt her. "Wait here."

Zack looked defeated but stayed at the threshold. "Don't be long."

She opened the door and shut it immediately behind her. "Honey, I'm home."

Matt was busily setting up in the living room. Beer and chips flanked the newly drawn map for the night's adventure. "Your stalker friend has been waiting outside."

"I know. He stopped me at the door."

"What does he want?" Josh asked. He stood vigorously whisking up his homemade dip to go with the chips.

"You boys mind if he comes to play with us?" she asked casually.

Matt looked up like a deer in headlights. "He's a vamp—"

"Yes. But I'll vouch for him. He's not one hundred percent evil." Sage looked over her shoulder. Zack could probably hear every word of her conversation with those bat ears of his.

Josh didn't look too convinced. He stirred his mixing bowl faster, splattering bits of dill on his apron.

"If it helps, he says he can play a warrior, and we could use another meat shield." Sage kept her tone light. She understood their worry, vampires could be pretty scary. If it were anyone else besides Zack, she wouldn't have bothered to ask.

"How do we know he won't… you know?" Matt cupped his neck with his hands.

"Because he is not completely without sense," Zack answered through the door.

"He's got a point." She fought to maintain her cool tone. Eavesdropping wasn't earning the vampire any points in her book. "Harming me or anyone in my family would bring down the wrath of ASSET on him."

"So not worth it!" Zack added. "Believe me. They'd string me up to watch the sunrise without a trial if I hurt the newbie."

"Really, that's your play here? Insulting me?" Sage glared at the door as if she could see him through it.

"I meant it as a term of endearment." Zack's laughter mingled surprisingly with Matt's.

"Such a cute little noob." Matt's chuckling shocked her nearly as much as seeing a vampire on her doorstep had. But the fact he'd finally relaxed a teensy bit was a good sign.

"Do we have a choice?" Josh sounded as if he knew the answer to that question.

"I'll buy pizza!" Zack sweetened the deal.

Josh blew out an exasperated breath. "Oh, just let him inside before the neighbors complain about his yelling."

Zack opened the door before Sage could turn toward it. "Thank you! I promise. Good behavior."

"I didn't invite you in yet," she protested.

"But he said it was okay." Zack walked in and whispered in Sage's ear. "That whole door thing…not true, by the way."

She groaned. Her noob-like ignorance was showing again, and it seemed that human and vampire alike were keen to take advantage of it. "Then why bother with it?"

"You mean being polite and waiting like you asked? I did say good behavior, did I not?" Zack allowed a moment of silence for his words to sink in before throwing another impish wink her way. "Unless you want me to be naughty. Please, let me know…"

She fought the urge to slap him for completely leveling her before game night had the chance to begin. "You want to keep those teeth?"

"Your house. Your rules." He bowed and twirled away as he came up, walking into the living room as if he owned the place.

"Don't make me regret this!" Sage whispered.

FOURTEEN

Hours passed in laughter and bad puns as they fought their way to the castle beyond the goblin city, slayed a dragon, and rescued the prince. Even Matt, who'd initially had seemed the most concerned about a vampire joining their campaign, lightened up as if he had forgotten who he was sitting next to.

The evening moved at such a frenzied pace that it was nearly sunrise by the time they were ready to call it a night.

"You going to make it to your coffin before bursting into flames?" Sage walked Zack outside. Silvery light had begun to peek through the veil of starlight.

"Don't you worry about me. I've been around for a very long time." He glanced quickly toward the horizon. "I have never failed to find a safe place to sleep."

"You'd better hurry then. Sun comes up fast." She moved to give him a hug, but pulled back suddenly. Somewhere during the hours of gameplay her guard had dropped, but they weren't on those kind of friendly terms yet.

Zack's eyes narrowed. He stood scrutinizing her for a moment before finding his voice. "Honestly, I'm more concerned about you. I meant what I said earlier: if you're dealing with a djinn…" His breath hitched in his chest. He coughed to cover his sudden hesitation, but Sage saw through the ruse. His eyes, far too blue to be mistaken for anything but otherworldly, met hers. There was something else buried deep within those icy depths that she hadn't seen before, but Sage didn't have the words to match the feeling they evoked.

"Djinn are tricksters; the worst kind. And you are so…" Zack cut himself off with a sigh.

He shifted on his feet and fiddled with his hands as if his internal war had chosen body parts to represent sides. Finally, with a growl of frustration, he spoke. "Please just give the assignment to someone with more experience."

Sage had nearly forgotten their conversation from earlier. Of course he had to go and ruin her good mood by bringing it up, not only reminding her about work, and pointing out her inexperience with his fearful plea. "ASSET wouldn't assign me something they didn't feel I could handle." She puffed her chest proudly. "And I've got good people in my corner."

"Grey?" he scoffed. "Do you remember how he introduced us?" Zack's tone took on an oddly jealous edge.

"His methods are unconventional, I'll give you that. But he gets results." She defended, feeling strangely wrong having to do so with Zack. "And Devon," Sage added. "He's always got my back."

Zack looked around, making a show of searching their surroundings. "Neither of them are here tonight." He met her eyes again, daring her to deny the truth.

His overprotectiveness was fast becoming annoying. Sage crossed her arms and stared back defiantly. "Why would they be? I'm off duty."

"You're a Terra and a brand new ASSET agent." He pointed straight down at her wrist. "You don't have off time."

"You're not going to start on me with the go live in the barracks crap, are you?" Sage stepped backwards, inching closer to her door, ready to make an escape if he tried to pull rank on her. "I've already heard that from the team you're so desperate to discredit." Zack had gone from zero to asshole with breakneck speed. But what bothered her more than the sudden misogyny was the shift in his posture. His muscles had tightened and his eyes dilated, growing darker the longer they stared at her. Something had changed in him, and it was no longer clear what his intentions were. Zack's focus on her had become more than friendly, and his kind were known to lust after one thing above all – blood!

"I would never tell you where to live." Zack launched himself forward with impossible speed, closing the gap between them before she could register the movement. His hand found her mouth, preventing her shocked gasp from escaping. Zack stood nose-to-nose with her, so close she could feel the heat from his breath. "Sweet girl. So naïve to the dangers surrounding you; innocent to the true nature of the world." His eyes grew darker, choking out all of the color that gave them their unnatural beauty. All predator, ready to strike, he pinned her against the apartment door. "Words lose their meaning with creatures like you. Headstrong. Impulsive... The only thing you learn from is failure." The timbre of his voice deepened; his breathing slowed to a determined rhythm of raw desire. "A tempting target, giftwrapped for anyone willing to snatch you up."

Zack let his hand fall from her mouth but kept her pinned to the door with his body. Close as he was, his eyes weren't the only thing Sage focused on.

Those teeth.

Sharp as daggers. She'd experienced the sting of a vampire's fangs once before, and that sudden remembrance made her scars itch. "You're acting like a real jerk right now, Zack."

"I know." He flashed those teeth at her again. "And don't think I can't hear how excited it makes you. Admit it. You're more than a little turned on right now."

A knot formed in her throat. She swallowed hard, forcing it down so she could speak. "Excited is not the word I would have chosen." Her voice cracked, betraying the panic she was so desperate to hide. This wasn't the Zack she knew; he'd morphed into something dangerous, and she couldn't tell how real his threats was.

"Pick a word then," he taunted. "Make it a good one."

"Stop." She pushed against him, but found his body an immovable wall. "You're creeping me out."

"Fear, is it?" Zack laughed coldly. "Good. You should be afraid. Most don't survive being bitten." His breath blew against her skin, surprisingly warm, but the effect chilled her blood.

"The last one who bit me didn't survive." She attempted again to mask the tremble of her voice with the threat.

"Grey, your great protector, was there to save the day. Where is he now?" Zack's words struck her like a slap to the face, but before she could respond, he bent his head to the crook of her neck.

She cringed, expecting pain that did not come.

"I could have you right now." Zack's lips hovered, tantalizingly close to her throbbing pulse. He inhaled slowly as if savoring every note of her scent. "But the real question is, could you" – He lifted his head and met her eyes once more – "would you try and stop me?"

Zack's words implied so much more than a simple threat…. She couldn't let that happen. But, being pinned against the door severely limited her options. Sage scrambled for the right words to stall long enough to find a way out. "I thought Terras were an acquired taste?" She reached down, toward her pocket.

Before she could dig for the knife she kept folded there, his knee came up, forcing her legs apart, and he growled possessively in her ear.

"One taste of you was such a tease. I need more."

More than just a bad boy, Zack was pure sin wrapped in a taut body with maybe centuries of experience. A very small part of her, welcomed the excitement, but self-preservation trumped desire. "Get used to disappointment!"

He nuzzled her neck and pecked a kiss at her racing pulse. "Don't pretend you aren't thinking about it. I can smell your arousal. I can see the way you look at me."

Her legs nearly went out from under her.

"You're going to get yourself killed. I would be disappointed if someone else got to the prize before me." Zack pulled back enough to meet her eyes again. "Rather than fall victim to the wrong sort," he whispered, "let me have you."

If he had wanted to, he could have ended her right there. She hadn't even put up a fight. Fear shifted to embarrassment. He'd done this on purpose. He was screwing with her. That had to be it. Showing off his speed; going full demon. Forcing her to look at him in that light to make her understand that predators were all around. Everyone had to remind her of how new she was.

Adrenalin kicked in, giving Sage strength enough to shoved Zack away. "When did you get so ... protective?"

"You wound me." He feigned pain, clutching at his chest where she'd just struck him. "Have I not been honest with you from the start? You know what I am. You know who I am. Why would you expect anything less of me?"

Always deflecting with a joke. He was the worst kind of playboy. So easy to talk to; so gregarious; while underneath it all he harbored deadly ulterior motives. "Stalking in the shadows and threatening to eat me – this isn't the Zack I considered a friend." Sage struggled to maintain her flippant tone. The worst thing she could do was let him sense how close she was to coming unglued.

"I'm a vampire. No matter what you'd like to think, at the end of the night, I am what I am." He licked his fangs, purposely flicking the sharpest one with his tongue. "But that doesn't mean we can't both enjoy some of the fringe benefits."

"Vampires are such assholes." Her heart continued its drumroll within her chest. If it kept that pace, she'd pass out. That thought alone kept her from allowing it to happen. Falling unconscious around Zack right now was a recipe for disaster.

"You don't know the half of it." Zack chuckled with the same ease he'd had all night, as if nothing truly bothered him. Or perhaps this was the game.

Sage narrowed her eyes, daring him with her most dangerous glare to move. Thankfully he remained where he stood. "So tonight was all about teaching me a lesson on the nature of your beast, then?"

"Oh, no. I've been dying for an RPG group to form, but none of my people are really into that sort of thing." He shrugged and sent his eyes skyward once more, perhaps gauging how much time he had or trying to avoid Sage's hateful eyes. "Call it a perk."

"Did Grey put you up to this? What did he pay you?" It wouldn't have been the first time her partner had tried to scare her into submission.

"No one is paying me. Certainly not… Grey!" That got his attention. Zack's casual posture stiffened once more, shifting back to the predator. "I'm genuinely concerned. You're still so new. So fresh. So….innocent." He took a defiant step forward.

"Easy pickings." His eyes flooded with insatiable hunger, zeroing in on their target. "What chance do you stand here? If I weren't such a gentleman, what could you possibly do to stop me?"

Goosebumps sprouted across her skin. His words sent more than one red flag up, and every internal alarm she had went off at once. Fight or flight; with nowhere to run. Zack outmatched her in speed and strength.

"I'd find a way to rearrange your manhood before you could kill me. So if that's your plan, get ready for a neutering." She stuffed her hand into her pocket, retrieving the knife she kept for emergencies.

Zack's eyes followed her hands. He smiled as he took a step toward her. "You'll go down with a fight, but you'll still go down. That's the problem."

"Personal space, dude!" Her hand flew out to stop him. "Unless you really want to spend what remains of your immortal life one nut lighter."

"You'll enjoy it more if you don't struggle." He made sure she could see all of his teeth. "And so will I…"

"Stop it!" she yelled. "Quit screwing with me. You know, for a minute there I thought you were cool. I let you into my home. I almost trusted you. And then you pull this crap."

"I'm a vampire, not one of the good guys." His eyes made a slow deliberate trail from her head downward. "I have needs and the beast demands to be sated."

Sage flipped open the knife, making sure he saw it.

Zack held his hands up in surrender. "A seasoned Terra would know that about my kind. We're beasts at our core. As are many other creatures. You're going to–"

"I know, I know. I'm going to get myself killed. We've already been through that part of the conversation."

"You're a poor judge of people. You don't understand the darker side of nature. It's a trick. The worst of us come in the best-looking packages."

"I judge people on their actions, not their" – she scrambled for the right word – "packages."

"You haven't seen mine yet." Zack waggled his eyebrows. "But you'll have to put the knife down first."

"See? That bullshit. You just killed any chance you had of ever being invited back here."

"A worthy sacrifice, if it makes you see the true danger." Hunger thickened his voice. "And you never know. You might enjoy learning all about the beast within."

"Get out of here before I show you how beastly I can be!" Sage growled. "I don't have the energy to deal with your crazy right now."

He took a single step backwards. The sun had more than peeked over the horizon. Zack's haughty expression faded as he saw for himself – his time was up. "As you wish!"

"Don't!" Sage reached around behind her to locate the door handle, but kept her eyes on Zack. No way in hell was she letting him out of her sight until she was sure he had gone. "You don't get to throw movie quotes at me like we're all good here."

"I meant what I said. You need protection." Zack turned and walked down the path. "From your own naivety." After a few steps, he picked up speed and in the blink of an eye, disappeared from view.

Her hands shook so badly she could hardly grip the handle. Afraid to turn around, Sage fumbled as she fought to catch her breath and slow her heart. The door opened behind her and she tumbled backwards.

Matt was there to catch her before her ass collided with linoleum. "You want to explain to me what that was all about?"

"I think he was trying to hit on me." Sage cringed, suddenly feeling the need to take a scalding hot shower to burn away the shame. Zack had creeped her out in the past, but this time he'd gone more than a step too far. It was as if he'd become a whole other person – dangerous, deadly, sexy. No. A beast more creature than man. If he'd pulled that crap around Grey, he'd probably be staked out waiting for the sunrise. But he hadn't. Zack had done it here. Without witnesses. Targeting Sage when he knew she was alone and defenseless.

What frightened her most was that a small part of her had enjoyed being the prey to his predator.

"No." Matt spoke the word like an order.

"Duh. He's a vampire," she replied. Her heart still refused to settle. She concentrated on taking slow breaths. In and out. Slow and deep. Filling her lungs with fresh, cleansing air.

"You sure you're okay?" Matt steadied her and returned to the kitchen, finishing up with the trash and tying the bag shut.

"Yeah, Zack just threw me off my game," she lied. He'd gotten under her skin. Her thoughts were all over the place. "I mean… how would that even work, right?" She hadn't meant to say it out loud. But the thought was there. Aside from being part beast, Zack was still very much a man. He'd caught her eye more than once. Strong. Confident. Sexy. She assumed all the parts were in working order. Experienced.

"No!" Matt said again, as if he knew exactly where her mind had wandered. "I'm as open-minded as they come, but if you're even considering what I think you are… no!"

"I need sleep." Heat rushed to her face, cheeks burning with embarrassment. How could she even think these thoughts? No. She had to get a grip, she couldn't let Zack or anyone screw with her like that. Sage wandered off into her room, struggling to think of anything other than Zack.

Matt's voice again found her ears. "No!"

FIFTEEN

A few hours of broken sleep left Sage feeling more exhausted than before. Too many questions swam in her mind. And on top of the mystery still needing to be solved, she couldn't shake the confusion left in the wake of Zack's odd behavior. Had he been making a serious pass at her, or was he just trying to scare her straight?

Between multiple missing persons reports and deadly one-night stands, a workout session with Devon was a welcome distraction.

But first, breakfast!

She dressed for the day and packed her duffel for training. A quick stop at the pub for their famous breakfast sandwich would fortify her for whatever hell the day would bring.

And coffee, black and full of sugar. That was absolutely essential to keep her upright after the night she'd just had.

Sage left the apartment as silently as she could to avoid waking her roommate. Outside, the day had brought a nearly cloudless sky and warm weather. But as she stepped onto the front patio, Sage sensed something watching her.

"Who's there?" she called out, as the prickle of unseen eyes made the hair on the back of her neck stand on end. Her tired eyes failed to see even with the blazing sunlight overhead, but she felt relatively certain Zack couldn't be waiting in the wings. He'd be dead to the world about now. If it wasn't the first troublemaker on her list, it had to be choice number two.

"Grey?" she yelled. "Quit messing with me. I've got no patience for games."

"He doesn't treat you very well, does he?" A disembodied voice floated on the wind, masculine and familiar. Where had she heard it before?

"This coming from the man hiding from view?" She circled slowly, trying to locate the voice's owner.

"Perhaps you're seeing the situation backwards."

"Show yourself," Sage demanded. "I've had less sleep than coffee, and my temper is on a hair trigger."

"Do you promise not to hurt me?" he asked.

"I don't make promises I can't keep." Sage summoned all her courage, trying to sound as menacing as she could.

"So many people underestimate how scary the Terra race can be." Luke came smiling from out of the shadows. "I humbly lay myself at your mercy." He lowered his head, bowing with his arms held in surrender.

"Are you guilty of something requiring mercy?" Sage asked, wondering if the missing people were about to be accounted for. "Who acts like that? Bowing and scraping like some medieval peasant."

"I've learned, through experience, that it's best to show appropriate respect for the law." He lifted his head and met her eyes. "Especially when you're like me… cursed for the mistakes of my past."

"So you're just sucking up, then?" She rolled her eyes.

"Yeah, I guess." He nodded. His silvery eyes glinted in the sunlight. "Your vampire friend told you all you need to know about my kind. 'Advanced level criminals,' I believe he called the djinn."

She glared at him. "Eavesdropping on me?"

"Voices carry so easily in the quiet of the night." He shrugged and sent his eyes skyward to the balcony of his apartment.

"What else carried up to your lair?" Too early. Way too early for this level of annoyance.

He glanced downward at his arms. She'd seen this look before. She'd made this same look when people noticed her birthmark. "You didn't recognize me for what I was, even after I told you, the first time we met." His smile faltered briefly. "I'm so grateful for that. It's refreshing, to be honest, that someone didn't hate me on sight. That's why I've worked so hard to befriend you."

"I know what you are." Her eyes landed on his arms, watching the tribal tattoo flames licking his skin, mesmerizing in the way they moved, like living beings. "I wonder if others can see your markings move like I can."

"When the gods have branded you with their mark, it is done so that all will see." Luke's cheeks reddened slightly. "Punishments in my case, and insurance against future criminal acts."

Zack had been adamant about her staying away from his kind. For a vampire to warn you off a magical being, it had to be serious. But, like every other time she had come into contact with Luke, Sage failed to register a threat.

"If you want to be a friend, then cut the eavesdropping." Sage hoped she'd delivered the statement with authority, and restarted her walk toward the parking.

"I am trying very hard to be a good boy. That's why I'm here." Luke's words stopped Sage in her tracks. "With information I think you'll find helpful."

"Speak." She turned to face him again.

"How willing you are to listen when you see it is to your benefit." He laughed, but it failed to register as true humor.

"And we're done here. Thanks for wasting my time."

"Wait. Don't go." Luke's expression hardened. "That was a bad joke. I'm sorry."

"I don't have time for bullshit. I have a job to do."

"The vampire can't tell you what you need to know," he blurted the words out before Sage could walk away again. "And that partner of yours doesn't respect you."

"Exactly how long have you been stalking me?"

"Not like that. Never." He backed up as if expecting her to strike him. "I've seen you guys around the apartment complex, and I hear things. You aren't exactly quiet about your comings and goings."

Sage's cheeks ignited at the thought of what had happened a few hours prior. Embarrassment of the highest caliber knowing her neighbor had listened to the whole thing.

Luke continued. "It's my business to know things."

"Why?" Her hand slipped into the hidden pocket of her mother's old leather jacket. She fingered the dagger sheathed there, ready to pull it if he so much as took one step closer to her.

"Keeps me alive." He shrugged. "People in my position aren't welcome in polite society, least of all around the Terras."

"For good reason, it seems."

"That's low. Even for a young Terra like you." He delivered the words like a punch to the gut.

"The more you talk, the less I want to listen," she countered.

"We're getting off on the wrong foot. I'm here with good intentions. I'm not your enemy."

"All evidence to the contrary," she fired back.

"People are disappearing all around town. No trace. No connection, right?"

Sage looked away, not wanting to admit he was right, and at the same time very interested in what he might say next.

"The connection is what you're not seeing," Luke suggested.

"You speak in riddles."

"Part of my curse. Being direct is not exactly in my wheelhouse." His voice took on a somber tone. Sage faced him again, seeing the same emotion echoed in his silvery eyes. "Magic can't hide from your sight." He reached out with one hand and took a step forward. "Unless you aren't looking at it."

After her encounter with Zack the night before, Sage wasn't about to let another potentially dangerous guy near her. She gripped the dagger tightly and drew it enough for the djinn to see the hilt. "Stay where you are."

"I'm sorry." His outstretched hand flew up submissively. "I only meant to show you."

"Use your words."

He left his arm hanging in the air so she could get a good look at his tattoo. Unlike hers, which was static, Luke's markings swam through his skin like a living being. "My curse is constantly working to bind me, a reminder that all magic comes at a price. Even magic that can steal from others."

He might as well have been speaking gibberish for all she understood.

"Those who have gone missing have not vanished. They exist somewhere. The threads of magic still link to them. You just have to know where to look."

"So is that one of my missing people, swimming through your veins?" She gave him the dirtiest of looks.

"Would I be so stupid as to show you my guilt?" A muscle in his jaw twitched. "No. Even if I had the power to absorb magic as my own, my curse prevents me from using it at will."

"So then what am I looking at?" Sage groaned with impatience.

"What has the power to trap magic? And bestow that power to someone for use at will?" He spoke the words very slowly. "When you can answer that question, then you'll understand."

So much for a straight answer. Sage blew out a frustrated breath.

Luke looked as if he wanted to say more, but as he opened his mouth, another voice called out for Sage.

Dammit! All she'd wanted was a bacon egg and cheese biscuit and some coffee. But apparently the universe had other ideas. She turned to acknowledge her partner. Grey jogged up to her from the parking lot at a pace way too speedy for this early hour.

"Don't you ever answer your phone?" Grey called out before he reached her.

She hadn't even heard it ring. Sage reached into her purse, fishing for it, and looked back toward Luke to tell him goodbye, but he'd disappeared. *Back to his magic lamp.*

She'd have to tell her partner about him. Good or bad, it felt like the right thing to do.

"I've called you five times!" Grey barked at her. "Why don't you answer? What the hell have you been doing?"

"Are you a teenage girl? Leave a message if I don't answer," she snarled back at him. Her patience had been tested one too many times this morning by surprise visitors and cryptic messages. She wasn't about to take this kind of crap from him, especially not on an empty stomach.

"Don't you take that tone with me, newbie!" He glowered at her. "What are you doing out here all alone?"

"All alone? In my apartment complex? Paranoid much?" She threw the words back at him. "If you're so worried about my safety, then why didn't you come join me for game night?"

"Children play games." Grey rolled his eyes. "I'm neither a child nor do I wish to babysit them."

"Could have fooled me."

Grey crossed his arms and stared down his nose at her. "You still haven't answered my question."

"I was heading to the pub for breakfast." Sage gave him an impish smirk. "Is that allowed? I mean, c'mon, it's broad daylight out here."

"You should know by now that means nothing." The hardness of his scowl softened into a disappointed frown. The look in his eyes said he'd been worried. But *why* was a question she needed more time to answer.

"Don't pretend to care or anything."

"I don't, but losing you would mean paperwork," Grey threw back at her, with a nonchalant shrug. "And I don't have time for that mess."

She wasn't falling for that load of crap. "Between you and Zack, there is no way I'm ever getting lost, so you can quit–"

"Zack was here?" Grey's tone shifted to curiosity.

"Yeah, he showed up for game night." Her mind replayed the way his breath had blown against her neck. Zack had crossed the line in more ways than one. A chill raced down her spine, and despite the morning's warmth, her arms erupted in goose pimples. She quickly folded her arms behind her back to hide them from sight.

Grey's eyes narrowed. Had he seen her reaction? He moved in closer than personal space allowed for and took her chin in his hands before she could stop him. "You invited him into your house? Did he stay the night? Is he still there?" Curiosity morphed into a possessive level of inquisition as he turned her head to either side, as if inspecting her for marks. "Did he touch you? Bite you?"

Confused as she was about Zack's walk on the dark side, Sage had not yet had the requisite amount of coffee to process her partner's sudden rage. Her brain errored out, leaving her with one simple conclusion: guys sucked.

"Say something!" Grey demanded.

"I'm fine." She backed away, swatting his hand like an annoying fly. "Where is this coming from?"

Anger burned behind Grey's eyes, a sight she'd never seen before. "You just…" Grey stumbled over his words. "Please don't let him in again."

"Something you want to tell me?"

His nostrils flared with heavy audible breaths. "Never let a vampire into your house. I thought at least you would know that." Grey turned away from her, muscles trembling in his arms. He balled up his hands into fists that had no target. "I let you out of my sight for one minute."

"Hey, I invited you to come hang out last night, remember?"

His jaw was clenched so tightly she could hear his teeth grinding. Moments of silent rage went by before he answered. "Had I known you'd go call a vampire…"

"Whoa, now. I didn't call anyone. Zack was already here, waiting on my doorstep. And where the hell is this" – she waved a hand at him – "coming from?" Protectiveness she could understand, but his actions and attitude smacked of jealousy. *What the hell was there to be jealous of?*

"Do I need to spell it out for you?" he growled.

"You want to keep your voice down? My neighbors don't need to hear you yelling at me." No doubt Luke was listening in. She hadn't seen him leave, but his balcony was in plain view. Another problem guy she'd have to deal with at some point, but after the way Grey had reacted to Zack, no way in hell was she opening that can of worms yet. Pain had begun to throb behind her eyes. If this continued, she'd have a full-blown migraine before lunch.

"He's a vampire, Sage!" Grey lowered the volume of his voice, but the anger still came through loud and clear.

"You're the one always pushing for us to talk to Zack and use his information."

"When *we* need him. That's it!" His face had flushed, but the heat there was far from embarrassment. Full-blown rage bubbled within him. "You think he's your friend? Do I need to remind you he attacked you the first time you met him?"

How dare he throw that in her face? Sage nearly lost it. For all the protecting these men in her life claimed to be doing for her, they were all guilty of causing more than their share of danger.

After a deep breath to tamp down her own mounting anger, she answered, "You paid Zack to hurt me."

"Exactly. He attacked you because I gave him money." Grey's reply came without even the slightest hint of remorse. "What if someone else wants to pay him for round two?"

"Are you mental? What does it say about you, that you willingly sent a killer after me?" Sage glared at him, daring Grey to find some defensible reply. When he couldn't, she laid into him again. "You're no better than he is. At least Zack came clean and told me what you'd done."

"He doesn't do anything without benefit," Grey let out an exasperated sigh. "Telling you my dirty little secret was in his best interest. It made you drop your guard. Now you trust him… You're a fool if you do. He's not a friend."

"He's as much a friend as you are right now." The pain in her head was increasing with each moment they continued to argue. With no end in sight, she'd officially entered the Twilight

Zone, having to defend the horrible actions of one guy to another just as guilty of being a prick, both of whom she technically worked with and would have to see on a regular basis. Not exactly what she'd signed up for. Ava might not have a soft spot for her, but as soon as Sage had the chance, she was putting in a request for a new partner.

"Vampires are dangerous."

"Says the man who dated one," she threw the words in his face. "Or did you forget I knew that little secret of yours?"

"I've got a few years on you, Sage. And you don't know the whole story. Listen to my wisdom and don't make the same mistakes I did. A vampire is not to be trusted."

Sage squeezed her eyes shut and took a deep cleansing breath before reopening them. Misogyny aside, she still had a job to do. "Are we done with the lectures? Because I was heading to breakfast, and if you hold me up any longer, I might consider cannibalism."

"Going to have to be fast food." Grey softened his tone. "We have another missing person, and this one might be the connection we've been looking for."

SIXTEEN

Food worked better than magic on Sage's mental state. By the time Grey had stopped in the parking lot of the Sortilege Staffing Solutions building, she'd all but forgotten the argument they'd had.

"You weren't kidding. There is magical Human Resources!" Sage marveled at how well magical society blended with the human world. A single sign above the door was the only indication of the business they were entering, three simple words in flat black, outlined in white: Sortilege Staffing Solutions.

Set inconspicuously between two call centers in the middle of large business development center, it didn't seem very magical at first glance. But Sage knew better, imagining the wonders that lay beyond what normal eyes could see.

"You work for the supernatural police force and you're surprised by this?" Grey responded with extra snark. "Where else would someone of magical nature think to get a job?"

"You know, it's okay to just answer with a simple yes every now and again. Those of us who are still a little star struck are allowed a teensy bit of awe every now and again."

"Damn newbie." He sighed.

"You sound like a crotchety old man," she threw back at him. His attitude was exactly the reason she needed to terminate their partnership.

"Get off my lawn!" His mouth twitched, not quite committing to a full grin, but revealing his amusement all the same.

Maybe there was hope for him yet. "Was that a joke? Did Grey Maddox try to be funny?" Sage exaggerated the shock in her tone. "Stop the presses – this one's going on the front page."

"And this is why I can't be anything but a crotchety old man around you." The smile died just as quickly as it had started. "You take everything too far."

"Which is exactly what a crotchety old man would say." For all she knew, he might actually be an old man. No one had really explained the whole immortal aging thing. "Just tone down the asshole a bit, and we'll be good."

"I'll try to remember that, but you know how us old geezers are with memory." He fixed his fedora on top of his head and gave himself a quick look in the rear view mirror of his bike.

"See? You're learning already." Sage fought the urge to knock the stupid hat off his head and settled for a playful punch aimed at his arm.

Grey dodged the blow. "Are we done playing now?"

"And the fun-slayer returns," she sighed.

"We do have work to do."

"Yes, sir!" She saluted.

"Fall in," he replied. "Your mission: keep that giant trap of yours shut."

"You say that every time. It's kind of becoming your catchphrase."

"Fine." Grey's nostrils flared with an annoyed huff. "Try not to act all, what did you call it, star struck. This is a place of business."

"Magical business." The prospect of delving deeper into new aspects of the magical world trumped any animosity she had toward her partner.

"Always is. You remember Sylvia, right?"

How could she forget the shadowrunner? A shadowy woman as beautiful as she was deadly who could kill with touch. "Yeah. Is she our suspect or a victim?"

"She's our contact."

"Oh." That took the wind from her sails. They hadn't really gotten off on the right foot the last time they'd met.

Thank goodness for magical immunity. Sylvia couldn't hurt a Terra, but power like that demanded a certain level of respect. "Gotcha."

"Be cool. Follow my lead, and…"

"I know. I know. Keep my damn mouth shut." Sage finished his sentence.

Grey led the way.

She'd expected Hogwarts or some form of the Ministry of Magic when walking into the Sortilege Staffing Solutions building. Maybe not owls flying around delivering memos; that could get messy. Instead she was greeted by a drab linoleum tiled waiting room. A perfectly normal-looking woman sat behind a wall of glass. Busy with paperwork, she didn't even look up when they entered. A sign with the label *Receptionist* had been fixed to the glass, multiple times by the way the adhesive outlines framed it. The dilapidated state of the place killed what remained of Sage's excitement. Chairs that had seen better days, worn clear through to the foam padding, lined the walls, and a locked door prevented them from moving further into the building. Not that she wanted to explore further. Her hope of being amazed by magical people in their own environment had all but died, much like the cockroach she spotted on its back twitching in the corner of the room.

"You sure we're in the right place?" Sage whispered.

Grey paid her no attention. He walked up to the glass panel and slid a piece of paper under the lip. "We're here to see Sylvia."

The receptionist on the other side continued to stare at her work. "Do you have an appointment?" She smacked her gum as she spoke, her fingers still busily typing on her keyboard.

Grey tapped on the glass and held up his wrist to the window. "Yes."

The receptionist's eyes lifted briefly, widening behind cat-eye glasses as she spotted the mark. Her hands moved to a button next to her keyboard. "Sorry, sir," she said, as she pressed the button and a loud buzz signaled the locked door had been released.

"This way." Grey led Sage into the back offices.

It continued to amaze her how the mark she'd hated all her life had become a literal door opener. Sage followed quickly behind her partner.

The office opened up into a sea of open-air cubicles. Creatures of all kinds buzzed around like worker bees flitting to and from workstations, pollinating them with papers while retrieving stacks to bring back to their own desks. Flashes of light arced from one station across the room to another. A folder materialized as the light faded away. *This is more like it.* Sage stopped to take it all in.

"Keep up, newbie." Grey caught her gawking and pulled her by the hand toward the back offices. Those were more traditional-looking, with walls rather than dividers.

Sage spotted the wispy form of Sylvia floating back and forth as if pacing. The angry look on her face said this meeting was not going to be any easier than their last had been.

"You take your sweet time when it's not one of your own at risk, don't you?" Sylvia greeted them with a sincere look of disdain.

Sage bit back her snarky reply, remembering how volatile Sylvia had been in the past.

"Apologies," Grey replied stiffly. He took a seat in front of the desk and pulled out a notebook. "Can you give me some details on the missing person?"

"You mean to tell me that your boss did not give you any information before sending you down to my office? The incompetence of your agency is astounding!" Sylvia's form faded in and out as her voice rose in volume. "I have already told what I know to whatever lackey it was I spoke with on the phone."

The last time Sage had encountered this shadowrunner, she'd expressed no amount of love for the ASSET agency. But here she was needing that very group she'd spent so much time badmouthing. Karma was funny like that. Sage tried to keep her face neutral. Laughing would most certainly invite more anger.

Grey gritted his teeth. "The best way for you to help us find your missing co-worker—"

"Assistant," Sylvia corrected.

"Yes, fine… We need you to confirm the details and let us have a look around." Grey's continued civility was impressive.

"I wouldn't have noticed she'd gone, except Thalia makes the most divine cup of coffee." Sylvia floated toward a filing cabinet at the back corner of her office. "Nearly lost her to a café last year, but I convinced her she'd have a better career here with us."

"That wasn't very nice," Sage blurted out.

"Barista." Sylvia glared back at Sage as if sizing her up. "How many successful coffee waitresses do you see out there?"

"What if she wanted to open her own café?" Sage replied weakly. Even Grey was glaring at her now. Open mouth, insert foot.

"Then she would need the business connections only I can help provide for her," Sylvia sneered. "Or would have if she hadn't poofed into thin air." She retrieved a file from the cabinet and floated back across the room, slamming the manila folder in front of Grey.

"That is your area of expertise, though, isn't it?" Grey lobbed the insult at her with a level tone.

"Am I being accused of something here?" Sylvia's form shifted from cloud to woman violently.

"I'm simply looking at facts," Grey responded. "Please, feel free to fill in the blanks for us."

Sage's jaw nearly dropped from shock. After an accusation like that, she expected Sylvia to fly off the handle, but rather than assault them with a verbal tirade or worse, Sylvia returned to her human form and let the haughty mask slip. "Thalia didn't show up for work yesterday. Her car is still parked outside. No one has seen or heard from her. I'm worried."

"So the last place she was seen was here?" Grey noted and continued his interrogation. "Is there any security footage we can look at?"

"We've reviewed all the video. She's not there." Sylvia wrung her hands as her answers continued to offer nothing helpful.

"I'm sure you'll understand that we need to look at the security footage ourselves. To see anything you might have missed," he added.

"You blame me, don't you? Is this how you operate? Insult your clients?" Sylvia looked as if she was one spark away from blowing a fuse. And Sage didn't want to be anywhere near that explosion.

"I don't need to remind you that Terras can see through magic," Grey continued, unfazed. "If that's what took Thalia, we might see something your eyes cannot."

"Shadowrunners see through magic too, you know." Sylvia faded into nothing and came back as if punctuating her statement.

"Be that as it may, we still need to see. Standard protocol. Take it up with the boss if you need to."

Sylvia materialized into her human form. She pressed a button on her phone and shouted, "Get me copies of the security footage for the last forty-eight hours."

"Thank you for your cooperation," Grey said. "Now, can you tell me what her class and talent was?"

"Kitsune," Sylvia said, after a slight hesitation. "It's all in her file." She shoved the manila folder at him.

More words Sage didn't know. She'd have to look that one up later, but clearly that designation was of some importance.

"No wonder you wanted to keep her around." Grey's comment earned him an icy glare from Sylvia. That must have hit closer to home than Sage's earlier remark about the coffee shop. Grey nodded to himself as he made a note. "How long had she worked for you?"

"She came to us a couple years ago." Sylvia replied. "She was young, only one tail, but sharper than all the flunkies here combined. I had hoped to groom her for success."

"And what did she do for you here? Besides make coffee?" Grey asked.

"She was my eyes and ears for newly hired. She kept tabs on those in their probation periods with new employers and acted as liaison for my department."

"So she knew who was where and what they were working on?" Grey clarified.

"Why does it sound like you're interrogating me,"– Sylvia threw her hands on her hips. A dangerous glare returned to her eyes – "rather than helping to find where she went?"

"Just being thorough," he replied. "Did she have any possessions? Trinkets she never went without?"

"Her essence, you mean?" Sylvia asked.

"Yes," he replied.

"I don't have it, if that's what you're implying."

"Why are you so jumpy?" Sage asked.

"Don't you take that tone with me!" Sylvia turned her icy stare on Sage. "You know very well how this works. I'm a Shade. Always first to blame."

"No one is blaming. I'm just gathering information to make a case." Grey's tone never wavered from the baseline.

"She never let her keys leave her sight. I assume her energy was disguised as one of her charms. There were at least fifty charms there. She jingled like Father Christmas when she walked down the hallway. But no, I don't know for sure. Why? Have other kitsune disappeared?" Sylvia asked, a little more calmly.

"We have to cover all the angles. If her power was taken, she'd go with it. Just ticking boxes on my list," Grey explained.

"Feel free to go through her desk and look at her car if you need to." Sylvia's tone changed. She stopped floating and took her seat behind the desk. "When you find her, make sure she comes back here."

"Hard to find a good assistant these days?" Sage asked snarkily.

"Contrary to popular opinion, I do have feelings," Sylvia replied with equal measure. "I took her under my wing. I wanted to see her succeed. And yes, I am worried about her. She's like you with a little less attitude; full of potential. Youth are often corrupted before they can see what's happening."

"If she had one tail, she had to have at least been around for a century," Grey added.

"As a damn fox. First tail, first transformation to her human form," Sylvia said defensively.

Clearly Sage had a lot more research to do. "So she was a newbie to being human?" she asked, knowing the moment the words left her lips she'd earn more newbie ridicule herself.

"Regular Captain Obvious, aren't you?" Sylvia beat Grey to the punch on that insult.

Sage chose to keep her mouth shut, rather than stick her foot in it again.

"We'll have a look around and see what we can find." Grey stood and pulled Sage's arm up. "We'll be in touch if we need more from you."

SEVENTEEN

Searching around Thalia's desk hadn't produced anything other than papercuts. Sylvia had said she'd only been recently unaccounted for, but based on the tipsy tower of papers in her inbox, the fox had to have been A.W.O.L. a lot longer. Either that or she was a serious slacker.

Grey had acted oddly closed off the entire time they'd been there. Sage watched him pick through papers, and more than once, he stuffed some of them in the file on Thalia that Sylvia had given him. He might have been onto something, but in keeping with his usual secretive behavior, he made no effort to clue her into his plan.

As far as she was concerned, they left Sortilege Staffing Solutions as empty-handed as they'd arrived – no real leads, no new suspects, and no connections, only the vague second-hand conversation about yet another magical being she didn't know.

"You're going to give me the details on the kitsune now, right?" Sage asked, as they walked out to the parking lot.

"You have the same access to the computer systems and libraries as I do." Grey shielded his eyes against the glaring afternoon sun. "Do some research of your own." He looked around the parking lot.

"That's a helpful attitude to take."

"Better than a lazy one." His attention shifted from the parking lot to the roof of the building. Clearly searching for something, but as usual not telling her what it was.

"You obviously know a bit about them. It might be beneficial to the case if you share so I'm not wasting time researching old information."

"It's all old information," Grey replied mechanically. He wandered through the parking lot, zigging and zagging through cars. Occasionally he'd stop to peer into one, but never for more than a moment.

Sage followed like a lost little puppy, grumbling. "So very partner-y of you."

"Sylvia seemed angry about her missing assistant," Grey commented, as he squeezed between two cars parked close together.

"She couldn't care less about Thalia," Sage replied.

"Why then do you think she became so agitated?"

Was this a test, or was he really interested in her input? Sage waited for her thoughts to gel before answering. The last thing she needed was more of Grey's ridicule.

"She's taking our investigation as a personal attack."

The corner of Grey's mouth quirked up. "Very good."

"That woman has too much pride," she added.

"That she does. But pride isn't fueling her attitude." Grey stopped next to an old purple VW Bug. "This is Thalia's."

Sage tugged at the handle. "Locked."

"We don't need to get in. Just give it a quick look. Any signs of foul play?"

They looked in opposite windows.

Definitely a girl's car. A pair of fuzzy dice and a set of Mardi Gras bead necklaces hung from the rear view mirror. The steering wheel was covered in a fuzzy purple material matching the outer paint job, and a fox decal sat dead center on the back window. Other than every cup holder in the car being filled with old coffee cups, nothing stood out as a clue.

Sage met Grey's eyes and shrugged, having nothing to say. The car looked like a car, but saying that offered nothing to the conversation.

"I didn't have much hope there either. But we had to at least look." Grey turned and began the slow march toward his bike, now on the other side of the parking lot from them.

"You never told me why you think Sylvia got all uppity," Sage called after him.

"She was quick to make sure we weren't pointing the finger at her. Did you notice that?"

"Why would we? She'd be stupid to draw attention to a missing person by calling us to investigate."

"Wouldn't be the first time someone tried that."

"So you do think she's a suspect?" Sage asked.

"Shadowrunners are the most feared of all the Shades. We have homework to do when we get back to the office." Grey moved faster now between the cars once his bike came into view.

"That still doesn't give us much to work with. Even if she did it, where's the body?" Sage wondered aloud.

"You're asking yourself the wrong question." Grey turned and handed the manila folder to Sage. "How does this case connect with the others?"

She opened the file and looked through the mess of pages Grey had swiped. Most of the file was Thalia's employment information: her address; her resume. None of that struck any chords with her until she flipped to the back. A page labeled Temporary Employment Evaluation had Marrin's name written on it as well as the gemini twins. The next page looked older, as if it had been around for a while. Staple marks and ripped corners made it look as if it had been roughly pulled from whatever file it had originally belonged to. But Sage recognized the Animal Sanctuary's logo on top of the contract for hire agreement.

"The missing assistant is the connecting point." Sage half-gasped as the realization struck. "Thalia had a hand in the placement of both Marrin's people and the brownie at the Animal Sanctuary."

"And now she's gone missing too."

A blur caught Sage's eye. At first it appeared like a small blip on the horizon, but it traveled with impossible speed. Taking the shape of a cloaked figure, it came careening into Grey's back before Sage could get a good look at it.

Grey tumbled forward, the file in his hands spilling out its contents as he came crashing into Sage.

Unable to stop his descent, Sage pivoted out of the way, managing to stay on her feet while Grey met the pavement with a loud groan.

Sage looked all around, searching for signs of the cloaked figure, hoping to avoid another surprise attack. "What the hell was that?"

"A sign. We're on the right track." Grey picked himself up. "On your guard."

He didn't need to tell her twice.

The shadow appeared again. "Behind that car," Sage whispered.

Grey balled a fist, ready to strike, and took a cautious step.

Sage held her breath and watched him inch closer to the slowly bobbing shadow. The hairs on the back of her neck prickled, and in a frightening instant, she realized Grey was after the wrong shadow. Something was behind her. Fight or flee? Her mind struggled to answer. Sage instinctively spun on her heel. The cloaked figure came into focus. Smaller than she'd expected. Childlike in size except for the brown cloak that draped to its feet. Where a face should be, she found only more brown cloth. Not a single bit of skin was showing. The moment that realization hit her, so did a tiny gloved fist.

Pain struck like lightning, racing in all directions across her skull.

Sage dropped to the ground and stuck her leg out blindly, hoping to take out an ankle or trip the cloaked figure before it had a chance to surprise her with another blow.

Her ears rang, muting all sound, but somewhere in the back of her head she heard Devon's voice like a ghost in her mind: *Don't be a victim.*

This wasn't training. There were no breaks. No mercy. *Do or die.*

A brown booted foot came up toward her. She dodged, rolling away. As soon as her hands found the pavement, Sage pushed herself up to her knees.

Grey had disappeared, and she had no time to look for him. Sage turned to the cloaked figure again. Tiny as it was, she hoped she could overpower it with sheer force. She lunged with a fierce roar and rammed into her attacker's abdomen.

They both came crashing to the ground, but Sage had the advantage. Landing on top, she unleashed a volley of punches at the cloaked figure. But where her fist should have collided with flesh, she found only air.

The cloak and whatever had given it shape evaporated into nothingness, as if it had never been there to begin with.

The pain however still rang in Sage's ears, so loudly she couldn't hear her partner calling out for her.

He placed on her shoulder.

She turned on him, fist cocked and ready, but relaxed when she met his eyes.

He mouthed something, but it was no good. She couldn't hear him.

Grey's face hardened. He pointed to the ground. During the fight, he'd dropped the file of Thalia's information. There should have been scattered pages, but not even a shred remained.

Sage sighed, defeated. That had been their best lead.

Grey took her face in his hands. The look in his eyes was something she had not seen before. Sadness? No. Concern. She had seen that look once before, when that vampire had nearly made a midnight snack of her on their first mission. Did she really look that bad?

The warmth of his hands felt nice. Soothing. He rubbed the spot where her pain seemed to be emanating from, and like magic, it lessened. The ringing didn't completely stop, but the volume lowered from ten to five.

"I think that little show of force just proved Sylvia belongs on our suspect list." He released her face and stood. "That thing that attacked us wasn't a shadowrunner, but damned if it didn't act like one. And they have the file."

"You think this was Sylvia's doing? But why?" For every answer she came up with, another question filled the void. Sage pushed herself to stand and dusted off her ruined jeans.

"*Why* is a question I keep asking myself. Those dots have yet to line up. But, while motive is important, we have something else equally valuable: a trail to follow."

"Which still leads us back to the question of bodies. Where the hell are they?" She didn't care if he called her Captain Obvious or not. They were chasing their tail. No evidence, no motive, and only a very flimsy connection between the missing people. It was a start, she'd give him that, but hardly the break in the case either of them had been hoping for.

"Each missing person vanished without a trace." Grey puzzled over it loudly. "No one poofs out of existence. There is always something left behind."

"I opened the Pandora's box with that question, didn't I?" Sage had said it as a joke, albeit a bad one, but the glimmer in Grey's eyes was more than amused.

"Newbie, you might just be on to something." He helped Sage to her feet. "We've got some homework to do!"

EIGHTEEN

Hours spent staring at computer screens, absorbing every word of knowledge she could find on shadowrunners, Pandora's boxes, and djinn curses, did not provided any of the answers Sage had been hoping for.

Grey had run with her offhand comment, convinced that someone had the mythical box and was trapping people inside its prison. The only problem with that theory was the lack of motive. As far as their records showed, the missing people were all squeaky clean, fly-under-the-radar types. No gambling problems, no bad debts, and no known enemies. Their bosses were all mourning their loss; even Sylvia, though she still firmly sat at the top of the suspect list.

On top of their squeaky clean record, all the missing people were of seemingly inconsequential power.

Sage flipped over her notes and wrote *kitsune* at the top of the blank side of the page. Her hand cramped, protesting the motions as she finished the word and took a good look at what she'd written.

Doctors' scrawls were more legible. Sage sighed and let her shoulders slump as she leaned back into the padded cushion of the office chair. The muscles all the way up her arm into her back ached. She'd been hunched over the keyboard and note-book all afternoon. The sun had gone down, and when she looked around the room, she noticed that most of the desks had emptied. Agents had either gone home for the day or were out on assignment. A peaceful quiet had settled over the office, but at the rate she was going, Sage would fall asleep at her key-board if she didn't get up and move around a bit.

She stood and stretched, reaching for the ceiling, lifting all the way up on tiptoes. Tension threatened to snap her like a rubber band, but she held the stretch through a few deep breaths. As she came back down, a wave of relief crashed so hard over her she couldn't stop the moan that left her mouth.

Sitting down was not an option, at least not at that point. "I'm going to take a lap, Grey," she said, still twisting in her full body stretch that brought more relief than it should.

If he heard her, she'd never know it. Grey had buried him-self so deeply into his computer screen he looked like the male version of Ava.

She doubted he'd even notice her absence. It wasn't like they'd said anything of substance to each other over the past few hours anyway. Caveman-like grunts didn't count. She closed up her notebook, shoved it into her bag, and headed out for some fresh air, or at least coffee in the break room.

ASSET Las Vegas was a whole different beast at night. Calmer. Relaxed. Maybe it was the lower number of agents on shift, or maybe it was the fact that only half the fluorescent lights were on, leaving the halls in a pleasant twilight-esque glow. Either way, Sage liked this low-key version. She wandered the halls, letting herself commit the map to memory, noting landmarks like the barracks wing and the break room. They had a game room she'd never seen before. A few people occupied this room, some playing video games, others at the pool table, getting ready to rack up for a new game. She stopped for a minute – tempted to go and introduce herself – gazing into the room like a stalker.

"You didn't show up for training this morning." Devon's voice nearly made her jump out of her skin.

She hadn't heard him come up behind her. "Don't do that!" she said, louder than she'd intended. Her heart pounded so fiercely it echoed in her ears.

"You're getting sloppy. Anyone could have snuck up on you while you were ogling those guys." Devon smiled and waved to the room.

"I wasn't ogling." Heat burned Sage's cheeks, and she moved quickly to take herself out of the line of sight. "Not cool at all."

Devon crossed his arms, amusement plastered across his face, as he watched her struggle to regain composure. "You deserved that. There are consequences when you miss training."

"Blame my partner. He absconded with me before breakfast." Her heart slowed after a few breaths, but the burn of embarrassment still remained.

"Break in the case?" One of Devon's eyebrows lifted curiously.

"Yes and no," she sighed.

"You look like something's bothering you." He glanced into the game room. "I doubt it's the missed connection in there. Let's walk and talk."

He didn't have to say where they were headed. She knew; and welcomed a little prayer and penance in the house of pain. Her mother had always said a good workout was the best path to a clear head. And none were better at putting Sage through her paces than the master of combat training himself.

Devon flicked on the lights as he entered the training room. "Grab some mat and start stretching."

She set her stuff down and began warming up while Devon disappeared into the back room and returned with bottles of water and towels.

"So, your first case… not going as expected?" He took a spot next to her and led with a butterfly stretch.

"Yes and no." She followed into a wide v, folding forward until her nose nearly touched the mat.

"Ambiguity doesn't help me help you. I'm going to need some specifics here, kid."

"I need answers." Sage groaned more from the stretch than her own frustration. The beat down she had taken earlier – combined with an afternoon as a desk jockey – left her muscles angry and tight. "So many questions. Nothing is making sense. And Grey and Zack…. great big douches."

Devon sounded as if he were choking on air. She couldn't see his face. He'd rolled onto his back and brought his legs up in the air. "I'm not going to touch your relationship problems, but I can try to help with answers of a magical nature." He moved into figure four position.

Sage followed, tight muscles protested the stretch at first, but as the heat simmered from her hips all the way down the back of her thigh, they melted in submission. "I don't have relationship problems. I have a jerk for a partner and a vampire as my primary eyes and ears on the streets."

"Did you expect something else?"

She sighed, realizing that she sounded like a petulant child. "Forget it. There are more important things."

"Such as?" Devon asked.

Sage switched legs, letting the burn heat up both sides of her lower body. "I'm seriously lacking in knowledge of magical beings."

"So you need me to be your personal database too?" Devon stood and stretched his arms over his head, reaching for the sky. "Knowledge comes at a price."

"Everything comes at a price."

"Way of the world, child!"

"So the kitsune. What do you know about them?" Sage came to her feet and shook out her arms, feeling warm and ready to begin.

"Foxes. Shifters."

"So they transform back and forth between fox and human?" Sage lowered into a fighting stance.

"The fox is their original form. They go through a type of metamorphosis around the century mark and begin to shapeshift." Devon threw a few quick jabs at her. Warning shots, easy to deflect. "More than simply shifting, they can copy themselves into any human form they wish when old enough."

Sage countered, dropping low to sweep his feet. "That's pretty handy."

"It is. And more than just a glamour." Devon hopped back just out of reach. "I don't believe Terras can see through it. I know I can't."

"So they become a true doppelganger?" She watched him closely, knowing better than to follow his fake retreat. Having been on the receiving end of a few too many surprise strikes while she was off balance, she chose to wait for his next attack.

"For lack of a better word, yes. Tricky little things. And they're wicked smart…fast too."

That would definitely be magic worth stealing.

Devon's eyes darted from her to the wall of mirrors and back again, just long enough to make her wonder if someone else had come into the training room. Last time, Grey had surprised her. But he'd set down some serious roots trying to figure out the unknown motive. It would take an act of the gods to get him to move at this point.

Devon struck fast. Before she registered the movement, he landed a nasty palm strike, knocking the air from her chest.

She crumpled to the ground, knowing another blow was coming, and used the momentum to roll away as she fought to regain her breath.

Devon sent a nasty kick, aimed at her knees. Struggling to get to her feet and doge at the same time, the full force of his foot found her butt cheek instead.

Pain with the promise of more helped her to focus. She narrowly dodged another strike as she struggled to get back upright and reset.

Devon was not in the habit of giving quarter to anyone. Tough love, he called it. But love had nothing to do with it. His fist came at her, moving as if in slow motion.

Sage reacted instinctively, executing a perfect deflection, and as Devon's momentum took him past her body, she landed a hard strike against his shoulder.

She took her momentary victory to completely fill her lungs and set herself back in fighting stance. "A kitsune can't steal or absorb power, can they? Grey mentioned something about a kind of energy ball."

Devon shook out his arms and took a moment to roll his head side to side a few times before turning to face her. "Their energy can be stored in a specially bound object that they keep with them. Kind of like a safety deposit box for their magic."

"Can anything else be stored in it?"

"Don't think so." Devon scratched his head. "No. It's tied to their life force. Only their magic can be contained. I have heard rumors that a kitsune could be controlled by someone else possessing their ball."

"Really?"

"If it's true, it rarely happens." He dropped low with a sweeping kick aimed at her legs. "Foxes are wicked smart."

Sage countered with a jump kick, nailing Devon in the same shoulder she'd hit moments earlier. "Our latest missing person is a kitsune. So…." She let that revelation hang in the air.

Devon's eyes watered as his back hit the mat. He took a moment to recover before he replied. "You're dealing with some serious evil if they outsmarted the fox."

"Evil like a djinn?" Sage held a hand out to help Devon up.

"That's a bit of a leap. Sure, they're in the spectrum of evil. But… I'm not sure they fit the profile." Devon walked to the bench and grabbed his water. "I take it you might have one in mind?"

"That's just it." She hadn't revealed her neighbor to anyone yet, mostly because they all had biases against the djinn, and she felt the moment she mentioned anything, she'd be on an even tighter leash than she had been. *Here goes nothing.* She crossed her fingers. "I do know a djinn, but he doesn't seem all that evil."

"That's kind of the point. They aren't going to come right out and say, 'Hey, I'm evil.'"

"I know that, but I just don't get the whole doom and gloom vibe from him."

Devon lifted on eyebrow curiously. "What *do* you get?"

"He seems like he wants to help." She picked at the nails on her left hand and shifted her balance from one foot to the other. "I don't know. Like he's trying to lead me toward something, but covertly."

Silence passed between them while Sage waited for Devon's reaction. Not only had she met djinn, she'd interacted with him… alone. Had she said this to Grey, he'd have berated her for putting her life in jeopardy.

"The djinn always have their own agenda." He hadn't yelled. Sage was thankful for that, but there was no mistaking the seriousness of his tone. "You don't get cursed into that life without a reason."

"No one has ever been falsely accused?"

"These are high-level magic abusers. Not petty thieves."

"So I should let Grey know about my new neighbor?" Sage blurted out the real reason she'd mentioned the djinn. Luke was nearly unavoidable, living in her apartment complex.

He mopped his head with the towel and blew out a loud sigh before replying. "Only you would have something like a djinn living next door."

"You don't sound surprised." *Or mad.*

"Why should I?" He shook his head. "This is you we're talking about."

"And yet, you don't sound terribly bothered either," Sage noted suspiciously. "Everyone else goes on red alert when I mention the djinn."

"They aren't known for running in the best of circles. But their danger lies in the use of their magic." His eyes narrowed as he met hers. "You haven't made any wishes, have you?"

"No, obviously. Do I look like a millionaire?"

"Good. Keep it that way, and I won't have reason to worry."

That had gone so much better than she'd expected. With the weight of that secret off her shoulders, she relaxed and joined Devon on the bench. "You don't think the djinn is re-sponsible for our missing people, do you?" She grabbed the bottle of water he'd brought her and opened it.

"You don't have any bodies?" Devon asked.

She shook her head and gulped down half the bottle in one go.

"Nothing just vanishes into thin air. And it takes powerful magic to entrap someone of magical descent into a talisman."

"Imprisoned?" Sage asked. "Like in a Pandora's box?"

Devon shook his head. "That's a one-in one-out kind of prison. Not really a multi-use method of trapping people."

"That's what I was thinking too after looking it up." She slouched, feeling defeated all over again. "It was the best lead we had."

"If there's nothing for you to find, then yes, maybe djinn magic is at play." Devon didn't sound entirely convinced of what he was saying. "The problem is, the djinn couldn't have done it alone. Their magic can only be requested."

"So someone is working with the djinn?" Sage wondered aloud. Her mind returned to the suspect list with Sylvia right at the top.

"If djinn magic is responsible, then it's possible they've tricked someone into wishing the bodies into other forms."

Sylvia was looking more and more likely as Devon continued to speak. She seemed just the type to want to wish someone dead and gone, and with a djinn right there whispering in her ear and stroking her ego, it would be all too easy for the djinn to start suggesting targets of their own.

"But the problem with djinn magic is that eventually the one making the wishes will have exhausted their soul's credit, and the djinn could no longer use them." Devon stood and stretched. "Think of the relationship like symbiosis. The one making the wishes is getting something they want, and the djinn is too. He may manipulate a bit, but ultimately the wish has to be made from free will to be worth the cost they'll eventually incur."

"Their soul, right?"

"Essentially, yes."

"And all creatures, even Shades, have souls, right?" Sage jumped to her feet, feeling as if she were near a breakthrough.

"Sounds like you've got your mojo back." Devon flung the towel around his neck. "Go on. Get out of here. Tomorrow we'll do some real training."

He'd all but confirmed everything she suspected. The dots were lining up, and with any luck the case could be closed in the morning. Sage threw her arms around Devon. "Thank you!"

"You and Grey did all the hard work. I just knocked some sense into you," he chuckled.

"That's not what Grey would say." She hadn't intended to sound so snarky.

Her comment earned a disappointed glare from Devon. "Despite what you think, Grey is on your side. Let him in. Stop being so pigheaded with him."

"Easy for you to say. He's not picking on you or treating you like a damn newbie."

"Annoying as it is, that's his way of being friendly."

"That's not how you treat your friends," she grumbled.

"He was raised differently. Survival of the fittest. Sarcasm to cover feelings. That kind of thing."

"You're not implying what I think you are?" Sage didn't want the answer to that question. Guys were an off-limit subject at the moment. Who had time for the emotional rollercoaster they created?

"What I'm saying is, if you want him to be a partner, you're going to have to be one too. So tell him about your neighbor before he finds out the hard way."

"Yes, sir," she called out, already bolting down the hallway heading toward the offices to fill Grey in on all she'd learned.

When she reached the desk, he'd already gone, having left a quickly scrawled note in the seat she'd previously occupied.

If you're not going to work, you can find your own ride tomorrow.

NINETEEN

Late as it was, Sage really didn't want to risk the bus, nor did she want to spend the night at ASSET. She fished her phone out of her purse and crossed her fingers, hoping Matt had worked the early shift at the bar. She sent him a quick message pleading for him to pick her up, sweetening the deal with the offer of free dinner and gas for his car if he'd rescue her.

She paced the office like a madwoman, waiting for his reply. Grey's note had been one strike too many against him. It was one thing for him to be a grump. She could even understand some of his overprotectiveness. But to have the audacity to act as if she wasn't doing anything at all?

Oh, hell no!

She'd sat there until her ass had gone numb, researching and going over the files they'd collected. Grey always made it a point to mock her newbieness, but the truth was she had a steep learning curve and was making the best of it. And frankly, as seasoned a detective as Grey claimed to be, he should have come up with the answer before her. It wasn't like he'd cracked the case yet. However, they had both landed on Sylvia as suspect number one.

She'd have words for him in the morning.

The gentle buzz of her phone helped to pull her from the edge of rage. And Matt's reply was the best news she'd had all day. She sent him the address and headed down to the parking lot level to meet him outside.

In the heart of downtown, surrounded by all things old Vegas, leaving the office of ASSET felt like stepping out into a truly magical realm. Neon in every color of the rainbow painted life onto the inky canvas of night, transforming old buildings and narrow streets into a wonderland of adventure for those brave enough to explore them. Alive even more so at night than during the daylight hours, downtown, much like the Strip, had its own uniquely Vegas allure. Older and smaller in scale than its Las Vegas Boulevard counterpart, Freemont Street and the surrounding Arts district were an homage to the city's origins. Capitalizing on the history and eclectic nature of what had made Vegas look great back in the Rat Pack days, it celebrated neon and vintage everything. Old signs had been retrofitted and relocated. New ones had been erected to match the same charm. Color splashed across every inch of downtown's canvas. Vivid purples and acid greens met with cool blues and fiery orange. Only a city like Vegas, known for being an adult playground, could get away with such an assault to the senses. Gaudy and loud in the best possible way; like falling down the rabbit hole to be greeted by the Mad Hatter, offering a cup that says *Drink me.*

"Don't mind if I do," Sage whispered to herself, as she stepped off the sidewalk, heading toward a giant slot machine three stories high boasting a zip line to take tourists down the heart of Freemont Street.

She watched the enormous one-armed bandit flash its jackpot lights before sending a series of screaming patrons down the line. Nearby, under the canopy, a band was announcing their upcoming performance.

Live music and a free show. Sage wondered if she'd have enough time to listen as well before Matt came to pick her up. She wandered toward the neon glow, promising herself just a quick peek. It was better than standing all alone at the mouth of the ASSET parking garage. Even Grey would have to agree. Given how much he sniped at her for being out in her apartment complex all alone, she'd never hear the end of it if he caught her standing in the shadowy parking garage waiting for someone to come kill her.

There were people under the canopy of Freemont Street, tons of them. And security. No doubt half a dozen surveillance cameras already had her on screen as she came up to the twinkling lights of the Four Queens.

"Haven't you learned your lesson?" Zack called after her.

His voice startled her into anger. Sage gritted her teeth. He was the last guy she wanted to run into, especially alone…and at night. After the day she'd had, Sage felt like Murphy's Law had some kind of punch card with her name on it. Screw her day up one more time and someone was getting a free ice cream.

Keeping her pace brisk, she continued to walk toward the sounds of the band announcing their set would start in five minutes.

"You're mad. Good," he taunted.

She couldn't hear his footsteps, but Zack's voice sounded close. Sage reached into her bag, fishing for something to defend herself with in case he was planning on replaying the previous night.

"Go away," she growled.

"I will. I promise. I just have one question to ask you."

He was right behind her. Sage didn't want to turn around to confirm it, but her sixth sense screamed that the vampire had invaded her personal space yet again.

"Please," he pleaded. "It will only take a minute."

Against her better judgment, Sage stopped and turned around. "What?" She glared at him.

"I don't mean to pry. But I have to know." Zack's eyes were once again icy blue, and the toothy grin he flashed at her was as playful as ever. No hints of the demon he'd showed her before. "You wouldn't happen to have six fingers on your right hand?"

Sage fought to hold onto her anger with him. Damn him. He didn't play fair. But she refused to let him off the hook that easily. She might not have had a sword in hand, but she'd go all kind of Inigo Montoya on his ass if she caught sight of his demon side. "Don't do that!"

"I haven't the slightest idea of what you're talking about." He feigned innocence with almost believable sincerity.

"The crap you pulled last night." Her hand trembled as she grasped for the dagger in her purse. "And then acting today like nothing happened."

Zack stepped toward her. The twinkling lights of the casino's old porte cochère highlighted the duality of his nature, flashing between shadowy death and friendly temptation. She wanted nothing to do with either at that point.

"Come any closer and you'll regret it."

He held his palms up. "Fair enough. We shall face each other like God intended. Sportsmanlike. Skill against skill alone."

Zack looked nothing like Andre the Giant, but the delivery of that line broke through her defenses. She cracked the smallest of smiles before reining it in. "So you put away those fangs and I drop my dagger, and we try and kill each other like civilized people?"

Zack licked his lips as the blinking lights sent him back into the shadow for the space of a breath. "I could kill you now."

"I don't believe you." She refused to be intimidated this time. "What's your game, anyway?"

"Is this the real you speaking, or your anger, Sage?"

"I don't like games."

Zack snorted. "Could have fooled me."

"You know what I mean." She kept her hand firmly gripping the dagger in her bag. "I might have been naïve about what you are, but I thought you were at least on my side." Her muscles trembled with an eagerness born of anger, but to the predator, it would show as fear. She compensated, putting as much vitriol into her voice as she could. "Then you pulled that crap after game night."

"Have you considered my actions might have been to your benefit? Look how alert you are right now. I can see it in your eyes, you're calculating every move I make, ready to strike if I take a step." He moved a step closer. Sage flinched, drawing the dagger from her bag, bringing it into view. "The blinders are off, and you're beginning to recognize danger."

Had he shown even the slightest remorse for crossing the line, lesson or not, she might have given him a chance to prove himself friendly. But his arrogance only served to drive home the reality that he had no respect for her.

"Congratulations – you've taught me that you're an asshole." She glared so hard her eyes burned. "I'd clap, but my hands are full. So go ahead and pat yourself on the back. And while you're at it, never darken my doorstep again."

"Don't be like that."

"Did I stutter?" Her phone buzzed, but she didn't want to drop the dagger to fish it out of her bag. This late, it had to be Matt, waiting to rescue her. His timing, impeccable. "Now I'm going to walk back over to the office. Alone. If you so much as sniff in that direction, I'll make sure ASSET sticks its nose into every aspect of your business for the rest of eternity. Got it?"

Zack bowed his head and took a slow step backwards. "As you wish."

He had to get in the final word. But she wasn't going to allow him to weasel his way back into her good graces. He was one hundred percent Dread Pirate Roberts at that point, no Westley to be found. Scratch that. He'd gone full Prince Humperdinck.

She kept him in view as she re-crossed the street and headed for the ASSET building. Matt's car sat idling out in front of the parking garage. With her nerves nearing the breaking point, she jumped in and shouted, "Go," with all the intensity of someone who'd just robbed a convenience store.

"Bad day at the office?" Matt put the car in gear and put both the lights of Freemont and the object of Sage's stress in the rear view mirror.

"Actually... it wasn't all bad." Sage fumbled with her buckle, trembling hands refused to work together, made the task utterly impossible. She closed her eyes and took a deep breath, allowing her heart to slow, and with that, exhaled out as much of the day's stress as she could. A few of those and her hands relaxed enough to click the buckle. "I think I might have a lead on our case."

"But..." Matt pressed for more, nervously.

She realized the way she'd entered the car, all crazy eyes and angry shouts, she'd probably set off all his internal alarms. "Everyone I work with is a douche." Sage sighed and let herself sink into the bucket seat. "Thanks for being my knight in shining armor tonight."

"Who was mean to my Sage?" Matt's tone perked up at the prospect of non-magical problems. "You want me to take care of them? Make them an offer they can't refuse?"

"Cement shoes and all! Take 'em to the mattresses." She giggled.

"Damn, girl. Who pissed you off? I was just thinking of a little roughing up, and here you are going all Godfather. What happened?"

She reached into her bag and found Grey's note. How could he possibly have thought she was slacking? "Newbie syndrome, I guess." She sighed. "Just not feeling appreciated for what I add to the partnership."

"That tool with the hat?" Matt asked.

"Yeah. How'd you guess?"

"You have any other partners I should know about?"

She shook her head.

"He's hard to read." Matt's eyes shifted from the road to Sage and back. "I see guys like that come into the bar all the time."

"Tough guy know-it-alls?" Sage said snarkily.

"Yeah." He nodded. "Usually compensating for something."

Sage laughed so hard she snorted. "Small penis syndrome?"

"Worse."

"What?"

"Intimidation."

That didn't sound right at all. Sage opened her mouth to say so, but Matt got there before she could voice her confusion.

"They want to appear the best, biggest, whatever it is they need the world to see. Their abilities are their identity. But…" he paused, his concentration shifting to the traffic they had to weave through to get onto the freeway. "When someone comes along that has something they don't, that makes them appear just as good, they get defensive. They go out of their way to be a jerk because they feel inferior. For all they can do that makes them important, there's someone else who can do the same, maybe even better."

"So…jealousy?" Sage asked.

"Yeah, there's probably a little jealousy there. But their approach is to overstate how good they are as compensation. I see it in the bar all the time, especially at the pool table. Bunch of guys playing – all laughs and drinks, round after round. There's a shark just killing it all night. Most guys are cool with it. Then out of the blue someone else shows up and ends their winning streak. Instead of being cool about it, the shark continues to challenge game after game, trying to figure the way to beat the newcomer."

"And do they eventually?"

Matt shrugged. "It's never that simple. Oftentimes it's the newcomer who determines the way it goes. If they're cool, a new round of drinks is bought and there's lots of back patting and friendly banter. But there's times where I have to forcibly remove both parties for escalating to blows."

"Why is it up to the newcomer? The only thing they did wrong was win. How can that be considered wrong?" Sage thought the female social hierarchy was screwed up, but from what Matt was saying, guys clearly won the gold medal in confusing personal interactions.

"I'm not going to pretend it's fair, but the shark was there first. It was his territory to begin with."

"What are you all, animals now? Want to go piss on something?" Sage snorted again.

"Admit it. You wish you could stand and pee," he teased. "Seriously, though. Just like when you go to someone's home, you have to be respectful of their rules. My bar is one of those places where the regulars feel at home. If you want to enter a new domain, it's always best done respectfully. Show the value you bring, sure, but don't be a douche about it."

Sage rolled that thought around in her mind as she watched the lights of downtown grow smaller. Goodbye adult playground, hello suburbia. One mile from the glow of the neon lights, Sin City turned into Anytown, USA. Sage welcomed normalcy, though her world was anything but. Grey still dominated her thoughts. Had Matt zeroed in on Grey's problem? Was he intimidated because she'd been so highly sought out after Miranda's death? He'd been assigned as her shadow from the very beginning. And for what it was worth, Sage had no extra special skills, only the legacy of her mother to live up to. He couldn't possibly know the secret she kept hidden in her locket. Guardianship over one of the most powerful magical items in existence was definitely something to be jealous of. But only Ava and Mark were privy to that secret.

"Did I say something wrong?" Matt asked.

"How could you ever? You're like my own personal Yoda." She nudged his shoulder playfully.

"Obi-Wan, please." He chuckled. "I don't look good in green."

"Either way, the force is strong with you."

"Funny. Josh says the same thing."

Sage rolled her eyes. "T.M.I."

"Did I see a smile? Yep. There it is. My work here is done!"

"Speaking of work, I do have something to let you know."

Matt's muscles tensed. He shifted lanes with a jerk of the wheel. "Yeah?"

The nervousness in his tone made her wonder if she should worry him, but knowing what she had learned about their new neighbor, it was better to play it safe. "Don't get all jumpy. I just want to let you know our new neighbor came up on the" – she hesitated, searching for the best non-threatening word – "magical registry."

Matt's vocabulary was reduced to one nervous "Yeah?"

Sage laughed as believably as she could. "I don't want you getting any crazy notions of wishing your way into millions, but we have a genie living across from us."

"Like Aladdin and the lamp?" The light returned to Matt's eyes.

"Pretty much. They call them djinn on the registry we have at ASSET. But yeah, they grant wishes. But nothing is free. Not even magic, so don't even try."

"You take all the fun out of everything. I was going to wish for a ride on the TARDIS."

"As much as I would love that, the Doctor does not come up on the registry, so don't go putting that on your bucket list, 'kay?" She stuck her tongue out at him, hoping the playfulness of her warning would be enough to make him understand without bringing up any new fears. He'd been understandably jumpy about all things magic. But, just as Devon had said, as long as no wishes were being made, then there was little danger with the djinn. That went for humans and magic users alike.

Matt pulled his car into the apartment complex and waited for the night gate to open. "If I can't have the Doctor, then there's no point in wishing for anything."

"How about this? The next time one comes to Comicon, I will pay for our meet and greet experience."

"You really did need a knight in shining armor today, didn't you?" He parked the car and cut the engine.

"More than you know," she sighed.

"Well, don't think you're getting out of buying food and gas."

"Payday," she replied.

"And the Doctor too. I'm holding you to that." Matt winked.

"As long as you promise not to go wishing for things. No genies for you." Sage held her hand out.

176

He shook it. "I'm totally getting the better end of this deal. You should have more bad days."

"There's always tomorrow." Sage was already dreading the next day of work and dealing with Grey and his shark-like temper tantrum. If Matt was right, and he usually was, then she'd have to be the bigger person. At least until they closed the case.

TWENTY

A night of uninterrupted sleep worked wonders on Sage's mental state. She woke feeling ready to tackle the day. And with the right amount of caffeine, she knew she could face Grey head on and put an end to the underlying drama between them.

Matt believed in the power of saying affirmations in the mirror. Law of attraction; send good intentions out and they will quickly return.

She hoped that would work as she looked at her reflection and confidently said, "Today will be a good day." It had to be. She didn't have the strength to deal with crazy and drama. One at a time or none at all, as far as she was concerned.

To add a boost to her confidence, she grabbed her mother's old leather jacket. Even though it was technically too hot to wear it, just having it with her made Sage feel like a bad-ass.

She popped a book into her bag, to keep her entertained for the long bus ride to work, and snuck out the front door, so as not to wake her sleeping roommate.

"Hello neighbor," Luke called out to Sage as she reached to put the key into the door lock.

Sage muttered a curse, nearly dropping her keys. Of course he'd have to be there. He was always there. Did he ever sleep? She steadied herself and finished locking the door.

"Not going to work today?" he asked.

She caught sight of him standing at the bottom of the stairs, smoking a cigarette. "On my way to the bus stop, actually." She waved politely and started down the path, hoping he'd get the message.

"You don't have your own transportation?" He stamped out his smoke and jogged over to her. A set of keys jingled at his waist with each step as he swiftly moved to catch up to her. "Need a ride?"

Either didn't get the message or didn't care. Sage had prepared herself to deal with Grey's turbulence, but she hadn't accounted for the questionable nature of her friendly neighborhood djinn. Luke hadn't, as of yet, been officially placed on the suspect list, but by nature of his curse, she knew she couldn't treat him with the same level of snark she reserved for creatures like Zack.

Civility was hard when caffeine levels were low. "Cars cost money. I'm good with the bus." It took all she had to keep her tone neutral.

"Surely ASSET pays you a decent wage." He unlocked the gate and held it open for her.

He might be a cursed criminal, but at lease chivalry hadn't died with his morals.

In the early morning light, the living tattoos on his arm appeared more vividly. She couldn't help but admire the way they waved and rolled across his skin. Like living flames made of ink, each movement was unique. Every wave touched on a different part of his skin.

Before she made a fool of herself, she forced herself to look away and walk through the gate. "Sorry. I'm a bit slow this morning. Yeah, the money's good enough, but student loans come first. So until then, it's the bus for me." She smiled politely. "Thanks."

She'd expected him to leave her at the gate, but Luke stepped through and continued to walk with her toward the main road. "I really admire you."

Go away. Go away. Go away! She practically screamed the words in her mind, but they never reached her mouth. So much for her morning affirmation. Sage's bullshit alarm was ringing loud and clear. "You hardly know me." She struggled to keep her tone neutral despite mounting annoyance.

"I know all I need to."

"You realize you sound like a total creeper right now, right?" Her hand moved down to her bag, instinctively reaching for a weapon, but a thought stopped her before she could find her dagger. Did djinn bleed? "And don't you have a girlfriend?"

His muscles tensed. "Yes."

She'd hit a nerve there. Sage made a mental note of that, and continued to walk, praying that when she found the bus she'd be free of him. "So… what are you doing?"

"I'm being friendly with my local law enforcement."

Did he actually get people to fall for cheeseball lines like that? "Sucking up again?"

"Shamelessly!" He flashed her a smile that might even rival Zack's brilliance. "Because one day I might need you in my corner."

That last statement rang true. He was hedging his bets through an attempt at friendship. "Isn't the point of law enforcement to protect those who need it, not those who try to weasel their way into favors?"

"See, that's exactly why I like you." Laughter followed his words, but she didn't believe he was truly amused. "You're fresh and unjaded. No prejudice. You shoot from the hip, and speak your mind."

As opposed to you feeding me spoonfuls of sugar-coated bullshit? She stopped herself from saying the words, but they were there, waiting to hop off the end of her tongue.

"And now you've gone silent." His tone shifted, softening. "I came on too eager, didn't I?"

"Eager?" Sage asked suspiciously. She looked around, spotting other people out walking, and felt safer knowing that if something happened, there would be witnesses. "What exactly are you eager for?"

Luke's hands flew up in surrender. "You totally misread me. I didn't mean it to sound like that." He stuttered, as if struggling for the right words. "I'm not the bad guy you think I am."

"That's exactly the kind of thing a bad guy would say. Trust me, I've met a few." Zack's face flew into her memory, causing her lip to curl slightly.

Luke's shoulders slumped. He sighed loudly and offered his wrists to her. "Cuff me and bring me in if you truly feel I deserve it."

"You have a crime you want to confess to?" she asked, hoping that he'd give her a real answer.

"Despite what you know of my curse, I do my best to keep my nose clean. I've suffered plenty for the wrong I did in the past."

Of all the things he'd said, that statement sounded genuine. But Sage couldn't just take him at his word. "Look, I believe people can be reformed. But trust is not something just given." She swatted his hands away.

"So then why are you actively pushing me away when I'm trying to be friendly and offer help when I can?"

"Okay, friend." She tested the word on her tongue. "What is the answer to the riddle you gave me the other day?"

He shifted from one foot to the other, and suddenly found the pavement much more interesting to look at. "I can't answer th–" An audible gulp that sounded more like a hiccup cut him off before he could finish his sentence.

"What?" She stopped and gave Luke her full attention, crossing her arms as she awaited his answer.

Luke raked both hands through his hair, dragging his fingertips all the way down to the nape of his neck. He opened his mouth more than once but failed to produce any words. Finally after silence had nearly exhausted Sage's patience, he let out a groan, and forced the words out. "I'm not allowed specifics."

"So much for being helpful." *And totally wasting her time.*

"Blame magic," he said through clenched teeth. "It has me in check as much as you."

He played the part well enough to be believable, but everyone had told her djinn were tricksters with their own agenda. "So you've got a magical gag order preventing you from telling me the answer to a riddle you gave me?"

"It's unfair, isn't it?" he confirmed with the question.

"It's a bit hard to believe." She picked up her pace again. The bus stop was in sight.

With any luck, the next bus would arrive immediately, freeing her of Luke and his cryptic messages.

"All of this magic surrounding you, and while you can see it, you can't be part of it," he called after her. "You're cursed. Sure, they tell you it's a blessing. You weren't chosen by the Mother. You just happened to belong to the family that swore eternal fealty to her. You might be immune to the harm that magic can do, but you're also left like a spectator, unable to understand its true power."

"Does this complete derail of our conversation have a point?" Her annoyance grew with each passing moment.

"Everyone's curse is different." He caught up to her. When his eyes finally found hers, the light had dulled some. Where there had been a sparkle to his silvery eyes, all that remained was murky gray. His face had paled visibly as well. Luke reached out, as if wanting to grasp her arm, but pulled it back at the last moment. "Sorry. Mine, for instance, does not allow me to use my own magic unless someone else commands it."

"So I've been told."

"I'm like you… in a way… surrounded by magic that I cannot use."

"For evil?" Sage asked.

"Or good," he replied defensively. "Just like you, I'm trapped. My skills are not my own to use. I am at the whim of others because of my curse. But what if I could change all of that?" His tone took on a nervous edge. Again he found the concrete of the sidewalk much more interesting to look at than her. "What if I had a friend guiding my magic?"

"We have to play the hand we're dealt." The words came out in her voice, but the conviction wasn't there. She'd always dreamed of casting spells and weaving magic to her own ends. Learning that magic was truly real had been a dream come true, until she realized that she could never use it. The cruelest of all jokes played on her. But she still had immunity. That counted for something. "Your curse was a punishment to teach you the value of the gift you abused."

"Yes. And you're right. Self-righteous bootstrap mentality and all. We must adapt to deal with the cruelties of this world." He raked his hand through his hair again, and switched to staring at the clouds. "But the truth is so few of the magical community have such honorable notions."

"Does this work on other girls?" She'd had just about enough crazy for the entire day, and it wasn't even nine yet.

"You think I'm playing." He lowered his gaze once again, meeting her eyes for half a breath before his face contorted into an expression that looked like pain. The moment she caught it, he averted his eyes again, settling on the nearby bus sign. "But whether or not you admit it out loud, you know my words are merely an echo of what you've thought privately. I understand. You must guard yourself. It's the smart thing to do."

"You hardly know me. Stop praising me so highly." Sage held her voice firm. "You're really starting to freak me out."

"I've known so many like you. Your instincts are what guide you. And despite what others say, instincts are right most of the time. You'll find what you're searching for, and I want to help. But because of my own curse, my hands are literally tied."

"I'll be honest here. I have no clue what you are capable of, magically speaking, but I do know that those cursed into your life were punished for abuse of magic. I have no reason to trust anything you whisper into my ear."

"Of course. Why should you trust me?" He sighed. "I'm just a criminal. But have you ever considered that some criminals are falsely accused?"

"You'll have to try harder than that lame excuse."

"I don't need you to trust me. What I offer is use of my powers to aid in your investigations."

"Why?"

"In service, I might one day have paid my debt and be released," Luke replied.

She couldn't determine whether he was speaking the truth or not. Either way, she wasn't about to blindly agree to anything he said.

"Consider how much more good could be done with both your immunity as well as my defensive magic." He rounded in front of her, and those silvery eyes of his again met hers. The color had returned. Whatever struggle he'd been having in the moments prior seemed to have ended. His whole face brightened, and the beginnings of a grin lifted the corners of his mouth.

"Magic comes at a price," Sage countered, with her best poker face.

"You're assuming the cost is too high."

"And that's where you lose me." Sage slammed hard into reality. The sales pitch he gave was too obvious. And the moment payment became part of the conversation, he'd lost.

"Consider your options," he said.

"What I'm considering is your guilt – trying to sell me on abusing magic I don't have. What did you really expect for me to say there?"

She expected him to reply in defense or anger, but the smile that had started only widened with her indignation. "I knew I picked the right Terra!"

Of all the things he'd said, that last phrase sent a chill down her spine. What did he mean by it? "Listen. I need to get to work, and you need to get back to whatever it is you do." She spotted the bus only one traffic light away and had never been more thankful to see it heading her way.

"If you won't consider my offer," Luke began, averting his eyes once again as he reached a hand out toward her. This time he was holding a small leather-bound book, wrapped tightly with a leather strap. "Please take this as a consolation prize." No title, no author, nothing on the outside gave her any indication what the book might be, though based on its small size, she assumed it was meant for note-taking. "It might be just the thing you need to connect the dots."

Her first thought was to ignore both him and the book and jump into the bus, but given the strange way he'd been acting and the clear shifts in his demeanor when he looked at her and when he didn't, she suspected that the magical gag order might be a real thing.

She took the book and skipped up the short stairway into the bus. In the back of her mind she heard the echo of Grey's taunting. She might be making yet another newbie mistake, but at that moment it seemed to be the lesser of two evils. She swiped her bus pass on the card reader and searched for a seat.

Luke thankfully hadn't followed. He waved as she took her seat and mouthed "Happy reading," as the bus pulled away from the curb.

TWENTY-ONE

"What took you so long?" Grey met her at the elevator, shit-eating-grin plastered across his face, clearly pleased with himself for forcing her extended commute to work.

"First bus I caught broke down." Sage fought the urge to smack that stupid fedora off his head. But before she sent her hand flying, she remembered her roommate's advice and wisdom. Grey was the shark, feeling inferior, and acting out of jealousy. It was up to her to play it cool. She nibbled at her bottom lip innocently for a moment and slowly lifted her gaze to his. "Sorry to inconvenience you. I'm here now. What's the plan, and do I have time to grab a quick coffee before we start?"

His brow furrowed. Grey stood speechless as if unsure how to react.

She chuckled to herself. He'd probably hoped his little stunt would give him a chance to lecture her on work ethic or whatever it was that made him a great agent. Not only had she robbed him of the grandstanding, she'd done it with a smile. And by the looks of it, that was an even better revenge than giving him a piece of her mind.

"Did you want some coffee too?" she added, with as much saccharine in her voice as she could manage.

"No." A muscle in his jaw twitched. "We need to retrace our steps today. I want to have another chat with Sylvia." He crossed his arms, still staring at her like a confused puppy. "And if we have time, Marrin."

"Excellent idea. I think you're on to something with Sylvia." She had to fight to keep a straight face as she praised him, even more so as her words caused Grey's face to flush. "But first, Coffee!"

"You go on ahead. Make it quick." He stepped backwards, leaving a wide berth for Sage to walk past him. "I need to grab the file. Meet you in the break room in five."

That had gone so much more easily than she'd anticipated. Who knew that killing with kindness could be so satisfying? Sage walked into the break room and found the coffee pot empty.

Just her luck. She grumbled at first, but stopped herself from falling into that trap. She'd told herself right from the beginning that this was going to be a good day. Weird, but good. And so far it was going exactly that way.

Shifting her perspective, she tried to focus on the bright side. Making a fresh pot meant she could brew it as strong as she liked, and enjoy it fresh.

She set her bag on the counter and started the ritual of rinsing the pot, loading the filter, and replenishing the water. Somewhere during all that motion she'd managed to knock her bag down, and the contents spilled all over the floor.

"So much for the bright side." She sighed.

"Bad morning?" Devon's voice caught her off guard.

"Just need more sleep and caffeine," she answered.

"Those two don't exactly work well together, you know." Devon bent down to help her pick up her bag.

"Without one, however, the other is more than necessary." Sage crouched down and grabbed her deodorant, wallet, and cell phone, shoving them quickly back into her bag.

Devon snatched up the old leather-bound notebook before she could retrieve it. "This yours?"

"Not really," Sage answered nervously. She hadn't had the chance yet to look at it, fearing some kind of magical retribution if she opened it in public

Devon, it seemed, had no such reservations. He opened it before she could stop him.

Sage flinched, but nothing happened. "Just a book," she whispered thankfully.

Devon's brow furrowed as he flipped through the pages, and the deeper he delved into the hand-written words, the more lines were etched into his features. "Whose is this?"

"Can you promise not to freak out if I tell you?"

"Don't play games, Sage, do you know what this book is?" His tone had gone darker than she'd ever heard before.

"Yeah. I mean, no. I mean…." The words were there, but putting them in the right order had suddenly become impossible. "djinn…"

"By the looks of this" – he held the book up with a hand-drawn picture of an amulet – "whoever your djinn is, they were using seriously forbidden magic."

"I think that was why he was cursed." Sage finally got her brain and mouth in sync. "He seemed all too eager to confess something, but wouldn't say exactly what."

"They're all tricksters. You can't trust what they say."

"That's the point." She nodded. "He gave that book to me as a clue."

Devon's jaw dropped. "He did what now?"

"He said he wants to help me solve the case." She chewed on her lip, not sure how to explain the unusual way he'd acted before handing the book over, as if two different people were struggling for control. "But he couldn't tell me the answers. One moment he'd be friendly and open, and then in the next breath he'd go Mr. Hyde and act all twitchy. But he did say this book will put the clues together."

"Magical gag order." Devon looked as if the light had switched on behind his eyes.

"That's what I was calling it," Sage replied proudly.

"Must be another part of the djinn curse. Whoever controls them might be exerting their will… to some extent. If they wish the djinn to keep their identity and intentions secret, the djinn cannot speak of it."

"Well, that makes so much sense," she agreed. "If you'd seen him… It was like watching a fight between two people in the same body."

The anger in Devon's expression had dulled, but he still looked deeply troubled as he thumbed through a few more pages in the book. "Remember that a djinn is a trickster by nature. They may be bound by a magical contract to whoever controls them, but even so, they'll find and use every loophole they can to make sure their own will is being carried out."

"So then you think he's tricking me by giving me this?" The longer the conversation continued, the more confused she became. Her instincts had told her to take the book, just as her instincts had initially told her Luke wasn't evil. He'd praised her for her instincts. But maybe it was all false, like the way she was buttering up Grey just to mess with his mind. If that were true, then she really was a stupid newbie.

As much as she wanted to take the train to depressionville, none of that rang true. Sure, she was impulsive and very new to the magical world, but her instincts stood apart from her head and her heart.

"I'm not sure what to make of all this. It's definitely out of the ordinary. But for him to have handed this over to you… does make me think he's being genuine about getting you to piece together the puzzle." Devon's lips pursed as he continued to scrutinize the pages. "But what will you find when the whole picture is revealed? Answers, or a trap?"

"Answers," Sage said hopefully.

The concerned look on Devon's face said it wouldn't be that simple. "Have you shown Ava yet?"

"Haven't even had my morning cuppa yet. Cut me some slack."

Devon handed the book to her. "Have Ava take a look at this, and report the djinn who gave it to you. Sooner rather than later."

The coffee maker gurgled, giving Sage the perfect distraction from their conversation. She pulled the pot and poured herself a mug of fresh liquid energy.

Grey appeared at the door as she was searching for creamer in the mini-fridge. "Please, take your time. We don't have anywhere to be. Maybe you want to sit and have some donuts with that coffee. Or how about a scone?"

Her charms had clearly worn off, and Mr. Passive Aggressive had returned with a vengeance.

"I thought you were pouring a cup to go, not having a leisurely breakfast with Devon." Grey crossed his arms, taunting her with a look that dared her to say something stupid and start a fight.

Sage let herself have a full calming breath, remembering to kill him with kindness before she responded. "You're so right, we have a lot to do today. Can I fill a to go cup for you? Sounds like you need one."

Her reply earned raised eyebrows from both men in the room.

Sage smiled sweetly as she held up the coffee pot.

"Busy day?" Devon asked curiously.

"Still on the missing persons case." Grey walked over and grabbed the cup Sage had just finished pouring. He mumbled "Thanks," and turned away, busying himself with adding sugar and creamer. "We need to get moving."

"Still no leads, eh?" Devon's question hung in the air as he eyed Sage.

She hadn't mentioned the book to Grey. After Devon's warning, she wanted to take it straight to Ava. But Grey was her partner. Shouldn't she inform him first? Her mind had not yet been given the proper dose of caffeine to problem-solve on that level. She snatched her cup from the counter and burned her tongue as she downed a gulp. Sputtering and moaning as her mouth went up in flames, she couldn't answer before Grey spoke again.

"I have some leads. We're taking a closer look at them to-day." Grey fixed the lid on his cup and took a sip. "Don't worry, man. We'll let you know if they start coming after ASSET em-ployees."

"Never had a doubt." Devon snatched the pot and poured his own cup. "But that wasn't my concern. The *why* is more important than the *who* at this point. Sage, I think you under-stand that, right?"

Sage feigned being unable to speak after burning her tongue. She mumbled as she waved goodbye and grabbed her purse to leave.

TWENTY-TWO

Caffeine had kicked in by the time Grey drove his bike into the staffing agency parking lot. Sage's mind was running a mile a minute computing all the details of the case so far. Sylvia still ranked as suspect number one, but her motive was elusive. As much as Sage wanted to believe that it was just Sylvia's new way of firing bad employees, she knew a Shade of her caliber would be far too smart to actually do it.

"See if you can get her talking this time," Grey suggested, as they walked into the dilapidated waiting room.

"Really?" Shocked by his suggestion, Sage curbed the snarky reply she had loaded and ready to fire. He actually wanted her to do something besides sit down and shut up? If this was the result of killing 'em with kindness, she'd do it way more often.

"She's all yours." Grey's tone carried a mocking edge.

Sage looked in the direction of Sylvia's office as they passed through the lobby door. A crying man rushed away from the Shade's office.

Never a good sign.

Sage gulped way the sudden fear threatening to stop her in her tracks. Terras were immune to magic. The worst Sylvia could do was yell at her. "Sticks and stones," she whispered to herself.

The door closed behind Grey with a loud slam, and from across the massive open floor of cubicles, Sylvia spotted them.

She rushed forward in a blur, appearing a moment later, two feet in front of Sage.

"Words can never hurt me," Sage finished the rhyme, as she fought the urge to back away. "Neither can magic."

"I hope you're here with good news to report." Sylvia glared impatiently at Grey and Sage.

With a steadying breath, Sage lifted her chin and headed toward Sylvia's office. "Still investigating," she said, trying to sound confident. "Let's continue this behind closed doors."

That thought sounded better in her head. The moment the door was shut behind them, trapping Sage and Grey in Sylvia's domain, the Shade laid into them. "I ask ASSET for help and they send me their best and brightest flunkies." Sylvia slammed a fist on her desk to punctuate the point.

The shadowrunner was in rare form. Fueled by anger, she maintained her solidity rather than hiding behind her normal cloud as she circled around them. "How dare you come back here with nothing to show? If it were one of yours that had gone missing, I'll bet they'd have been found by now."

"I understand you're upset, but we're doing our best with the limited information you've provided." Sage paused for a moment, scrutinizing Sylvia's face for a reaction. Someone had sent the cloaked figure after them the last time they'd been here. But Sylvia's expression failed to betray any guilt. "Thalia was not the only missing person reported this week." Sage held her head high, doing her best to keep her voice level. "We have reason to believe they are conn–"

Grey nudged her with his elbow, and when she looked at him, he shook his head. Was she not supposed to have said that? Oh well. The damage had already been done.

Sylvia's eyebrow lifted curiously. "You think there's a connection to my missing girl?"

"For us to be sure, we'll need more information from you." Grey jumped in before Sage could stick her foot further in her mouth. "Other than your professional relationship, were you close?"

"I couldn't care less about what happens after hours," Sylvia huffed.

"Humor us," Sage said innocently. "Did she have any friends? Any relationships outside of this office? Close family?"

Sylvia bristled. Her annoyance held the room in silence as Sage waited to see if she would reply at all. The Shade might as well have had guilty stamped across her forehead the way she fought to keep secrets. Finally, after an eternity, she said, "There was a boyfriend. A recent thing."

"I thought you didn't care." Sage let the sarcastic comment fly before she could stop herself.

"I don't," Sylvia sneered. "I wouldn't have even noticed if not for the gaudy necklace she started to wear around the office." Her lips pulled back into a snarl. The moment Sage noticed the change, Sylvia's expression returned to complete neutrality. "I told her the necklace was fake, but she was over the moon because *he* gave it to her. Puppy love, or whatever it's called for foxes."

The missing brownie had a necklace too. Recently acquired from a new boyfriend. Sage pulled out her phone and jotted down a quick note. "Did you ever see the boyfriend?"

"Why would I? I don't do after hours with my staff." Sylvia's reply had more jealousy than scorn layered in her tone.

Sage noted that as well. Maybe it was a clue to her motive. "You said before that you were grooming her for management." *What if the student had suddenly begun to shine brighter than the master? All this posturing and anger at ASSET for not working fast enough would show that Sylvia had done all she could to find poor Thalia.*

"And you somehow took that to mean that Thalia and I were bosom buddies going out for drinks and girls' night?"

"Were you?" Sage asked.

"No!" Sylvia countered indignantly. "It would be improper for management to fraternize with subordinates."

Sage glanced quickly over to Grey. He hadn't interrupted her or tried to shift the conversation. If he had any feelings on the direction she was taking, it didn't show on his face. He stared forward with tired eyes as he stood with his arms crossed.

The room had fallen silent. Sylvia's posture matched Grey's in all but the eyes. Where his were dull and bored, her sharp eyes were locked and loaded on Sage's face.

"The boyfriend never came to pick her up?" Sage asked.

"This is a place of business!" Sylvia's reply struck as hard as a viper. "Boyfriends can wait in the parking lot."

Grey seemed to snap out of his trance. "Well, as usual, you've been extremely helpful." He tipped his hat, nodded to Sage, and pointed at the door.

If only mind-reading were one of their special abilities. That would make this whole process so much easier.

"As helpful as you are competent." Sylvia struck the final verbal blow.

Grey might have been ready to leave, but Sage felt so close to a breakthrough.

The jealous tones; the mention of a boyfriend; the jewelry… There was something there. It felt right, but she needed to have time to connect the dots, which wouldn't happen if Grey pushed Sylvia into an explosion.

"Before we go, can we have one more look at Thalia's desk?" Sage asked sweetly, hoping to temper Sylvia's annoyance.

"If you must. I cannot guarantee it has been left as it was since you last came by. We do have work to do here. Even when some of our little worker bees go missing, files must be taken care of. Employers need people, and our clients need jobs." Sylvia waved a dismissive hand to shoo them off. The shadowrunner had more than just a boss-level relationship with Thalia. The jealousy Sage sensed was off the charts.

Motive – it had to be.

Sage was first out the door, thankful to have escaped Sylvia's unpredictable temper unscathed. She headed straight for Thalia's desk, on a mission to find out more about the mysterious boyfriend and the jewelry.

Grey followed behind. "You have a plan, I assume?"

"Just a hunch," Sage replied. Grey had been surprisingly quiet in Sylvia's office, far from his normal snarky self, but the mystery of his newfound silence would have to be solved later. "I want to check for the boyfriend's name. It has to be written somewhere."

"Why?" He stared blankly at her, his head tilting sideways like a confused puppy.

"You've probably never experienced it," she snickered, "but when you actually like someone and have a relationship with them, their name pops up a lot."

"Must be a girl thing." He'd failed to take the bait. Every other time she'd thrown snark his way, Grey responded in kind. But this time he simply shrugged.

"Just look on her desk for sticky notes…reminders of dates, names, or phone numbers, that sort of thing."

Grey took the area around Thalia's monitor.

Sage dove into the drawers. The top drawer was always a junk drawer. If it were Sage's desk, that would be the first place she'd stash errant notes, especially ones with memorable dates and anniversaries. Whoever this boyfriend was, he had to have been a charmer and worked fast, meaning Thalia would have been swept off her feet. Dinners, movies, maybe some shows on the Strip. Sage shuffled everything around – pencils, pens, some old lip balm tubes, crumpled notes with sketches of foxes on them. On first inspection, the drawer didn't appear to have anything important. Just like the last time they had looked through it. But something had to be there. Sage refused to accept defeat again. The brownie had had a spotlessly clean house, but this was no brownie. Thalia was a low-level Career Assistant who'd just landed a boyfriend who could afford lavish jewelry. Where were the notes with last names scrawled over and over in pretty handwriting?

She dug deeper into the drawer, feeling around all the crevices and corners where papers might have gotten jammed when opening and closing. Her fingers caught the edges of something thicker than paper jammed up against the top of the drawer. She pulled the whole thing out of its insert and reached up and inside the belly of the desk.

Her heart was beating like a drum as she pulled two thin strips of card stock free. *Jackpot!* A torn pair of tickets for Marrin the Mentalist. Comped tickets, at that. Sage pumped a fist in the air triumphantly but kept her victory squeal silent. Unlike Sylvia's office, Thalia's was out in the open where anyone could hear.

Finally a dot connected. She and someone else, possibly the boyfriend, had seen the show. Judging by the date on the ticket, recently, too.

Sage pocketed the ticket stub and continued looking. When the top drawer did not reveal any more secrets, she moved down to the next, hoping to find a datebook or something. Her initial excitement was short-lived. All she uncovered were manila folders with client names on them, none of them men, and none of the ladies' names matched her missing person's report.

The bottom drawer wasn't much more help. A few more large files, some instructions for filing by magical class, and a secret stash of candy. Thalia wouldn't miss any of that. Sage swiped a couple of snack-sized chocolate bars and closed the drawer.

"Anything?" she asked.

Grey shrugged. "She likes these notes." He pointed to the colorful array around the monitor. "But none of them have little hearts drawn around them."

Sage rolled her eyes. "Move." She shoved him aside to take a look herself. Just like with the drawers, the notes offered little more than a glimpse into Thalia's day working at the employment agency. A want list of magical attributes looked promising, then another listing the four magical family branches. They almost added up to a clue, until the note below it had job duties to match each class type. Below that one, another note listed job openings. Hardly the diabolical list of a serial killer.

"Pretty much par for the course in this line of work," Sage mumbled to herself. At the top of Thalia's screen were non-magical contacts within the city government: the assessor's office, inspectors, and animal control.

The last note, was almost impossible to read, seemed to be a phone number. Sage clipped a picture of it on her cell to get a better look at later.

She turned to face Grey hoping he'd found something, but the blank stare he'd adopted told her all she needed to know.

"It was a long shot. No name for the mysterious boyfriend, but I did pick up this." She held up the ticket stubs.

"Now that is something." Grey's eyes lit with curiosity. He inspected them, turning the tickets over in his hand before returning them to her. "Looks like it's time to go pay another visit to Marrin."

TWENTY-THREE

The second time through, the labyrinth that made up the casino's back of the house didn't hold the same level of intimidation for Sage as her initial run. Thought it still seemed very institutional, she appreciated the sense of neutrality it offered compared to the sense assaulting casino floor they had to travel through to get there.

Walking like a man on a mission, Grey wordlessly led the way straight to the door with Marrin's name on it.

He knocked, and Sage listened carefully for Mr. Magnificent to answer.

"Good cop, bad cop?" she asked.

"Grow up," he replied, curtly.

They'd gotten along so well up to that point, she'd almost forgotten he was a jerk. "Never." She stuck her tongue out, hoping to get a reaction.

Grey ignored her and knocked a second time, but did not wait for an answer. He grabbed the handle and shoved the door open, shouting, "Marrin, you in here?"

Sage spotted him lying on the couch across the room. The stench of alcohol mixed with bile wafted up to her nose before she had a chance to cross the threshold. "Don't think you're going to get much out of him today."

If it weren't for the soft cat-like purr of his snores, she would have thought him dead. His chest barely rose and fell with each gentle rumbling breath.

"Someone's been hitting it hard." Grey chuckled.

He came right up next to the sleeping siren and nudged him sharply with his knee. "Rise and shine!"

Marrin groaned and mumbled, but his eyes didn't open.

"On your feet." Grey shoved him harder the second time.

"I've got your money," Marrin shouted as his eyes flew open, before he realized who he was speaking to.

"What money?" Grey stared down at the siren with interest. "Who are you in debt to?"

"No one. It was just a dream." Marrin shot upright and attempted to smooth out his wrinkled clothes. His hands jerked around as if he were struggling to control them. "Horrible dream. Nightmare, really." He blinked repeatedly as his eyes darted between Sage's face and Grey. "I'm fine. All good here. Did you find my girls?"

"You haven't been completely honest with us, have you?" Grey plopped himself down next to Marrin, throwing a friendly arm around his shoulder.

Sage moved to stand in front of Marrin. Grey might have balked at her quip of going good cop bad cop, but he was certainly playing the part.

"What? I told you all I know." Marrin scooted sideways and shoved Grey's arm away. "My girls disappeared off the face of the earth. Their car was towed this morning from the employee lot."

"Who's trying to shut down your show?" Grey asked, sounding oddly sympathetic.

Sage folded her arms and stared down at Marrin. "Someone you owe a lot of money to?"

"I told you already." Marrin's expression darkened. "My problems do not extend to my employees. If I have debts, it's my legs that get broken." He stood and pushed past Sage's flimsy blockade.

"Did your girls follow you into debt? They didn't have your powers of persuasion." Grey followed Marrin to his feet, keeping annoyingly close to the nervous siren.

"Am I under investigation?" Marrin shuffled sideways to free himself of Grey's shadow. "I hardly knew the girls. They were new. They'd been with me for maybe a month. The agency was pretty mad about my last assistant requesting reassignment."

"You deal with the agency a lot?" Grey continued to match every step Marrin made.

"I make a call, they send a list of potential employees." Marrin continued to two-step across the room.

"Who do you call?" Sage asked.

"It's just a general number. I don't know who answers. It's different every time," he replied quickly.

Grey stopped chasing and matched Sage's folded arms. "You've called a lot, I take it?"

Pinned between the two Terra pillars, Marrin had nowhere to go. "My powers of persuasion make people uncomfortable," he confessed. "But I swear I don't use my voice on the staff."

"I don't even want to go there," Sage said, praying that their investigation would not lead them down that rabbit hole. "Keep it professional!"

"I have a tiny black spot on my reputation." Marrin's face reddened. "*You* try being a siren. It's not always easy to know when people are being honest or just under your spell. That's why I love you Terras so much."

"Flattery is unnecessary. Stick to the facts." Grey glared at the siren. "If you have a contact at the agency and you don't tell us who it is, we'll have to bring you in for further questioning with our boss."

Ava must have had a reputation outside of ASSET. Just the mention of her and Marrin threw up his hands in surrender. "Fine," his voice broke. "Look. I don't know every person I talk to. But on this last round, I sweet-talked one of the placement coordinators, and she located the perfect assistants. Gemini twins are damn near impossible to find in this town, you know."

"Thalia?" Sage asked.

"Yea, that name sounds familiar, now that you mention it." He nodded eagerly.

The dots were starting to line up. Sage felt a break in the case was within reach. "You comped her tickets to your show as a thank you?"

"I do that a lot. You want come tonight? I'll sit you up right up front. My favorite table," Marrin replied.

"Thalia," Sage barked in frustration. "Do you remember comping her tickets?"

Marrin stood quiet for a moment before shrugging. "I can't remember them all. I see so many faces every day."

"Too bad." Grey let out an exaggerated sigh. "Because we have reason to believe that the man she was with, the night you comped those tickets, is the guy who nabbed your girls."

Marrin's eyes widened. He opened his mouth to speak, but no words came.

"Too bad. We were this close," Grey added, with a disappointed snap of his fingers. "But as he said, he can't remember them all."

"Wait. I might… Hold on." Marrin held up a finger as he crossed the room to his desk. "What day was the show she came to?"

Sage pulled out the ticket stubs and handed them to him.

"There's surveillance all over this casino, and in the showroom too. Let me see if I can get security to pull the recordings for that night. We might be able to get a look at him. And I'll get credit for helping the investigation, right?"

"Credit of what type?" Sage asked.

"You know, maybe you ignore some of the less savory things being said about me in the future." Marrin waggled an eyebrow.

"Just get the security footage." Sage had to remind herself that the siren was a client; punching him wouldn't help their investigation.

"How long will that take?" Grey asked.

"Maybe 48 hours, tops," Marrin replied.

"You have 24 hours before we come back and I let Sage here work her own magic." Grey tugged at her arm as he headed toward the door.

TWENTY-FOUR

The best part of riding on Grey's motorcycle was it gave her an easy out when it came to small talk. Sage spent the entire trip back to the office working the pieces of the puzzle in her head. Everything was right there in front of her – the answers, the motivation, the guilty parties. But nothing fit.

"So, what's your read, partner?" Grey broke through Sage's pensive silence once they'd pulled into ASSET's parking garage.

"I really wish I could tell if you're mocking me." Frustrated at her own failure to connect the dots, Sage let her sarcasm fly before she could stop herself.

"Depends on your answer, really." He shrugged and looked away quickly. "Could go either way."

Sage set her helmet down on the seat of the bike and went to work tying her hair back into a clean ponytail. "With motivation like that, you can see why I'm so eager to reply."

"You've been acting a little odd today." He busied himself digging through the saddle bags, and didn't see the face she made at his eye-roll-worthy remark.

"I could say the same for you. Especially after your little temper tantrum last night."

Grey slapped his fedora on. A satisfied smile spread across his face. "Oooh, we are still prickly, aren't we?"

"Not in the slightest." Sage shouldered her bag, fighting the urge to snatch his hat and shove it down his throat. *Kill him with kindness*, she reminded herself, before finishing her reply. "Just commenting on the maturity level of our partnership."

"Big girls can be responsible for their own transportation."

"Fine." She'd known it would come to that sooner or later anyway. "I'll ride the bus. Are we done with this conversation?"

"You don't have to take that tone. I didn't mean... It's easy to take advantage..." He pinched the bridge of his nose and sighed. "It's fine, really. I just can't always be counted on to be a chauffeur."

His sudden shift had her head spinning. What was he playing at? She crossed her arms and glared at him. "I never expected you to chauffeur. Nor did I plan on taking advantage of you. But kudos on the misogyny. You nailed it with that little love note you left me."

"Is that what you thought?" Grey cocked his head to the side, his brow furrowing.

She was certain they spoke the same language, but the confused look on his face said otherwise. "How did you expect me to take it?"

He shifted uncomfortably from one foot to the other. "Partners have to do more than just work side by side." His voice gained conviction as he continued. "They need to be able to lean on each other and confide in each other." Grey met her eyes head on as he punctuated his speech with, "They must trust each other."

Sage took a step backward, as if the force of his glare had pushed her. "That's not–"

"Shut up and listen for once," he threw the full weight of his voice into the command.

Shock held her tongue. This was a different side of Grey, one she'd never thought to see from him.

"Whether or not you want to be partnered with me, we are. Which means we have a responsibility to work together…for the case."

"I *was* working!"

"Whatever you think you're doing, doesn't matter. You're arrogant, obstinate, and entitled." He growled the words. "I can deal with that. But what I can't handle" – he took a deep breath, as if needing the moment to calm his mounting anger – "is that you're secretive."

"I'm an open freaking book." Sage threw her hands up in the air. It didn't matter what she did. She was always wrong. "Problem is every time I try to open my mouth, you shut me down, telling me how stupid or childish I am."

"You have a lot to learn."

"And I would if I had a partner who helped me instead of being a bully" Sage squared off against him, planting her feet as her hands found her hips. She arched an eyebrow, daring him to refute her statement.

He should have been intimidated. She'd thrown that look at Matt many a time before with excellent results, but Grey only laughed.

"Devon kicks the crap out of you, and you go to him for everything. You confide in him."

"Don't try to cover jealousy with pretty words. Devon is my trainer. It's his job to spar with me." If he wanted to bring other people into this, she'd willingly oblige. "But let's not forget that you employed a vampire to attack me in order to trick me into following your orders."

"I'll admit that wasn't my finest moment." Amusement faded from Grey's face. "But since then I have done everything in my power to protect you. And as partners, we have a duty to be honest with each other."

"Is this about Zack showing up at my apartment?" She let her hands fall from her hips. "Seriously? I told you he did that on his own, and it would have been rude of me to shoo him away."

"He would have understood." Grey looked away, pretending to fix his hair, and adjusted his hat.

"Remember I invited you to stay. You declined."

"I don't want to play stupid games."

"You could have just hung out and gotten to know me and my family better."

"You mean the roommates?" His nose crinkled.

"Yes! Matt and Josh are like brothers to me," she said, with enough force to ensure he understood they were not to be disparaged. "You want trust? That's earned. We might be partners, but that doesn't take away the things you've done. You call *me* arrogant? Take a look at yourself. You don't want to listen to me because I'm a damn newbie who doesn't know anything. You're the expert, and I should just shut up and listen while the big people talk. "

"That's taking my words out of context."

"Your words." She pointed a finger at him and herself in turn. "My ears."

"You have so much to learn."

"I don't deny that. But I'm not an idiot. I might have a thing or two to bring to the table. You want to know why I talk to Devon and not you?" She glared at him, waiting to see if he would come back full snark or not.

Grey sighed and waved his hand as if to say, "Go on."

"He listens. He might not agree with me, but he listens. He lets me lay it all on the line without name-calling or belittling of any kind."

Grey rolled his eyes so hard Sage expected them to pop out. "Easy for him to do; he doesn't work in the field."

She might as well be speaking to a brick wall for all the good it was doing. "You know what? I don't think this is about me at all. It's you. No matter what I say, you're going to have a comeback. So what is it? You don't want a partner? You didn't have one before I came along. Are you just a lone wolf, pushing everyone away so you don't have to share the glory?"

"Glory?" He choked on the word. "This job isn't about glory."

"What is it, then?"

"We're not here for medals or recognition. Get that out of your head right now. We protect the world from the destructive forces of magic. It's not pretty. It's not fun. But It is dangerous. People die every day in our line of work. Especially arrogant newbie agents like you who get all doe-eyed over how cool magic is."

For the second time in as many minutes, the force of his anger pushed her back a step. Sage hadn't realized she'd struck a nerve. A raw one at that. Of course, as closed off as Grey was, how could anyone know what really bothered him? She gave herself a moment to cool off and approached softly.

"Is that what happened to your last partner?"

Grey turned away. "Don't do that. We're talking about you."

He didn't have to confirm the obvious. She saw him in a new light. Misguided as his methods had been, his intentions were good. And she had to admit she'd been nothing short of a brat in the way she'd dealt with him.

Neither of them had really taken the time to understand each other. "Fine," Sage sighed. She needed to be the bigger person and offer the olive branch. "Let's talk about me, then. You want to build the trust between us? I've got something serious to tell you."

Grey opened his mouth.

"I need you to hear me out first," Sage cut him off before he could speak. "And when you feel the urge to lecture me on being a stupid newbie, just bite your tongue." She held her hand out to shake. "Can you do that?"

Grey glanced suspiciously over his shoulder. "I'm really not going to like this, am I?"

"Probably not." She waved her hand, reminding him they needed to shake before she revealed anything. "But remember I'm coming to you with this. I'm trusting you, knowing it's going to be potentially fatal for me."

"Are you in danger?" He faced her again, suspicion shifting to concern so quickly it made her head spin.

"Bad choice of words." She smirked at him impishly, hoping to diffuse his temper before it had the chance to go off again. "I'm just expecting the standard verbal bashing from you."

"That bad, eh?"

"Oh yeah. But If I hear the word newbie, come from your lips, I'm knocking that stupid hat straight off your head."

Grey's jaw tightened, and Sage began regret opening up to him. She waited in silence, hand still extended. The comment about the hat might have been a little mean, but she needed him to understand how badly his constant belittling was.

He let out a sigh as he took her hand, squeezing as he shook it. "Fine. I'm listening."

Her throat suddenly went dry at the prospect of letting her secret slip. But she'd committed to telling him. No going back now. She swallowed hard. "We've been going round and round trying to put this puzzle together. And as close as we have come, we still feel like there's a piece missing."

"Go on." He held her hand hostage, his grip tightening.

"I have a source. One very much dubious in nature, who might have given me a way to connect the dots."

"You're speaking in riddles." His brow furrowed deeply.

"You mentioned the djinn being a potential suspect. And while I haven't ruled that out completely, I do have reason to believe they might also be able to help us break this case wide open. Well, not *they*, one djinn in particular."

"You know a djinn, and you didn't tell me?" Grey growled. At any moment he was going to start calling her a damned newbie.

"Hold your tongue, remember?" She yanked her hand from his grip before he crushed it. "I'm telling you now…partner… let me finish… without the lecture."

Grey's chest rumbled with each angry breath, but true to his promise he did not utter another word.

"My new neighbor," she continued. "He just moved into my apartment complex. I can't stress this enough. Meeting him was totally out of my control. He gave me a book and said it could help with the case."

Grey stood as still as a statue, his body so tense Sage could see veins throbbing at his neck. One wrong word might set him off, and like a coiled spring, he'd shoot straight up into the ceiling.

Sage waited, cringing, knowing she was in a world of trouble for not telling him sooner about Luke.

The more she thought about it, Luke could easily be involved in the case, if not the culprit. Being a djinn automatically qualified him for the dark side; not that anyone admitted to their being one.

It's the person not the magic that does evil deeds.

But even people who spouted that ideology agreed the djinn were inherently bad.

If that were the case, why would Luke give her the book? Maybe he was dark, but like Vader, he felt conflicted, and it was just enough to make him do something for the light side. If only life worked as easily as Sci-Fi.

"Djinn do things for their own personal reasons." Grey's reply came on a surprisingly level tone. "What could this one get from giving you potential evidence against him?"

Sage had spent the entire ride from Marrin's back to ASSET trying to figure out how it all fit together. She shrugged. "I was thinking we have a look together. Maybe *we* can come up with the answer."

"Show me when we get inside." Grey looked around as if checking to make sure no one had heard them, and started walking toward the elevator. "You really think my hat is stupid?"

His question stunned her speechless. In truth, she hated that hat, but Sage hadn't intended to wound his pride with her off the cuff remark. He couldn't be that fragile, could he?

The elevator doors opened and Grey stepped in first. When he looked at her she could see he wanted an answer.

"Do you really think I'm just a dumb newbie?" She deflected.

"Not every day."

"Same goes for your hat." Sage smirked, hoping that would be enough to placate his ego.

They rode the elevator to the top and headed straight for and open office. Soon as they were behind closed doors, Sage pulled the book from her bag and started thumbing through the pages. Grey pulled up a chair next to her.

Hand-written, definitely a journal of some kind, it had recipes of all kinds for manipulating magic. No wonder Devon had been upset.

"Whoever wrote that book was into some serious power-grabbing," Grey commented as he read over her shoulder. "Wait. Stop there."

The Amulet of Emmuri

*The great gods before the dawn of man had blessed
the earth with their creations.
Ethereals were connected to the heavens and
knowledge.
Elementals were connected to the physical realm.
Shades were connected to the world unseen.*

*Each claimed supremacy, believing their destiny
to rule over all who dwelled within their realm. But
none had enough power to rule.
Their hubris led to the creation of the Terra.
But even the Mother's new creation failed to be
superior.*

*To claim true superiority, one must harness all
powers for their own.*

A few crude drawings with labels too faded to be read appeared to describe the cut and shape of a crystal that could be turned into the Amulet of Emmuri.

Four pages followed the drawing, filled with spells in a very specific order meant to create a magical prison within the stone. From what she understood, once fully imbued with all the blessings and spells, the stone would be capable of housing the four different elements of magic, and use them as a type of battery. Each quadrant of the diamond-shaped stone had unique spells to trap a different power.

The following pages had been dedicated to explaining how to obtain the magic, each page focused on a specific branch of magic, with their own requirements and special rituals.

Sage focused on the underlined notes.

Infusion of the magical elements must come from living sources.

One member from each magical family must be sacrificed to the stone. Their magic, held in a facet, can be drawn upon as needed.

Physical contact with the stone must be established to attune vibrations before infusion can be initiated.

Transfer of all elements must happen within one moon cycle.

Cannot imbue stone with my own magic. I feel it draining my power with each attempt. External magic needed to facilitate transfer.

Once Sage reached that line, she noticed more scribbles and words that had been crossed out, as if the person who had written them had tried various methods but failed each time. One word, however, she recognized even with the fading, tight script.

Djinn.

Separated from their own magic, they do not appear to feel the power drain. Their curse removes their will to fight orders given. Facilitators.

If that were true, then it meant Luke was innocent. Sage breathed a sigh. Her instincts had been right, it seemed. But rather than gloat about it, she continued to read.

The Amulet of Emmuri is able to harness the magic held within: Ethereal, Elemental, Shade, and Terra and allow the wearer use of these powers as their own, even before all four elements are imbued.

The amulet had been used before, but if Sage was reading it correctly, the creator of this magical artifact had not completed the transfer of all four branches.

Sage pulled out her notes. The gemini twins were members of the Elemental family. The brownie was a member of the Ethereal family. The kitsune belonged to the Shade family. Which left only the Terra family line.

If someone was loading the stone, and she was ninety percent sure that was the case, then…

Her heart leapt into her chest. A Terra was next.

She continued to read.

Djinn magic…not immune to the stones pull. May need alternate facilitator. Drained magic.

Some of the writing had been scratched out, and in place of the old words, new ones had been written with a modern pen. The handwriting was smoother, with less flourish. If she had to guess a gender, it appeared to be male. One thing was for certain: it had been written recently. The darkness of the pen clashed against the yellowing pages and faded browns of the ancient-looking scribbles.

The magic of the djinn would be exhausted upon completion of the stone.

Did that mean the djinn would die? Or just lose access to his magic forever?

If that were the case, then Luke clearly couldn't be the culprit; unless he would gain all the magic in the amulet instead. There were too many variables. Sage's head ached as she tried to work through the problem.

Who was the djinn really working for?

Who was wishing djinn magic into action?

Could it really be Sylvia? She didn't seem the power-hungry type; she had enough of that already. Marrin looked guilty enough, but why would he cannibalize his own people for it?

He'd already said his powers of persuasion kept his legs from being broken well enough.

The Animal Sanctuary? No. They were at risk of losing everything because someone called the city inspectors on them. Why hurt themselves?

Even now she was stuck at square one.

"So, exactly how long were you planning to wait to tell me your neighbor was a djinn?" Grey asked with a surprisingly level tone.

Sage shrugged. "Honestly, I didn't think you'd listen to anything else once I said the word *djinn*."

"Because you pull secretive crap like this." He pointed at the book. "Someone has to protect you from yourself."

"Like I said before, if you'd stop acting like I'm clueless... you know, give me the benefit of the doubt every once in a while—"

"Didn't I just do that?" Grey asked.

"And yet, I feel there's a lecture coming."

"No. I keep my promises. I'm just pointing out facts. It's pretty clear you've known about this djinn for a while. Especially if he gave you the book."

"See, that's where you're wrong," she countered. "I hardly know the guy. I've done my best to stay away from him, too. He was the one to shove this thing in my face."

"I'd trust you more if you'd tell me what's happening. Especially at your house," Grey said.

"Still prickly because Zack came to hang out with me?"

"ASSET agents don't invite predators into their homes." He was dangerously close to breaking that promise.

"Says the man who used to date one?" Sage cut him to the quick. Grey never spoke about the mysterious vampire ex of his.

"Don't —"

She'd wanted to shut down his high and mighty attitude, but the sudden choked silence between them spoke volumes. She'd overplayed her hand and struck a tender nerve with him, one she hadn't intended to.

"Zack is not the real issue here," she spoke cautiously. "This was my olive branch. I hoped that you would see my intentions are good. I can't live in fear that everything I do is going to be graded so harshly. We're supposed to be partners."

"You don't yet have the experience needed to make some of the decisions you've been making alone."

"And ridiculing me for everything I do is going to make me less likely to go it alone?"

"No," he sighed. "But you have to appreciate the danger."

"I'm not trying to get myself killed. Contrary to popular belief, I do like living."

"Then don't hide things from me, please." He sounded so sincere.

"I'm telling you something pretty freaking big now. How are you going to react to me, and what are you going to do with the information?" She glared at him, waiting to see if he could handle being nice for a change.

"You think your neighbor wants your help?" Grey's eyes narrowed as he looked from the book in Sage's hand back up to her face. "He's a djinn."

"He didn't have to tell me anything. He could have let this happen right under my nose."

"He told you that a Terra was next on the list. Probably to frighten you before he was forced to magic you into the stone."

"But how can that be if we're immune?"

"He might not need to do anything magical. It might be something as simple as using your blood. Or the blood from any Terra, for that matter, to bathe the stone in our magical protection. The book called for an infusion."

"I believe he warned me for a reason." Sage laid the book on the table and stood. "He's telling me he needs us to stop him because he can't stop himself."

"And how are we supposed to do that?"

Good question. One she hadn't even considered. But since Grey asked, she took a moment to think about it rather than blurt out the first words that came to mind. "Bring in the djinn and keep him safe here. And recall all the Terras in town until further notice."

"You need to clear that with Ava first, and explain to her why you waited until now to reveal your new neighbor and his magical plan."

"You hate me, don't you?" she asked. Sending her in alone to tell Ava she screwed up? He might as well let her face the djinn alone; she'd have a better chance of survival.

"You withhold evidence. Ava will want answers." Grey threw a dirty look her way.

"Very partner-y of you, throwing me under the bus. I thought you were supposed to have my back?"

"I do. Way back here in the nose bleeds, eating popcorn and watching the show." He laughed.

"Whatever. I can take my lumps alone. I'm not scared." She scowled at him, trying really hard to hold the angry look. "But when she asks why I didn't follow procedure, I'll tell her I didn't really know what to do. I mean, I tried to ask you about djinns, but all you said was they were evil and to stay away."

"You know Ava won't fall for that line of crap."

"Do I?" She batted her eyes innocently. "It's not a lie."

Grey sighed. "From now on, we listen to each other. Had I known about your neighbor, I'd have had an investigative team out there ASAP looking into him and his connections."

"Speaking of. How are we going to learn who he's working for?"

"One problem at a time. Now that we know who he is and what he's doing, let's bring him in. If we gift wrap him for Ava, she might go easy on you for taking your time reporting him." Grey nodded toward the door.

That was a plan she could get behind. Maybe Grey could be a good partner after all.

TWENTY-FIVE

They'd borrowed an ASSET car to retrieve Luke. Sage found herself missing the wind in her hair and the feeling that she had cheated death once again when they arrived back at her apartment complex.

As usual, she found Luke standing out on the stairs smoking his cigarette. He spotted her before she could open her mouth and call him down.

"It looks like someone did their homework." Luke smiled, congenial as always. He stamped out his cigarette and descended the stairs to meet them. "I had a feeling you'd be back today. But did you have to bring him along?"

"You have a problem with my partner?" Sage asked.

"Hard enough as it was to find a Terra willing to listen to me, dealing with her overbearing partner who clearly has no respect for the position he's in makes things infinitely more complicated."

Grey's expression caught in a scrunch somewhere between confusion and anger. "I've been an agent here for a very long time. Don't presume to lecture me on my duty."

"You misunderstand me." Luke held up a hand to stop him. "I have no doubt you're a crack agent, but your partner here has been left in the dark. When she questions you, she's ridiculed. When you take her on assignments, you keep her from speaking. These are learning experiences. Pass or fail, every opportunity is a teaching one, and you have failed Sage in the worst possible ways."

Sage's cheeks flushed. She averted her eyes hoping to cool the burn of embarrassment before anyone made a comment.

"She gets more information from the vampire than I have seen from you," Luke added.

With that statement, he crossed the line from a knight defending her honor to a stalker. And that left a bitter taste in her mouth. "Exactly how long have you been following me around?"

"Most of what I hear has come from that very patio." Luke nodded toward her apartment.

"You can twist the truth however you like, djinn." Grey's expression finally settled on anger. "It only proves what we know to be true of your kind."

"What do you know of my kind?" Luke's tone turned threatening.

"You don't get the djinn curse unless you're attempting magic of the darkest variety."

"Touché." Luke winced. "No accounting for time served and good behavior; a life sentence for one mistake is a literal eternity. But please, go on about something done thousands of years before you were born."

"This is getting us nowhere," Sage interrupted. "The amulet in that book – is that what your master is trying to recreate?"

"I'm afraid I cannot give a definitive answer to that question, but I'm willing to bet all the dots lined up for you when doing your research."

Confirmation enough for Sage. "Have you seen the amulet?"

Luke pressed his lips together tightly. His breath came long and loud through his nose, nostrils flaring wildly.

Magical gag order manifesting, Sage wondered. Either way, his actions alone had pretty much confirmed what she suspected, but still she waited patiently for him to verbalize it.

"I have recently seen a necklace." Luke's words came strained through tightly clenched teeth. "It held a stone so big it would cause the wearer to hunch over."

"How did you come across this?" Sage held out the book he'd lent her.

"It was mine." Luke's response came much faster and more easily than his last.

Sage gasped at the truth bomb he'd just dropped.

"Forbidden magic has its consequences. My research was incomplete, but my eagerness to press on led to my curse." His cheeks reddened slightly. "But my new master is smart, and realized the missing pieces needed to succeed."

"You sound a little too proud," Grey commented.

"It's rewarding to see the evolution of one's work. But after years of service, I understand my curse was a necessary punishment for grasping too hard at magic that didn't belong to me. However, it is that curse which prevents me from acting in ways that might prevent it from happening again."

"Who is your master?" Grey demanded.

"You of all people know I cannot say." Luke grimaced. "So long as my master possesses my talisman, I am bound to their will."

"And yet you sought out Sage?" Grey folded his arms. "I'm not buying it."

"Sage was a happy accident. I just moved to this neighborhood."

"I don't believe in coincidences." Grey's lip curled into a sneer. His muscles tensed. "If this master didn't want you dealing with Sage, they would have stopped you. I sense a trap."

"Protecting your assets would be wise," Luke agreed.

Sage knew it was a trap, but just like the djinn, she felt unable to prevent springing it as long as they were out in the open. "Then I'm going to ask for you to follow us back to ASSET."

"You did read the notes in that book I gave you." Luke's expression darkened.

"Why do you think we're here?" Sage asked.

"Due diligence. Interviewing suspects." Luke waved his hand flippantly. "You're the law. I'd expect nothing short of you doing your job."

"And bringing criminals down to the station," Sage said, and immediately regretted the cheesy sitcom-esque line.

"You are the final piece of the puzzle." Luke's eyes widened fearfully.

"Me?" Sage pointed to herself. Why the hell was she so important?

"Terras," Luke clarified.

"Are you threatening us?" Grey balled up his fists.

"A friendly warning. Should my master wish—"

"We're better protected behind ASSET's walls," Grey said.

Luke smiled wickedly. "You can always return alone."

"Not without more information, which you seem to be unable to give," Sage added.

"And you think behind your protective barrier that you can somehow negate the magic binding my tongue?" Luke raised an eyebrow as if genuinely curious.

"If anyone can make a miracle like that happen, it's Ava." Sage hadn't meant to say the thought out loud, but the words still rang true. She looked over her shoulder, making sure there were no other neighbors within earshot. Thankfully, the apartment complex was relatively quiet at mid-day. Most people were still at work, and the few she saw out were in the pool splashing loudly enough to avoid hearing their conversation.

"I do love a good experiment." Luke held his hands out as if waiting for cuffs. "Am I under arrest? Do I have rights? A phone call?"

"Just walk." Grey refused to laugh at the djinn's joke. "Ava is going to have a fit with this one."

"Should we apologize in advance?" Sage meant it as a joke, but no one seemed to get it.

"I want you to understand I am trying to help, but I can only reveal so much." Luke followed along as they headed to the parking lot.

"You know everything in that book, right?" Sage asked.

"I do," Luke answered warily.

"So if your master completes their work, your magic will be absorbed too," she added.

"Meaning I will no longer be tied to cursed magic." Luke filled in the blanks.

"That can go either way, you understand. You could die, or you could be rendered mortal," she clarified, drawing a finger under her throat for emphasis.

"Either is fine." Luke shrugged. "I've lived many lifetimes. Served many masters. Seen civilizations rise and fall only to rise again."

"So by that logic, you sound like you almost want your master to succeed," Grey commented.

"I said *either* is fine," Luke clarified. "Any outcome for me is acceptable. However, knowing the cost of my master accomplishing their goals is unfortunate. Which is why I have done all I could to alert the local law. It's out of my hands now, and off my conscience what happens next."

"He swings from nice guy to jerk just as fast as you do, Grey." Sage tried joking again; the tone of the conversation had become way to somber for her liking.

"You've got a point there. Perhaps he deserves a little time locked in a room with Ava. Master or not, she'll extract the truth from of him," Grey replied, in rare form.

Sage giggled, refusing to tamp down her amusement. Laughter felt good. How long had it been since she'd had a real laugh with Grey?

Luke stared at them both in utter disbelief. "How can you two make jokes, knowing your situation is dire?"

"Because laughter is often necessary. Rather than let the stress shatter us," Grey replied. "Every day my people square up against magical abusers with world-altering machinations. You're far from the first or the last. Those in my line of work who can't deal with the stress soon find themselves out of the agency… in a body bag."

Goosebumps prickled all over Sage's skin. She gulped back a knot that had suddenly wedged itself in her throat.

Luke's eyes darted back and forth between Grey and Sage, but he did not open his mouth to speak.

"You think I'm mean to Sage because I don't tell her everything and ask her to stop talking so she can listen?" Grey aimed his words like nocked arrow, straight at Luke's head. "I'm teaching her the best way I know… through experience. There's a lot of really scary shit out there. Reading about it in books is nothing compared to experience. Even then I have worked, perhaps too stringently, to mitigate that experience."

"It's fine, really." She hoped to derail this conversation. They'd already gone rounds with each other on the topic. No need to bring others into it.

"Bottom line is…We're a team," Grey continued his defense. "You can stand there, high and mighty, with your magical gag order stopping you from giving us the information… that's fine." He nudged Sage's shoulder and gave her a mischievous wink. "We have our own ways around that. And while our boss is tearing into you, we will find your master."

"You're free to try." Luke held his hands out again to be cuffed.

The gesture didn't match the tone of his voice, nor the strange look Sage caught in his eyes. She'd seen it the last time they'd talked, as if he were not truly in control of himself. That thought worried her.

ASSET had its own safety measures in place. They had to, in order to house the prisoners that were brought in for questioning or sentencing. Since he was a suspect, it was procedure to bring Luke in. But that odd glint in his eye had her second guessing it. He'd said it himself not a few moments before: they needed a Terra. Would bringing him in set off the trap his master had planned?

"Wait!" Sage said, before they headed to the car. "We need some collateral before we go."

"Smart thinking," Luke praised her.

"Unless we have his talisman, there's no collateral we could collect to hold him," Grey replied with a frustrated sigh.

"But you cannot be anything but impressed by your partner's train of thought." Luke nodded to Sage. "Sadly, my talisman is under the control of my master. I can offer my word, if that would do."

"The word of a djinn?" Sage glared at him.

"A djinn I may be and a trickster by design, but my words always ring true – that cannot be denied." He bowed with a flourish of his hand.

"Was that absolutely necessary?" Grey all but rolled his eyes at Luke.

Sage wasn't sure how she should respond.

"He can bend the truth to its breaking point." Grey nodded at Sage. "But he cannot lie."

"Okay, Luke, what word can you give?" she asked.

"I like you, Sage. You have a true heart. I wouldn't dream of harming you. And it is my promise that behind the walls of ASSET all agents are safe from my magic."

Sage thought long and hard about his revelation. It seemed they had no choice. If djinn magic was needed to work the final infusion of the amulet, and his promise was safety from his magic behind ASSET walls, then that was where they needed to be… quickly.

"You'd better be telling the truth!"

TWENTY-SIX

They marched Luke straight up to the top floor of ASSET. The elevator doors parted and Grey pressed forward, pushing Luke toward the receptionist desk.

Sage's gut tightened every time she saw someone sitting at there. She'd avoided getting to know the new receptionist. Nothing against the new girl, but the ghost of Rina haunted that desk, and even though the two didn't look a thing alike, all Sage could see was Rina's face and the false smile that had lured her into trust.

As they marched past, Sage did a double take. The little pixie of a girl had tears in her eyes.

Before she could stop herself to ask, Grey cleared his throat to get Sage's attention. He opened the door and all but shoved Luke inside.

"Do you treat all your prisoners so well?" Luke asked.

"Yes," Grey replied.

Sage had expected to see Ava's nose buried in her computer, but the office was empty and her laptop closed. "You're lucky – the boss is out."

"Am I?" Luke scrunched up his face, confusion creasing his brow.

"Is there something you need to tell us?" Sage's heart skipped a beat. "Did you know she would not be here?" *Had they already completed the amulet?*

"You know my tongue is held in check by my master. I have said all I can." Luke sank down, onto a chair in front of Ava's desk.

He looked like a man without a care in the world. And yet, that had to be a lie. His fate, whether he admitted it or not, was tied to the amulet, and the last one attempted had cursed him. *Maybe that was it,* Sage hoped. *If he knew the end would result in his freedom and some other master being cursed into his life, he truly would have nothing to fear.* And that was a far better outcome than the alternative.

Sage nearly said as much, but Ava stormed into the room, carrying a great axe in one hand, resting on her shoulder, and a thick file in a green folder in the other. Some papers had been roughly shoved inside and looked as if they had been rained on.

"I thought I could trust you two to solve this case quickly!" She rounded the corner of her desk and slapped the file down. "You now have another missing person to add to your tally… and this one's much more high profile. I have the whole Shade guild up my ass…" Ava's voice trailed off as she noticed Luke in the chair opposite. "What is this?" She thrust her axe at the djinn sitting quietly in his chair.

"This is Luke," Sage chirped with pride. "And he's the djinn being employed to–"

"Unless he's going to make our missing people materialize here in my office, I don't care what his name is."

"He's got information we need, but he can't tell us," Sage replied.

Ava's gaze fell to Luke's arms, zeroing in on the living tattoos. "Tricky, tricky, tricky." Her brows pulled together causing fine lines appeared above them. Ava set her axe down on the desk next to her laptop and took a seat. "Obviously you're no closer to learning the truth of why Sylvia has now been added to the missing persons list?"

"We sort of thought–" Sage cut herself off. "Did you say Sylvia? No. We just spoke with her."

"Impossible. Her husband reported her missing this morning!" Ava all but growled.

"We were just there at her office. I swear!" Sage replied.

"But were you talking to her?" Luke commented casually.

"What the hell is that supposed to mean?" Sage turned to Grey, hoping he'd have an answer, or at the very least back her up. But her partner stood mute, stroking his chin while thoughts percolated in his mind. "We were there, getting the full brunt of her temper for not solving the case. I'm pretty sure I didn't dream that."

"I need this case closed now," Ava demanded.

"He's the key to helping us close it," Sage offered, patting Luke on the shoulder.

"A djinn, especially one directly involved in the case, is not a reliable source of information. Throw him in a cell and keep him there while you two continue your investigation."

"But we know his master is the one taking people." Sage reached into her bag and pulled out the leather notebook Luke had given her. She tossed it in front of Ava. "This is what they're being used for."

Ava glanced at it curiously before taking the book in hand. She quietly looked over the pages, her eyebrows arching with interest as she flipped to the amulet's information.

"When we spoke to Sylvia this morning, did you notice anything odd about her?" Grey's whisper broke the quiet that had fallen over the room.

"No," Sage answered, without thinking.

"I can't recall seeing her shift the whole time we spoke with her this morning," Grey continued, prompting Sage to change gears and have a look back at her memories.

Had Sylvia morphed into her usual black cloud of doom? She had certainly employed her cheery demeanor. Sylvia's words had been as sharp as ever. But Sage hadn't paid that much attention to what she looked like. Terras were supposed to be able to see through magic. If someone was impersonating Sylvia with a glamour either she or Grey should have been able to tell. Or would they? Sage remembered how easily she'd been fooled at the Animal Sanctuary. Shifters were of two forms. On the surface she only saw one at a time. But when she paid closer attention their shadowy other half became apparent. Was Luke's master a shifter?

"We have to do is learn who his master is," Sage demanded. "He is the key. The missing piece."

"Put the djinn in a cell," Ava directed the order at Grey. "Now."

A look of pure satisfaction spread across Luke's face. He held his hands up as if waiting for cuffs. "As you command."

"You see. He's participating willingly." Even as Sage said the words, a bad feeling prickled at the back of her neck. Something was off, but she couldn't quite figure out if it was Luke triggering it or Ava. "We don't have to lock him up."

"It doesn't matter what he wants," Ava said.

"I know. He's a dirty trickster who can't be trusted." Sage groaned.

"He's not in control of his own mind," Ava countered. "All his master has to do is recall him and he'll poof away. Where would that leave you?"

"What good does it do us to stick him in a cell, then?" Sage asked.

"You expect me to reveal our secrets here in front of him?" Ava glared back at Sage as if daring her to speak another contradictory word.

"Do you want me on guard duty?" Grey asked, his tone cautious.

Ava set the book down and pointed her finger straight at the page with the amulet. "No!"

Sage looked at the spot where her boss's finger had landed. The list of magical ingredients needed to complete the amulets power: neutral magic from a Terra.

"He's to be quarantined. And if he manages to escape, following him is exactly what his master wants. Whomever they are, they need one of us to finish the job." Ava pressed the button on her desk phone. "Recall all agents and have them check into the building ASAP. No questions asked. Quarantine the building as well. All personnel of magical lineage other than Terras are to be sent home until further notice."

"We can't hide in here forever." Sage had thought of that exact scenario but knew it wouldn't solve their problem, only put a bandage on the situation.

"We don't have to. The master will eventually come for their djinn when he doesn't return. And I think he knows that." Ava's nose crinkled as she turned her attention on Luke.

His smile never faltered. Nor did he show even the slightest sense of unease, even under the scrutinizing eyes of Ava. "I suspected you had some tricks up your sleeve here. I'm ready to see my room now."

"Can we really keep him here?" Sage asked. "Sever the connection between him and his master?"

Ava's expression darkened as Sage became the latest target of her frightening glare.

Grey took Luke by the arm and lifted him out of his seat with an eagerness that bordered on fear. "Let's go, genie."

"As you command," Luke replied.

The door slammed behind the men as they left. Sage gulped, realizing she'd drawn the short stick being left with Ava, a person far scarier than the djinn had proven to be.

She waited anxiously in silence, hoping Ava wouldn't decide to pick the axe back up and use it. She'd been so confident that her boss would be the one to sort this mess out. But as she lifted her eyes, Sage found Ava looking just as worried as she was. Ava pinched the bridge of her nose and collapsed onto her office chair.

"We don't have a magical prison cell, do we?" Sage asked.

"Not one that can hold back a djinn being called to his master."

"So that was all for show? A trick for the trickster?"

"Precisely. Stalling for time."

"Fake it till you make it," Sage added with a giggle to break the tension.

"This is hardly the occasion for levity, Miss Cynwrig. Do you understand the severity of what we're up against?"

"Yes ma'am." Sage's voice cracked.

Ava saw straight through the lie. "How could you?" She lifted the book and set it back down with a sigh. "If this book… if this amulet…" She took a few breaths. Her eyebrows knitted together and deep creases appeared across her brow, teasing age that had been blurred by immortality. "No one should have this kind of power. Not only does it throw the natural balance off, but one person having that much power is bound to cause chaotic disaster. Tyranny, wars, destruction… it all goes hand in hand."

"And because the Terra are part of the spell, we lose our ability to protect the world?" Sage guessed.

"Yes. The whole reason for our people's creation becomes moot." Ava cracked the smallest of smiles.

Her approval meant the world to Sage at that moment, instilling a sense of hopeful pride that she hadn't realized she needed.

The moment ended as quickly as it came. Ava's eyes found Sage's neck and her expression brightened beyond approval and straight to guaranteed victory. "We do have one thing that can negate all magic."

Sage's hand moved instinctively toward her necklace. Although she craved the feeling of purpose and pride for continuing her mother's legacy, the resolution Ava was insinuating cheapened it. "That's supposed to remain a secret. Not to be used because of how dangerous it is." *Was she being tested?*

"Have you read this book?"

"I looked it over, yes."

"Then how can you argue against stopping the creation of something that threatens the balance we're charged to protect?"

Framed in that light, Ava's words made sense. "I'm not arguing with your point. But it just feels wrong to use something you entrusted to me to keep a secret."

"Desperate times," Ava replied without hesitation.

"To use it would reveal the secret of its whereabouts. Won't that cause other issues?"

"Leave mitigating the damages to me. You just do as you're ordered."

"You think my using the seed on the djinn will stop this master from completing the amulet?" Sage asked.

"Djinn magic is part of the equation." Ava didn't sound completely convinced, but at the same time, she had no other suggestion.

"I'm not sure I like the sound of this." Sage stood and paced the room. "We could possibly kill Luke. And what if this master finds another djinn later? Do we kill them too? Maybe next time we won't find out until it's too late and this master completes their work. Then what? We can't fight an unstoppable force."

"If Luke is as honorable as you think he is, he wouldn't have come here if he didn't think you had a chance of helping. If his intentions are less than honorable or motivated by his master, neither of them could possibly know about the ace we're hiding up our sleeves." She pointed at Sage's necklace. "Either way we have the upper hand, and you and Grey have more time to track down the master while they're scrambling to find a new djinn."

"But you're asking me to kill him," Sage countered.

"Collateral damage is expected in war."

"We're not at war yet." Sage grasped for anything that might help her case. Ava might have grown accustomed to death over the long years she'd been alive, but Sage was still coming to grips with Rina's death, and being asked to end another life so soon felt like a Herculean task she wasn't ready to wrap her mind around.

"Give me the necklace, and I'll do it if you don't have the courage." Ava reached out her hand.

"No. This isn't right. I was made guardian over this weapon because it needed to be in the hands of someone who wouldn't use it."

"Can't," Ava corrected.

"Won't. A Terra can't use the magic, but all I have to do is let someone else hold it. You know that."

"I do. And I also know when exceptions must be made for the greater good. Sage, we cannot let this master complete the amulet. We have a duty to protect magic at all costs." Ava stood, looking more terrifying than ever. She held out her hand and demanded that Sage give up the necklace.

"No," Sage answered with a defeated sigh. "I'll go and talk to Luke."

"I'll come with you," Ava said.

"No!" Sage added strength to her voice. "If you want me to do this, I have to do it my way. Alone."

"You know I'll be watching on camera."

"Watch all you want." Sage turned and headed out of the office, not sure what she would do when she reached Luke's cell. His death wasn't the answer; that she felt certain of. Other djinns could be found to complete the master's work. But, maybe just the threat of the end for Luke with devastating consequences would be enough to help him fight his master's control and at least give her a clue where to find the real baddie.

TWENTY-SEVEN

How exactly does the angel of death greet their victim? Quick and painless? Sage could throw the seed at him, and when he caught it…poof!

Would it be kinder to have a conversation before the deed was done? Explain herself and apologize before ending him?

The weight of duty pressed down on her with each step she took. With any luck, it would crush her before she could reach the elevators.

How could Ava ask this of her?

She had offered to do it herself, but the way Ava had jumped so eagerly to take control of the seed had been just as unsettling as asking Sage to do it; maybe even more.

Ava wasn't evil. A micromanaging overlord, sure, but not evil.

However, in the presence of ultimate power, even the best can be turned.

Her phone buzzed; one distraction too many to deal with. She left it in her pocket without answering as she pressed the elevator button.

There had to be some other way to avoid killing Luke. That just felt wrong on so many levels. But unless she found the answer before she reached his cell, she'd have to.

Her phone buzzed again as she rode the elevator down toward the prison level. She pulled it out far enough to see it was Matt calling. "Not now," Sage groaned, and sent the call to voicemail. Worst time ever for her to get a phone call. He'd hear all about this adventure later – if she could look him in the eye after being forced to assassinate a djinn who'd come to her in search of help.

The elevator doors parted. Sage nearly collided with Grey as she stepped out.

"What did Ava say?" he asked.

"That we should take shifts watching him. I'm first," she lied, but failed to nail the casual tone.

Grey planted his feet and crossed his arms. His eyes narrowed as he stared at her. "I don't think that's exactly what Ava said. How about we try again?"

"Why? Because I'm not capable of standing guard?"

Grey sighed loudly. "I thought we were going to stop this."

"You started it," Sage threw back at him.

"You're hiding something." He was an impassible wall, preventing her from heading down the hallway toward Luke's cell.

"With good reason, okay?" She tried move, but he took her by the shoulders.

"I can worry about my partner, can't I?"

She shrugged free of his grip. "Is that what you call it?"

"In my own way, yes. I don't want to see anything bad happen to you."

"What about having to do bad things?" she mumbled.

Grey's expression darkened.

"Whatever. Just stop being such a jerk," she huffed. "Might make working together a bit easier."

"Then be honest with me. What's going on?"

It became painfully clear that Grey wasn't taking no for an answer this time.

"Magical gag order. Talk to Ava if you want those details."

The moment the words left Sage's lips, Grey's posture changed. His angry eyes softened. "Can you do what she's asked?"

"Sure," Sage lied, more confidently this time. As much as she hated Grey's cocky swagger, his pity was far more off-putting.

"Whatever she asked you to do, it's probably for the best." Grey put a hand on her shoulder, this time in solidarity. "Serving the greater good puts us in positions we never wish to be in."

His reaction not only confirmed he understood the magnitude of what she'd been ordered to do, but proved he'd been in her position more than once himself. And as he turned to let her pass, she realized he hadn't asked her to tell him more.

Her phone buzzed again. Why was Matt calling her? Something deep down said she should answer, but talking to him would kill her resolve to complete the task she'd been assigned. He'd have to forgive her and be prepared for the emotional flood she'd come home with.

Sage pocketed her phone and made the long walk down the cellblock filled with heavy doors. Luke had been placed in the cell at the far end. The walk felt endless, like every step she took added two more to her journey.

When she finally reached the end and opened the door with a scan of her hand, she found Luke lounging comfortably on a cot against the wall. His face was the picture of serenity, as if he were completely content to be locked away.

"More comfortable than a magic lamp?" Sage asked with a nervous laugh.

"Is it to be torture, then... before I'm executed? Or were you actually trying to be funny?" Luke sat up. "The rack is far less painful than amateur hour."

"Touché," Sage replied.

"I am surprised they sent you. I expected your partner to be the one to do it." Despite the seriousness of his words, he still appeared content.

"I wish I knew whether or not to trust you." Sage took a step closer, scrutinizing his face for any tells. No one looks their murderer in the eye and smiles, and yet that was exactly what he was doing.

"What does your gut tell you?" Luke patted the spot next to him on the cot.

She shook her head at the gesture; kind as it was, she didn't feel like sitting. "My gut doesn't feel like you deserve death."

"Death comes for us all. I have to admit, I am glad it is you and not the grumpy one. You make for such a bittersweet end." He spoke with the same natural charm Marrin the Magnificent had.

"You knew all along that if we brought you in, it would mean death?"

"I had my suspicions." He shrugged. "Though I'm still uncertain of the method. We djinn are hard to kill."

"Your death severs the master's ability to wish the amulet into completion."

"A valid theory. One I have entertained myself. And if that is the judgment of your boss" – he held out his hands and winked – "then hack away at my magical chains."

Sage's phone buzzed again. She tried to ignore it. "Why are you so eager?"

"My intentions confuse you?" he countered.

"Obviously."

"Because under the control of my master, I can never be sure when my intentions are truly mine. Many times they are the will of my master as their wish is uttered into my talisman." He winced and doubled over. With his head between his knees, Luke's breathing suddenly stuttered.

"Are you okay?" Sage asked, unsure if she should go help him or not. Her phone buzzed again, and she nearly chucked it across the room.

As if her frustrated growl had awakened him from his fit, Luke rose and met Sage's eyes. "You really should answer that."

"Okay," she said slowly. This was the kind of moment she really wished she had her partner. Luke was up to something. Or he wasn't, and she was looking into the eyes of his master. Either way, answering the phone felt like opening Pandora's box, and yet she was powerless to stop herself. Sage pulled the buzzing phone from her pocket and answered. "Kinda busy, Matt."

"It's not nice to play with other people's toys," a woman replied.

Sage's heart nearly stopped. She'd never heard the voice before, but it had all the hallmarks of Sylvia's haughty temper.

"Who is this?" Sage snarled into the phone. Her eyes flashed to Luke with a deadly promise of retribution.

"I'm so very sorry, Sage." Luke faded from the room, leaving behind the empty cot he'd been sitting in.

"You play with my toys, now I play with yours!" The woman disconnected the call.

"Matt," She wailed. She had to save him. Somehow.

TWENTY-EIGHT

If not for the soundproofing in the prison cell, the entire building might have heard Sage desperately screaming for her roommate. She frantically redialed Matt's phone, only to end up reaching voicemail.

Of all the times to be magically immune! If she were anything but a Terra, Sage could have hitched a ride with an Ethereal and rushed to Matt's rescue in the blink of an eye.

"What's the use of magic if you can't use it to save the ones you love?"

She couldn't bear to think of what that woman might be doing to her roommate at that moment. Anger burned the tears in her eyes, evaporating them before they had the chance to drip down her cheeks.

As bait, Matt would at least be kept alive. That small speck of hope was the only thing keeping Sage from flying completely off the handle.

Who the hell was the mystery woman? Sage needed a face to give focus to her rage. Without it, she kept picturing Sylvia but as much as she wished for the easy answer, but the voice did not belong to the shadowrunner. Who was Luke's master? The question had plagued her through every encounter she'd had with him. He was guilty by proxy, but the puppet master had to have been within arm's reach the entire time.

The strange woman's voice replayed in her mind.

Definitely cocky.

Completely mean.

Surprisingly young.

But none of that helped Sage identify the owner of the voice. The mystery woman remained just that.

She might not kill the bait, but her choice of words – *You play with my toys, now I play with yours* – was a threat not to be ignored. A terrifying vision of Matt tied and gagged, completely helpless, tortured to the brink of sanity, sent Sage's heart racing.

She fought to fill her lungs with air as panic threatened to cripple her where she stood. Why hadn't she seen this coming?

This was her fault. She'd left Matt a sitting duck. She should have protected him. She'd promised not to bring her work home. If anything happened to Matt, she'd never forgive herself.

Stupid, stupid, stupid Sage!

Luke, innocent or not of intention, was their neighbor. Of course his master would know of her human roommate. The master would undoubtedly know all of Sage's pressure points. And instead of warning Matt about the potential danger of a djinn's master, she'd only told her roommate about the genie.

She had to save him!

Sage clenched her fist so tight her nails broke the skin of her palm. Pain short-circuited the panic attack, freezing her in place. She focused on the sensations: skin ripping, throbbing, blood rising to meet the offending nails. Breathing with purpose, she forced her heartrate to slow.

Calmer, for the moment, she called Matt's phone one final time, praying someone would answer. She'd even settle for another conversation with the mystery woman if it meant confirming proof of life for Matt.

No one answered.

After a few more moments of focused breathing, she unclenched her fist and brought her hand up to the pendant around her neck.

Sage hadn't wanted to use the weapon on Luke, but fate had just forced her hand. She whispered an apology to her mother's memory for what she was about to do, and then turned her attention to the upper corner of the cell. Glaring at the little domed camera, knowing Ava would be watching, she said, "You want me to be the angel of death? So be it!"

Racing to the elevators, Sage planned her route: Down to the parking garage, borrow an agency car, and then she'd break every speed limit in the city to get home to Matt.

She could do this. And if anyone tried to stop her….

Grey's face appeared as the elevator doors parted. "Going somewhere?" he asked, as if he already knew her plan.

"Out of my way." Sage tried to shove past him, but like a brick wall, he stood tall, blocking her escape.

"I thought we weren't doing this anymore." Grey sighed. "No secrets. We're partners."

"Probably not after I'm finished." She futilely tried to push her way through his blockade.

"I know what she asked you to do was unfair."

"I don't have time for this." If she hadn't been in such a rush, Sage might have appreciated his non-judgmental tone, but time was not on her side, and she had too long a journey ahead of her. "Move!" she snapped at him.

"Only if I can come with you."

"You're not—" She stumbled over the angry reply teetering on the edge of her tongue as her brain struggled to comprehend his offer. "Wait. What? You want to help?"

Mocking and contempt were the usual armor he donned when heading into a battle of wills with Sage. But as she searched his face for signs of ulterior motives, she found only the reflection of empathy in Grey's eyes.

"It never gets any easier. I'm sorry. Ava asked you to do something awful, right?"

"Maybe." Sage shrugged, arming herself with cool detachment to shield her unease. Smart-assed comments she could handle, but this sudden softness in Grey's manner left no target for her to unleash her overflowing rage on.

"Obviously, tough girl." Grey let slip a small hint of the real him peek through his Boy Scout façade. "And here I find you running, but not from fear. You've got that insane look you get when you're about to go do something brilliantly stupid."

"I don't have a look." She bristled at his insinuation. He hadn't known her long enough to assign motives to her expressions.

"Really?" Grey replied without missing a beat. "You had the same look the night we went to go interrogate the vampire coven. Maybe a little less leather this time, but just as determined to head into hell, guns a-blazin'."

He had her there. But if she admitted it, he'd never let her go. She scrambled for something to tell him but came up short.

"If I were a betting man," Grey began, and folded his arms. Narrowing his eyes, he looked her up and down, as if searching for clues. "I'd guess that the deed Ava demanded isn't done yet because you found another way around it."

"Not completely true." The tough girl look wasn't working on him. She should have known better. He wasn't the type to be intimidated. And they *had* agreed to start acting like partners.

Coming clean might even buy her some time; something she desperately needed.

"You tried and it backfired?" He cocked his head sideways, worry creeping into his expression for the first time.

"Am I that transparent?"

"Like a ghost, only paler." The forced smile he plastered across his face failed to mask the fear reflecting in his eyes. "Let me help you."

"Can I trust you?"

"We're partners, right?" Grey stepped to the side, a gesture of good will, allowing her to pass.

"I'm about to do something extremely stupid," Sage admitted with a heavy sigh.

"Obviously."

"And dangerous."

"Captain Obvious." He saluted her. "I've got your back."

"So you can have a good show of me getting my ass kicked?" Laughter was the best medicine, or so they said. "Maybe we should pick up some popcorn along the way." She refused to admit it out loud, but knowing someone was on her side, even if they couldn't join her for the final battle, did help. "Unfortunately, when the time comes, I have to do the deed alone," she added.

"That's not happening, partner." He punctuated the last word with laser-like focus, staring Sage down with a look that could rival Ava's in intensity. "Truth time," Grey demanded. "Let's hear the plan!"

Cameras lined the hallways, and the walls had ears. "Step into my office." She urged him into the elevator.

Grey followed without protest. They rode down to the parking garage in silence, and walked casually toward his bike. She kept her eyes peeled, looking for signs of alarm. She was hoping to avoid a fight, and at the same time wondering why no one had stopped her or Grey from leaving. Ava had called for all Terras to return to the building. Something was off, but time was of the essence, and the longer she waited to act, the closer Matt might be to death.

"Code word." Sage restarted the conversation before they mounted his bike. She hoped he would remember their last mission and the important artifact everyone had been so keen to kill each other to get their hands on.

Confusion played across Grey's brow, aging him beyond his normal youthful appearance. Sage struggled to find a way to say what she needed without actually speaking the words.

"How do you terminate a djinn?" she asked.

"Destroy their talisman," Grey replied almost immediately.

"Didn't you find it odd that Ava sent me in to guard Luke, if we both know he came here willingly?"

"She wanted you to end him." Grey scratched at his chin. She could almost see the wheels turning in his head.

"And how could I terminate a djinn if we we're not in control of his talisman?"

Thinking always looked like such a painful experience for Grey. Sage expected to see smoke rising from his ears with all the mental effort he seemed to be exerting. "You couldn't…unless–" Realization sparked behind his eyes. "Code word… You mean the spo–"

"Don't say it." Sage glanced around to see if anyone else might have heard. There were fewer cameras here in the garage. She turned away from the one she could see and purposefully patted the spot where her necklace lay under her shirt. "Guard duty." She then pointed at him: "Babysitter."

Anger narrowed Grey's eyes, but he nodded all the same. "Makes perfect sense now."

"So you understand why I was assigned this job?"

"No. You're a newbie. We have hundreds of capable agents who could handle a job like this."

"But the secret would be revealed if Ava asked anyone else to take this on. After what happened with Rina, it's my full-time job as guardian."

"How long have you had it?"

"Hmm-mmm," she shook her head. "No more questions. And you have to promise me: this goes no further than you and me. I'm not even supposed to tell you."

"Didn't we agree to be partners?"

"This goes beyond partners. You take this to your grave." She hoped she hadn't just made a huge mistake by telling him. But what choice did she have?

"I know nothing. I say nothing. I swear." He crossed himself and held up a three-finger salute.

"Back to being the Boy Scout?" If not for the stress threatening to break her, Sage might have laughed at his attempt to be funny. "Okay, partner." Sage mounted the bike and pulled on her helmet.

"So since I'm the babysitter, what's my role in your plan?" Grey fixed his helmet and brought the bike to life.

"I have to go in alone." Sage urged him to agree without asking too many questions.

"Nope." He revved the bike and sped out of the parking garage before she could protest.

TWENTY-NINE

Grey pulled into the visitor parking lot just outside of Sage's apartment complex. Evening was in full bloom with a half moon shining down from a cloudless sky. All seemed business as usual, but Sage knew better. Her gut churned with worry for Matt. They'd ridden down from ASSET at breakneck speed, but had that been fast enough? Had the master tired of waiting for her and taken out her aggression on Matt? That thought made her blood boil.

"I mean it… alone," Sage warned Grey, as she pulled off her helmet, ready to bolt through the night gate, guns a-blazing. The hairs on the back of her neck prickled. She stopped dead before taking her first step. Unseen eyes were on her already. The master? Luke? Or worse? Goosebumps spread down her arms. Sage turned around slowly, scanning the shadows for a hint of anything out of place.

Grey cleared his throat, but before he had the chance to speak, she held a hand up to shush him.

"You sense that?" she whispered.

The parking lot, she realized, was unusually packed with cars for a weeknight. Nearly every space was taken. Dread festered in her belly, threatening to explode up her throat. "Something is out there…waiting for me or you, maybe both." The streetlights failed to illuminate the whole parking lot, leaving too many places in shadow.

"This isn't a good idea." Grey yanked her arm back before she could take off. "We need backup."

She couldn't deny his truth, but the trap had already been sprung. They were here. For better or worse, it was time to face the music. "No time." Sage pulled free of his grip. "They've got my roommate."

Grey sighed, sounding as though he had already accepted defeat. "I know you love Matt–"

"I'm going to stop you there before you say something you can never take back. He does not die on my watch. He means more to me than anyone else. Understood?"

"We do this together." He cut the engine and pulled his own helmet off. "I'm not letting my partner walk into a trap alone!"

"Fine. Whatever. But hurry." She looked over her shoulder toward the far end of the parking lot. Something glinted in the darkness.

Grey dug into his saddle bags and pulled out his favorite twin machetes. "Trap or not, we'll at least have some protection."

Had she thought about weapons before leaving, Sage would have brought a few extra shiny pointy things herself. Her pocket knife would do little good in comparison

A reflection caught her eye again, only a few car lengths away this time. Whatever it was out there, it was on the move. But like a trick of the mind, when Sage focused on the last place she saw the shifting of the light, it vanished into shadow.

"What?" Grey asked suspiciously.

"You ready?" Sage shouldered her bag, ready to head into the apartment complex.

A trick. It had to be a stupid trick. Luke was using his magic or something to distract her and keep her from making it to the apartment. She refused to look again, though the weight of those unseen eyes pressed down on the back of her neck, taunting her.

Machetes in hand, Grey took the lead. Not wanting to be left behind, Sage nearly beat him, racing to the gate.

A blast of cold wind hit Sage like a tornado. She struggled to keep her feet planted on the ground as the angry air swirled around her. One of Grey's weapons sailed through the air, narrowly missing her head. Grey hit the ground next to her, still holding the other machete.

"What the hell?" Sage spun with the wind, hoping to finally glimpse the thing stalking them, but found only disappointing shadows as the cyclone abated.

Frustrated and more than a little scared, Sage let out a growl loud enough to rival any werewolf. "Show yourself, Luke!"

"The djinn isn't so friendly now, is he?" Grey retrieved the fallen blade. With practiced precision, he swung the machetes around, adjusting his grip, and by the time he found his feet, he looked ready for a fight.

Sage nearly called him Captain Obvious but thought better of it, seeing as he was the only one with weapons.

Grey circled around quickly, giving the parking lot a once over. Based on the growl that came from his throat, he had come to the same conclusion she had.

"We're being played," Sage whispered under her breath.

"Thank you, Captain Obvious." Grey held out one of the machetes for her to take. "Back to back formation. You keep watch on your side, I'll take mine."

"Aren't you both adorable?" A female voice, the same one that had baited Sage to come, taunted them from the shadows. "Watching the two of you work together has been such fun.

But I must admit, it's so much more entertaining when you bicker."

Who the hell was she?

"Not sure if you're going for cowardly or intimidating with this whole hiding in the darkness crap." Sage matched her tone as best she could. Her nerves on edge, it was all she could do to keep her voice from cracking. "Either way, your methods are really annoying."

"You are so cute. I could just eat you up." The woman giggled.

"Hope you like heartburn," Sage quipped.

"Oh, we're not at the main course yet. I set this all up for maximum dramatic impact." The voice came from a different angle, but Sage failed to see any shifting in the light or shadow to match the movement. "No tears. No pleading. I just don't think you're properly motivated to continue this game."

"Just ignore and keep moving." Grey took Sage's hand roughly and pulled her toward the apartment complex gate.

Sage bit back the snarky comment she had locked and loaded to fire. Matt was the goal. Ensuring his safety was all that mattered. After that, she'd school the disembodied voice in the ways of the troll.

"Did I give you permission to walk away?" The woman's voice grew louder.

Sage finally caught sight of her. From a distance, she appeared like a small brown blur. Small as a child, from what Sage could tell, the little creature's form hadn't quite come into focus. Cloaked from head to toe, even as she came closer, their enemy remained completely anonymous.

"Brownie?" Grey didn't sound entirely sure as he spoke the word. "You've been warned. Attack us and we will end you. Prisoners just mean more paperwork I don't have time to file."

The cloaked woman disappeared as soon as Sage had spotted her. Childlike giggling surrounded them, but Sage guessed it was another trick. She'd already shown her speed. Sage stopped turning around to get a good look. There was no point in wasting anymore energy to play a losing game. It was time for Sage to become the Game Master.

"I think this little trickster is scared of you, Grey."

"If she was smart, she would be," he replied.

Standing back to back, Sage felt every twitch and tremble of Grey's muscles. Coiled up like a spring, he'd burst into action at the slightest attack. A fight on open ground would be best, but the way this woman was playing in the shadows, Sage wondered if she could provoke her enough to come out and play.

"I wouldn't go as far as that," Sage scoffed. "Smart people don't provoke a Terra in the first place."

The woman appeared again from the corner of Sage's eye. "This one has spunk." A brown blur darkened to russet red as it swept past Sage's hand, knocking the machete from her grip. "I might even keep her around a bit longer. Seeing as how she's brought me another sacrifice."

Sage slid her hand down and retrieved the small pocket knife from her bag. The way the woman spoke sounded as if she were talking to another person – Luke, most likely. As much as he had tried to help her in the past, in the presence of his master, Sage could count on Luke being her enemy now.

"You want Grey?" Sage forced her voice to remain steady. "Take him. He's a pain in my ass anyway."

Grey bumped against her back with a grunt of frustration.

"Already bargaining for your life?" The woman sounded truly amused by that prospect. "All in good time. But let's not rush the fun. I want to savor it. It's not often I get to play with Terras."

"Well, you should have said something earlier. I might have invited you to game night. It's kind of my thing too," Sage said.

"You play at magic, little girl. No reward for all the effort you put into these games of yours." The woman's laughter turned sinister. "I play for keeps."

"Not nice to play with other people's toys though," Sage warned. "People tend to get angry and take them back."

"Let them try," the woman answered.

"Show yourself and I will." Sage put all the strength into her voice as she delivered the threat.

"You must think so little of me to suggest I'd fall for a ruse as simple as that." The voice surrounded them again. "Which tells me you still haven't figured out my identity."

"Only because you're too scared to reveal yourself," Grey said, before Sage had the chance to.

"Since you adore games so much, how about we play something fun?" the woman teased.

"I don't have time. Busy schedule and all. I have to kill you and save my friend. Rain check?" Sage quipped.

"So cute!" The woman giggled again, sounding more pleased with herself than Sage's reply. "But this game I think you'll like. Answer my riddle, and I'll release your friend."

If only it were that easy! Sage struggled to see the angle, knowing it had to be a trap, but she would do anything to save her roommate. "Eager to give him up? I know how you feel. Men are such funny creatures. I'd be happy to take him off your hands." Sage held her breath, waiting to see how the woman would reply. All that mattered was saving Matt.

"Eager? No," she scoffed. "There's no need for the extra baggage now that I have you here. And besides, I'm bored with him. I have two new play toys right in front of me."

Anxiety formed a knot in Sage's throat. She swallowed hard and set her jaw, determined to fight the good fight to the bitter end. "Fine. What's your riddle?"

"Simple… Who am I?" She surrounded them with cackling laughter, and once the sound faded, an eerie quiet settled over Sage and Grey.

"Not Sylvia," Sage whispered to herself. No mistaking that haughty tone, though the woman taunting them did remind her of the Shade in personality.

"Not the brownie," Grey suggested. "But similar in size."

"It has to be someone we've come across. She wants us to figure it out. She's toying with us. Her identity is an unimportant detail." Sage didn't care who heard her as she jumped through the mental hoops of deduction.

"The gemini twins, or at least one of them," Grey suggested, but immediately shook his head. "No. That doesn't seem right. They're tall and slender. It couldn't be them."

"Glamour?" Sage said and immediately rejected the idea. She could see through that kind of magic. "Nevermind. Give me more clues," Sage demanded.

"Female," Grey replied. "Small. Quick. Tricky."

"Trickster!" Sage almost shouted the word. "What was Sylvia's assistant?"

"Kitsune…Yes, that does make sense." Grey nodded.

"Thalia!" Sage called out.

A flash of light nearly blinded Sage. In the haze that followed, clapping echoed around them. "Very good! You can have your friend now."

When the light blindness faded, Sage pushed her eyes to focus on the figure struggling on the ground at her feet. It was a man, but not one she considered a friend.

"Zack?" Sage groaned, disappointed at her prize. "Where's Matt?"

"Did you think I meant the human?" Thalia giggled with pure amusement. "Silly me. I forgot to specify which one off your toys I'd grown tired of."

"Where's my roommate?" Sage demanded. "No games. I want him released now. Safe and alive."

"Oh, honey, haven't you learned? No man is worth getting that worked up over." She continued to taunt with laughter. "But if you must, we can bargain. You already know exactly where he is. But my price for that toy will be much higher. Why not take what I have generously given you and leave while you still can?"

"You know I won't do that." Sage had had enough talking and playtime. She needed a target for her anger. As soon as she came face to face with the tricksy little fox, she'd muzzle that beast permanently. "Cut the crap and let's settle this right here and now."

"My game. We play by my rules." Thalia clicked her tongue dismissively. "If you're ready to move up to level two, you know where to find me." Her voice faded into the breeze.

THIRTY

"I'm not even going to ask how you got caught up in this." Sage bent down and untied Zack.

"You sure? It's a harrowing tale filled with mystery and intrigue." He rubbed at the raw spots where the ropes had bitten into his wrists. The raw angry marks faded almost instantly, leaving no trace of the injury he'd just sustained. "And I hear it ends with a kiss." Zack puckered and leaned toward Sage.

She made a fist and held it up to Zack's lips. "I prefer stories with more action."

"That's the best part. The brave heroine saving the poor defenseless vampire." He made a show of kissing her knuckles. Standing with a smile so wide he couldn't hide his teeth. "I'm forever in your debt."

"Don't let it go to your head," Sage grumbled.

"What? Your noble sacrifice to come and save poor little me." Zack winked at her. "I'd never read more into that."

"Good." *Insufferable flirt!* That man just didn't know when to quit, and she'd had just about enough. "Because I thought I was saving Matt."

The man who always had a witty remark locked and loaded stood with his mouth gaping. She'd stung him good with that one, but fun as it was to take the wind from Zack's sails, there was no time to waste with her roommate still in danger.

"How did you get messed up in this, vampire?" Grey broke the uneasy silence. "Stalking around Sage's home again?"

"Funny you should say that." Zack chuckled nervously. "I had come by to speak to her. Our last meeting didn't go as well as I had intended."

"I believe I said I didn't want to see you again," Sage clarified.

"How long has he been bothering you?" Grey inserted himself between Sage and Zack.

"No." Zack seemed to shrink. He took an unsteady step back. "Nothing like that."

"Actually, he did threaten to bite me." Sage smirked. Grey wouldn't kill the vampire, but he would definitely be able to take him down a few pegs; humble him a little. "He said he wanted to show me the dark side."

"What?" Grey's fist tightened around the handles of his machetes. The muscles in his arms tensed and trembled, ready for action.

"Taken completely out of context, I assure you," Zack replied.

Grey stared down at the vampire as if wondering which body part he'd like to dismember first. "Give me one good reason."

"She needed someone to make her see the truth." Zack glanced down to the weapons and back up at Grey. The implied threat seemed to trigger his darker half. Zack rose up to his full height and stood his ground. "Tough love."

"Not your place, vampire," Grey growled. "She's my partner. Mine to protect."

"Should I congratulate you on the smashing job you've done thus far?" Zack's reply came quickly with a heavy dose of snark. "If you'd paid any attention at all to Sage, I would never have had the chance to get close to her."

"If you were the gentleman you pretend to be, you'd know better than to get close to her...alone." Grey looked to Sage as if checking to make sure she was still there. "She's innocent."

Sage had only intended to embarrass the vampire, but the way the boys were working themselves up to a fight made her feel ashamed. She opened her mouth to interrupt, but couldn't manage to get in a word.

"Which is exactly why I had to make her see the danger. You haven't properly prepared her, and you've left her vulnerable." Zack stepped in closer, jabbing a finger at Grey's chest. "For god's sake, she was living right next to a damned djinn, and you didn't catch on until it was too late."

Sage held her breath, waiting to see if Grey would retaliate. As tense as he looked, when that man started swinging his blades, heads would roll.

"I'll give you that one." Grey heaved a heavy sigh. Not the response Sage had expected, but far better than bloodshed. "Touch me again and you lose the finger."

"Save your threats for the real villains." Zack rolled his eyes, but dropped his arms to his sides all the same.

"While you swoop in to take advantage of the vulnerable and innocent women?" Grey lobbed the insult at him with an almost lazy drawl.

"I don't have to take anything; women give it willingly." Zack didn't have a chance to finish. The moment he'd uttered the wrong words, Grey dropped his machetes and threw a punch like a cannon blast at the vampire's face.

Lost in their testosterone-filled pissing match, they'd either forgotten or didn't care that the mission had not ended. Sage wasn't about to wait for them to realize their mistake. She used the diversion to sneak away. Matt was still in the hands of Thalia, and Sage knew exactly what that little fox wanted in exchange. Her life for his… no question asked.

THIRTY-ONE

The lights looked normal in the windows as she walked up to her apartment. The door was closed, and there were no signs of forced entry or sounds of a struggle inside. All looked as it should. The only thing missing was the sound of Matt's voice. He wasn't the quiet type. Even being held against his will, he'd have something snarky to say. What did his silence mean?

A lump formed in her throat. Sage struggled to swallow it down as she reached for the door. "Please be alive. Please be alive. Please be alive," she chanted to herself, and turned the knob.

Light from the kitchen welcomed her into the apartment as usual, but beyond that, only the soft glow of the TV kept the rest of the living space from cave-like darkness. Her favorite madman with a blue box sat frozen on screen, paused, waiting for someone to bring it back to life. Sitting opposite the screen's glow, Matt mirrored the doctor. Still as a statue, his body filled the usual space on the couch, but his posture was all wrong. Like a mannequin, he sat rigid, his eyes open but not seeing, his mouth gaping, but no movement in his chest to indicate breathing. Sage refused to entertain the thought that he might be dead. Frozen in time she could handle, but nothing more.

"I'm here to storm the castle," Sage called out, more to give the illusion of courage than from true bravery. Her knees threatened to buckle with each step she took toward her silent roommate.

"You're late." Thalia stood from her position in the recliner. She came face to face with Sage, smiling as if she'd already won. "Dinner's gone cold. You want me to nuke it for you?"

Up close, Thalia could have passed for a ten-year-old, as small as she was. Sage wasn't exactly a giant, but she'd never had to look down to anyone. Thalia's face had an ageless quality that added to the deceptively childlike appearance. A pair of erect ears sat atop Thalia's head. Tipped with black fur that transitioned into long ginger hair running midway down her back. Not one but two tails wagged behind Thalia's back, each swaying with their own rhythm.

"Ready to make a trade?" Despite Thalia's size, the voice that came from her little body left no doubt she was a woman, and one who was confident and very much aware of the advantage she had.

"I'm done with games, and seeing as you're in my home, maybe it's time you leave." Sage whipped a finger toward the door.

Thalia laughed so hard it caused a large amulet hanging around her neck to bounce free from the folds of her cloak. A gaudy thing hanging from a heavy silver chain, the stone was as large as a child's fist. The deepest red she'd ever seen, it reminded her of blood, but as she moved and the facets caught in the light, Sage caught glimpses of people imprisoned within. Very much alive and struggling to get free, the prisoners beat their fists against the impenetrable crystal. They opened their mouths, screaming and shouting, but Sage heard nothing.

Thalia's smile turned wicked. "You think you're pretty cute, don't you?"

"I'm at least a five, as is. But add a touch of lipstick and liner and I'm a solid seven." Sage countered with her best impersonation of Zack's narcissism. She regretted leaving the guys back in the parking lot, but since they'd been bickering like children in the schoolyard, they hadn't left her much choice.

"Don't flatter yourself." Thalia's lips twisted into a scowl. She radiated a dangerous blend of power and self-confidence that went well beyond hubris. Attitude like that came from a place of assurance. "You might have all these boys wrapped around your finger, but that doesn't work on me."

"Funny. I hear that's the only way you've managed to accomplish this jewelry scheme." Sage swallowed hard, trying to force her anxiety down. No good would come from allowing herself to be intimidated, even if Thalia had all but called "check and mate" in this little game she'd orchestrated. "Got a little boy toy wrapped around your little finger?"

"Boys have their uses." Thalia held out her hand. Around her left thumb, she wore a thick ring made of black stone. Etched into the band were runes in gold. Sage remembered seeing symbols like those before. Ava had similar markings on her arms. "Luke, it's time for you to come out and play."

He blinked into the room and took Thalia's hand, placing a chaste kiss on the ring. "What is your wish, my master?" His face betrayed no emotion nor did his eyes hold any sense of recognition as they landed on Sage.

"There are advantages to having some men wrapped around your finger." Thalia's voice softened. She wrapped her arms around Luke. "But you will never fully realize them."

"You can have him. As I understand it, you've nearly spent the value of your soul to finish his work." Sage crossed her arms as she delivered the words. "And when he's left you a dried-up husk, your precious boy toy will move on to something newer and prettier."

"If I were mortal, your pathetic taunt might bother me." Her tails wagged in unison, aggressively swaying from side to side.

Sage had struck a chord. Thalia's snarky denial confirmed it, and now Sage knew the tune to play to throw the kitsune off her game. "You sure about that? Any use of magic not belonging to one's self requires payment." She winked at Luke, hoping he'd wake from his zombie-like trance and acknowledge her.

Thalia turned to her djinn. "Is this true? Answer me, now!"

"I do not control the rules of magic," Luke answered mechanically. "I am only bound to serve whoever holds my talisman,"

Thalia's tails swished furiously, side to side, like windshield wipers combating a torrential downpour. "I command you to speak only the truth to me."

Luke's jaw tightened. He was in there somewhere, hiding behind the mask of indifference. "Once you hold universal power, you are not bound to the laws of repayment."

Thalia turned like a snotty teenager to face Sage. "You see? It's good to have the right man at your beck and call."

He was playing his own game, and in her delusion, Thalia had failed to hear the key words in his truthful statement. There was still a chance Sage might beat her. But it wouldn't be pretty. "Awesome for you," Sage snarked right back at the cocky kitsune. "You want a cookie or something?"

Anger boiled up to Thalia's cheeks. "I'm tired of playing."

"You mean losing, right?" Sage teased.

Thalia faced Luke again. "Time to add her to our collection."

"Is that your wish?" Luke asked quietly, but the look in his eyes screamed *No*.

"Yes. Now do it," she demanded.

Luke took hold of the amulet in one hand. His other waved over it with tight circles, as he mumbled words Sage could not hear. The jewel ignited as if lit by an internal fire. He lifted his free hand, and the glow came free of the stone. It took the form of a ghostly hand, mimicking every movement Luke made. He extended his arm and reached for her, and the ethereal hand extended toward Sage.

Innate neutrality, don't fail me now! Sage stood her ground, but as the fingers of light grazed her face, she realized they were not any normal kind of magic.

She could feel those ghostly fingers as real as if Luke himself were trying to take hold of her. She reached under her shirt and took hold of the locket. With a small press of her thumb, the tree trunk opened and the seed of destruction fell into her hand. She grasped it tightly in her fist and threw a punch at the ethereal hand.

The moment the amulet's magic connected with Sage's fist, it evaporated.

"What did you do?" Thalia shrieked.

"This was not me, master," Luke replied with uncertainty. "The Terra has some kind of defense."

"Good game." Sage put as much authority into her voice as she could muster. "If you're a smart little fox, you'll lose gracefully before things get much worse."

"Terras have no magic," Thalia snarled at Luke. "Do something."

Sage held up her wrist bearing the mark of her people. "You don't know as much as you think about Terra magic. You cannot harm me. But continue on this path and you will end up just like your djinn friend here. There's eternal punishment for those who abuse magic."

"What are you waiting for, djinn? Finish this," Thalia demanded.

Luke's tattoos glowed as brightly as the amulet around Thalia's neck. Again the magical hand reached for Sage.

She stood ready, her own hand in a tight fist around the seed. The magical hand grew in size, fingers wrapping themselves around her whole body. She should have been gasping for air as it tried to crush her ribs, but tight as it squeezed, Sage felt nothing but gentle pressure.

Sage brought her clenched fist to her chest. The seed ignited within her palm. All the magic surrounding her, fed its fire. Her own hand began to glow white hot. Sage scream as she struggled to keep hold of the seed.

Luke pulled back. His magical hand retreated, but caught in the pull of the seed's destructive force, brought Sage along in its wake. Her feet dragged against the floor, as she tried to hold her ground. The amulet glowed red hot around Thalia's neck like a homing beacon.

That same intense fire burned within Sage's palm as the seed continued to absorb the magic drawing her in. The hand around her flickered but didn't extinguish.

It took everything Sage had her to keep hold of the seed. She cried with pure agony as her skin melted, but dare not open her palm to confirm the damage. Searing heat traveled straight to her bones, echoing all throughout her body.

Thalia cackled with delight. "Oooh, she is strong! What an excellent choice for the collection." She rose up on her tip toes and kiss Luke on the cheek. "You're nearly free, my pet."

Sage's only hope lay in the power of the seed of destruction being stronger than the amulet. If she let go, it would all be over.

Deep breaths. In and out. Sage counted the seconds as she filled her lungs with air and then expelled it.

The tethers of magic began to loosen. The pressure in her chest lightened with each cycle of her breath.

Just a few more minutes. Hold on! Magic isn't without some limits.

Luke's book had said it could be exhausted. All she had to do was outlast it.

"Why do you need all this magic, anyway?" Sage grunted with the effort it took to ground her feet and hold her position.

"Because life isn't fair, and those without active power always pay the price." Thalia snarled.

"Seems like I'm the one paying a price. I have no active magic. Not very fair, is it?" Sage ground her teeth, not sure how much longer she could hold on.

"Your family wasn't hunted to extinction for their magic."

"My mom…was killed…protecting magic." She lost control for a moment and the ethereal hand pulled her closer. "She was the only family I knew."

"Not the same. What are you doing? Why isn't this working?" Thalia snapped angrily at Luke.

"I do not know, my master. I'm afraid I don't have enough power to complete the transfer." He waved his hand harder around the amulet. Its strength bolstered and Sage tripped, falling face forward to the ground.

Fear threatened to undo her the moment her hands slapped the floor. She pawed at the linoleum, thinking she had lost the seed in her tumble, but as she lifted her hand she saw it glowing from within her palm. The burn had been more than magical; the seed had embedded itself into her skin. She scrambled to her feet and searched for something to help anchor her. Luke's magic had yet to exhaust itself, and his ethereal hand was still tugging her closer. If she touched the amulet before that, she might end up trapped inside. Seed or no seed. She couldn't let that happen.

She gripped the kitchen table with her free hand, and when that failed and chairs provided no help, she clawed at the wall dividing the kitchen and living room. She held for a moment before the wood splintered and sliced her fingers.

Thalia extended her own hands to welcome Sage home with a deadly embrace.

Sage spotted the ring, Luke's ring, a black stripe on her pale skin. His talisman. She gave in to the pull of his magic, and her pain faded. Sage's body floated as if riding the waves of an ocean current toward the shore. Sage smiled and reached for the ring on Thalia's hand.

Heat started again, deep inside Sage's palm, and like wildfire consumed her entire body. She screamed, but all had gone silent. An explosion of light washed everything from Sage's vision, and then her world faded to black.

THIRTY-TWO

Sage opened her eyes to the angry sight of Thalia standing over her, clutching the glowing amulet around her neck.

"What have you done?" the kitsune snarled.

"Stopped you from completing that." Sage didn't dare turn to confirm what had happened to Luke; if the pain in her hand were any indication, he was probably ten times worse off. "I've neutralized your djinn. It's over."

Smoldering rage burned deep within Thalia's eyes. "You took away my toy. Now I'll take yours." One hand on the amulet, she stretched out the other and pointed to the splintered wood.

Before Sage could utter a protest, Thalia sent the splinters flying through the air at her roommate, who still sat paralyzed on the couch.

His body remained frozen as the shards of wood sliced through his skin. There was no sound; no flinching. But there was no mistaking the blood dribbling down his neck.

"Matt!" Sage screamed. She jumped to her feet and lunged at Thalia.

The kitsune dodged Sage's blind rage. Claws grew from the ends of Thalia's fingers, her teeth elongated, and her skin began to take on a rusty glow. "You're next!" She snarled and slashed a clawed hand at Sage.

The seed had burned itself so deeply into her palm Sage no longer needed to clench her fist to hold it. She dodged the claws and spun away from Thalia's attack. "Your magic is useless on me, you know that." Sage held her arms out open. "But if you think you can take me one on one, come at me!"

"I have more magic than you can possibly imagine," Thalia taunted.

"All but the most important." Sage looked for an in. She was desperate to get her hands on the amulet before the kitsune used it again. "Don't you know why we Terras are so feared by other classes?"

"ASSET has an excellent PR department," Thalia scoffed.

"Innate neutrality. Lay a hand on me, and all your stolen magic goes bye-bye." She waved her hand to drive the point home. "I would have thought a kitsune would know better. Aren't you all supposed to be so smart?"

"You're bluffing. I've never heard of a Terra able to steal power."

"Steal? No. Neutralize. Say goodbye to all that immense power. I can't use it, but I can make sure you never do again either." Sage circled around Thalia, casting quick glances at Matt, whose body had begun to slump slightly, growing paler as his blood stained the couch. She wondered if she touched him with the seed if he would wake up.

"Luke, I wish you to immobilize her," Thalia shrieked.

Luke rose from where he'd fallen on the ground and lumbered to Sage. His expression lacked the life she'd come to know. His eyes had lost their slivery luster. Still he moved as commanded, and magic or not, he had her in size and strength.

She met his eyes with look that said, *Don't*, but unable to resist a command from his master, Luke reached his hand out to touch Sage.

The moment his fingers connected with her body, he shuddered. Luke's eyes widened and he moved to pull his hand away, but he found himself stuck.

The seed ignited again, deep within Sage's ruined hand. She reached out and placed that hand open-palmed on Luke's chest. What little magic he had left tethering him to his master began to flow from him, feeding the seed all his power.

When she looked into Luke's eyes, she expected to see pain or fear, but he surprised her with a look of complete serenity, as if he welcomed the end of his magic and possibly his life too.

Eyes watering, Sage struggled to keep her composure as she turned to face Thalia. The ring on her thumb glowed too. But the glow faded with each second that passed until its light finally extinguished.

Luke crumpled to the ground.

"You see?" Sage pointed her other hand toward Thalia. A little superhero theatrics, to give her words more power. "Come at me."

Thalia gripped the amulet tightly around her neck. Her gaze turned from Sage to Matt and back. "What if I save him? Will you let me go free?"

"Give me the amulet."

"He's going to die," Thalia replied.

"So will you. We can either do this the easy way or the hard. You choose."

Thalia bolted, heading for the front door. She opened it and ran smack into Grey. Who knew how long he had been waiting on the other side?

"Don't touch me," Thalia screamed, throwing her hands up in the air as if afraid to touch Grey. She spun around to face Sage.

"Remember…" Sage walked slowly over to Thalia and reached out her hand. "I gave you a choice." She placed her palm up to Thalia's forehead. "You chose wrong."

The light of Thalia's magic glowed brightly until the seed had absorbed it all. Her human form shank as she faded back into a fox, her first form.

Grey scruffed the squirming little beast and quickly shoved it onto Matt's gym bag sitting by the door.

The amulet fell, shattering as it hit the ground.

Wind exploded from the amulet as it broke, and the force it unleashed blew out all the windows in the apartment. Swirling like a cyclone in reverse, it expelled angry clouds of magic within the apartment. Sparks of lightning and thunder claps belched from the swirling cloud. Two gorgeous women with eyes like glittering tourmaline and hair as rich as spun gold materialized in front of Sage. Dressed as if they had been taken the moment their show ended, both still sported showgirl feathers and skin-tight leotards. The gemini twins.

Before they could utter a word, Sage yelled, "Run. Get out of here!"

Zap! Another thunderous burst of light belched out of the shattered stone and a tiny creature, like a living doll, appeared. The brownie. Sage made the mental tally.

The tiny brownie woman seemed to understand what had happened. The moment she had her freedom, she scurried toward the open front door of Sage's apartment.

One final blast of energy released a shadow dark and angry as any Sage had ever witnessed. Sylvia belted out a cry to match the fury of the storm that had brought her. She met Sage's eyes the moment her shadow materialized into physical form. No words needed to be said; not that Sage expected any thanks from a shadowrunner.

"Leave now," Sage shouted the order. "The danger has not yet passed."

Based on the sneer, Sylvia didn't take well to being ordered around, but she left all the same.

The windstorm died as suddenly as it came, and all that remained of the amulet were shards of black glass. Sage breathed a sigh of relief for that small victory. There was no chance of some other opportunist picking it up and trying to finish its work. Luke's book and the research inside would be safely locked away in ASSET's vaults.

"Good timing." Sage finally acknowledged Grey. "You boys certainly took your time finishing your dick-measuring contest."

"You should know better than that, partner." Grey dropped the squirming bag of kitsune, and helped Sage to her feet. "We've been here the whole time, watching you work from the window." He winked. "I knew you'd handle business, but I had to distract fang-boy long enough to avoid awkward questions."

"Speaking of blood. I need a medic for my roommate." Sage turned. Zack was already at Matt's side, taking interest in the blood that had ruined their couch. How he'd gotten past her was a mystery until she saw the shattered window. "You keep away from him." She panicked. Vampires and blood were never a good combination.

Zack straightened and turned to give her his full attention. Hands up in the air, he made a valiant effort to show her he was not a threat. "I'm sorry, Sage. He's too far gone." His voice held no hint of sarcasm. "She got him good."

Her whole world came crashing down. This wasn't how things were supposed to go. She'd fought so hard. "No. He can't die!" Her legs threatened to give out. Tears flooded her eyes. All that pain, everything she had endured fighting Luke and Thalia, couldn't hold a candle to the agony of her heart shredding to pieces.

Matt's body flopped over on the couch, landing with a wet *sploosh* on the cushion.

Wanting to rage and at the same time crumbling under the weight of her sadness, Sage found herself frozen in the moment. Her eyes locked on Matt's dying body and their blood-soaked couch. All the power in the world, but she had none to save him.

"Do something. Someone." She forced the words from her mouth with all the power of a mighty roar, but her strength had left her with only a mouse-like whisper.

"I may have a solution," Zack offered cautiously. The muscles in his face tightened. She caught the flare of his nostrils. He was no doubt tempted by the smell of blood, but there was no pleasure to be found in his eyes, only sympathy. "But this is not something to choose lightly."

She knew without explanation what that meant. "Why would you do this?"

"Not for him, I assure you. He's nothing to me. But you..." Zack's eyes mirrored her pain. "I can't see you like this. Maybe..." He dropped his gaze and picked at his fingernails. "If Grey or I had gotten in here sooner, perhaps this situation could have been avoided. If I can help make things right, I will."

Grey had done a good job of keeping Zack out of the loop. His admission sounded genuine enough, and that heaped more guilt on top of the weight already pressing down on her shoulders. Between the uneasy feelings his admission brought up and her desperation for Matt's safety, Sage couldn't get the words to move from her brain to her mouth. What he was offering went well beyond a favor. *Making things right* was a stretch as well. Turning Matt to keep him from dying came with consequences of its own. Matt might not want this life.

"Will he…" Sage wasn't even sure how to finish that sentence.

"He'll be the same Matt you've always known. Just with a slightly different diet," Zack answered as if he'd already rehearsed the speech.

Grey cleared his throat. "That's putting it lightly. He's sentencing your roommate to a lifetime of darkness."

"There are consequences, yes, but compared to the alternative…" Zack inhaled a deep breath and blew out slowly. Even in her current state, Sage could see how hard this was for Zack, being so close to all that blood. "Just… take a moment. But not more than that." His eyes closed as he took in another breath. "He doesn't have much time left."

Sage turned to Grey. How could she make such an important decision like this with no time? Selfishly she wanted to scream *Yes*. Losing Matt would be like losing a piece of her soul. But cursing him to extend his life… That could just as easily backfire and cause her to lose him for all eternity. "What do I do?" Her voice cracked.

"He would live." Grey's face blanked of emotions, but behind the mask she saw the tense muscles holding strong. Had he faced this decision once before? Did he know something he didn't want to say? She opened her mouth to try to give her thoughts sound, but he beat her to it. "If life is all that matters to you, save him."

"Would he hate me for it?" she asked, pleading for absolution, even though she hadn't committed the crime yet. "Would Joshua? Oh, God! What do I do? Josh would kill me."

"Decision time, please; we're nearing the deadline," Zack reminded them, his tone darkening with each word.

"For Matt, only time will tell if resentment will fester," Grey answered flatly. "He'll need a babysitter in the beginning, through the new bloodlust. Especially with the human boy-friend."

"I can't let him die," Sage sobbed.

Grey pulled her close. He surrounded her with all of his strength and warmth, a connection she desperately needed. "Since you single-handedly saved the world tonight, I can't let you be the bad guy. I'll take the blame. Do it, Zack."

She couldn't remember the last time someone had held her. The weight of all her emotions crushed her, but as she crumpled, it was Grey who held her up. The sound of his steady heartbeat called her back from the depths of despair.

She clung to him, sobbing, "Forgive me."

"Hey." Grey lifted her face and met her eyes. "We still have a job to do. I need you to focus, okay?" Where she was a hot mess, he was the picture of strength, the rock she needed. "Can you pull it together for a little longer?" He held her face in his hands, keeping their eyes locked as he spoke, distracting Sage from the sounds of struggling behind her. "Matt is being taken care of. I'm the bad guy, okay?"

She sniffled and tried to nod. "Yep." Part of her understood why Grey was aloof most of the time. The job was brutal. This was still technically only her first week as an agent, and she'd been chewed up and spit back out by it. In the space of a month, she'd lost her mother, killed someone, nearly died twice dealing with vampires, and was now cursing her roommate to an extension of this life. At some point, tears had to stop falling. No one could remain sane constantly feeling all the emotional pain for eternity.

How long would it be before she turned it all off?

Matt's duffel bag squirmed at her feet.

Thalia.

Focusing her negative energy helped pull her from the darkness. Taking her magic and human form were just the beginning. That little beast deserved so much more payback for the problems she'd caused. "What do we do with that?" Anger turned up the volume on Sage's voice.

"Cage her up and take her back to ASSET," Grey replied.

"That's too good for her," Sage growled. She turned her head to look toward Matt, but Grey grabbed her face. "Look at me, not him. We're agents first. No revenge. Do our duty. We take her in."

"If we have to."

"Trust me, she's not going to have it easy. She's probably wishing she were dead, being trapped in that sweaty gym bag."

"Is that supposed to make me laugh?" She failed to see the humor.

"Yes. This job is going to suck sometimes. Not everyone lives. If you don't learn to appreciate the small victories sometimes, it will eat you alive."

"I lost my mom. I lost Matt. Is that all there is? Losing people?" she asked.

"Sometimes you gain people, too." Grey threw an arm around Sage's shoulder. "We do have good days too."

"How many have you lost?" she asked.

"Oh I'm not drunk enough for that conversation." Grey let his arm fall.

"And you never will be." Sage would give just about anything at that moment for a good stiff drink that actually numbed the pain.

"One day, I'll tell you about the woman I loved and had to..."

Matt let out a painful moan, and Sage snapped to attention. She was at his side in a flash. "Talk to me. Say something." She hovered over him, afraid to touch him. Her hand itched where the stone still sat buried in her palm. "Please don't hate me."

"What happened?" Matt rasped, as if he'd spent a week in the desert with no water. He brought his free hand up to his head. "Am I dead?"

Sage looked at Zack, pleading with her eyes for him to give her an answer that Matt might accept.

"You're going to want to take it easy there, buddy." Zack pressed a hand to Matt's chest to keep him from sitting up. "You had a bit of an accident. I'm here to help you through it, okay?"

"You promised you'd never bring your work home." Matt's tone turned angry, but his voice did not rise past a dry whisper.

"You can hold that over me for the rest of eternity if you want. As long as you're alive to hate me." Sage reached a hand out to him and immediately pulled it back, slapping it over her mouth. Matt might be alive-ish, but with the seed buried in her palm, one touch would certainly kill him.

Zack tilted his head curiously, his eyes narrowing as he looked her over.

"We are going to have serious words, you and I." Matt strained to speak. His breaths were labored as if he were struggling.

"We may need some quiet time here," Zack whispered. "There's a lot to process."

"Sage," Matt whimpered painfully.

"You're going to be okay. We'll talk later." She stood and looked at Zack. "Take care of him!"

"I know. Or you'll have my head," he replied.

"Thank you!" She wanted to reach out and hug him, but the itch in her palm stopped her with her arms out wide. She pinched her eyes closed and growled, frustrated with this new complication. She dropped her arms and spun back to face Grey. "We need to get out of here."

"Right… We still have to get back to ASSET." Grey picked up the duffel. "Ava's probably already set up a cell for us next to foxy here." He shook the bag, making Thalia chitter loudly as she tried to claw her way out.

"Take care of him," Sage gave the order to Zack. "If we survive Ava's wrath, I'll be back."

THIRTY-THREE

"What happened to the weapon?" Grey asked, as they took the path down to the night gate.

"I think I'm the weapon now." Sage held out her hand. The seed had burned through layers of skin, and in the time that had elapsed since she'd last used it to reduce Thalia to her original form, the skin had grown over the wounds. All that remained was a small discoloration where the seed sat just under the surface.

"Well, that's one way to hide it." Grey reached out as if scared to touch her at first, and then took her hand in his. "You're one of a kind. For more than just this."

"Was that a compliment?"

"Don't let it go to your head."

"Are you kidding? I'm blasting this out to anyone who will listen. I might even take out an ad, or have one of those sky-writers draw it up in the heavens. Grey Maddox said something nice!"

"I knew I'd regret that." He winked. "But at least I got a smile out of you."

"I shouldn't be smiling."

"You saved the world and your roommate all in one night."

"What happens if I touch him?" Sage held her hand up.

"I thought he had a boyfriend." Grey smirked, but the time for jokes had passed.

"I couldn't take his hand and comfort him. He's probably going through hell, but I'd probably kill him with a single hug."

Grey seemed to consider her words. They walked silently for a few moments before he finally spoke up. "Ava knows about the... thing?"

"Yeah." Sage let her shoulders slump. "So she'll want to keep this whole situation on the hush hush."

"What explanation are we giving then for your new super power?"

"Just that... I'm a special kind of Terra. No one saw how I did it. Anyone watching would have only seen me touch Thalia and Luke." Sage hadn't even thought of Luke. She'd taken his power; that much she knew. And she'd broken the connection between the ring and him. But didn't remember seeing him lying on the floor as they left. She stopped in her tracks and glanced back toward the apartment.

"What?" Grey asked.

Under the shadow of a stairwell, she caught the miniature explosion of hot ashes being flicked from a cigarette. A pair of silvery eyes blinked and vanished into the darkness. She couldn't be sure it was him, but it no longer mattered. Luke had earned his freedom, in whatever form it came.

"Hey." Grey snapped his fingers in front of her face to grab her attention. "You sure no one saw you use the weapon? I saw Sylvia when she came out. She was looking at you with serious suspicion." Grey tossed the duffel with Thalia on his shoulder and mounted his bike.

"You don't think she realizes?" Sage wondered aloud.

"We need to make sure Ava gets a complete report. And maybe, you should consider keeping that weapon where it is for a while longer. Safety first."

"Until *I* start to be used as a weapon," Sage warned. "That was the reason I was chosen as guardian. I didn't want to use it, ever. I had no choice here. But once word gets out that it or I or whatever can use it, then more will come to try and claim its power, and by extension, me."

"When did you grow up?" Grey asked with genuine shock.

"Back there, when I had to destroy the life of my best friend, all thanks to magic." She mounted the bike and held tightly as Grey took off.

THIRTY-FOUR

They rode silently back to ASSET. All the while Sage silently prayed to any gods that would listen that Matt might forgive her.

Her boss's wrath had nothing on the disappointment in Matt's eyes.

Sage walked numbly into Ava's office. She stood while Grey gave his report. Words were said, but she couldn't remember what they were. It was only when Ava stood and called out her name that she finally woke from her stupor.

"While I cannot condone your actions or your blatant flaunting of my orders," Ava said, as her turquoise eyes seemed to look straight into Sage's soul, "I am happy to see both you and Mr. Maddox here have recovered the missing people and brought the criminal to justice."

"Just doing our jobs." Grey shrugged the duffel bag off his shoulder and let it fall to the ground. Thalia whimpered inside.

"Take that one to a cell. I'm sure there's a zoo somewhere we can donate her to." Ava pointed a manicured nail towards the door.

"Will she ever return to her kitsune form?" Sage asked.

"If her magic has been taken, no. She'll live out her days as that little creature."

"And what of Luke?" Sage asked. "We didn't see him after all the commotion."

"Inconsequential." Ava waved the question away as if it were an annoying fly. "He's either magic-less and living as a mortal, or he's taken his talisman and returned to the shadows. Djinn can only act on other people's wishes, so unless someone else gets ahold of this..." – she held up the old journal – "we should have nothing to concern ourselves with."

"I'll go ahead and make my reports then," Sage said mechanically.

"One final thing." Ava glared at her. "There is the matter of your... necklace." Her eyes flitted to Grey for a second before returning to Sage.

"I'll deliver this one to her cell." Grey excused himself with excellent timing, continuing the ruse of not knowing about the seed.

Sage held her hand out to Ava. "There was a small problem with the necklace. It appears to have dirtied up my hand."

"Quite dirty." Ava scrutinized the darkened spot at her palm. "Still effective, though?"

"You saw the effect it had when I touched Thalia." Sage sighed, knowing that she couldn't touch anyone magical if she had now become the universe's Hoover."

"How are you with the pain?" Ava seemed more curious about the mechanics than interested in offering a solution to its removal.

"I've had enough of that for a while," Sage replied. "It would be nice to remove the cause."

"Does anyone know how you managed to neutralize the kitsune?"

Sage shrugged. "I've become a super Terra, it would seem."

"Interesting. That we can work with. I'll need you to creatively word your report when you and Grey enter it into the database."

"Understood."

"And you realize that since Mr. Maddox knows... he's now your permanent partner." Ava lifted an eyebrow as if she knew how close Sage had been to requesting a transfer.

But after all they had endured together, especially seeing how he'd come to her aid when Matt was being threatened, being his partner no longer seemed like a punishment. "I wouldn't have anyone else." Sage smiled weakly.

"Good. And as for the dirty palms... Gloves, perhaps?" Ava suggested. "At least until we can find a solution to scrub them clean."

"Chainmail?" Sage replied sarcastically. She'd cut the thing out herself if need be.

"That silver locket seemed to shield the weapon before." Ava's tone held no compassion. "I'm sure you can find some type of silver-lined gloves in our archives. Improvise until we can find a solution. Without understanding the nature of the bond that thing has created with your body, we can't just slice it out."

"Thank you." She breathed a sigh of relief, knowing that Ava intended to have the seed removed. She'd hate to be strapped down with that power for the rest of her life. If the silver gloves worked, at least she'd be able to manage until then.

"We'll discuss surgical options when things have cooled down a bit. For now, go home, rest, and take care of your domestic issue. Dismissed!"

More Magic to Come

The Agents of A.S.S.E.T. will return
Christmas 2018
with

MAGIC IN DISGUISE

Please Review

Your opinion matters! When people first look at a book, beyond the description and the cover, they pay close attention to what others **like you** have to say.

If the book is getting overwhelmingly good or bad reviews, it can weigh heavily on that readers decision whether or not to click that purchase button.

It does not have to be a book report.
It does not have to be 5 stars. *I would never ask for any special favoritism.*

A book review is simply sharing what you thought of the book. It answers two very simple questions:

Did you like it?
Would you recommend it to someone else?

That's it. Your opinion matters. Most importantly to me, because I want to ensure you are enjoying the books I write. But beyond my hope for your satisfaction, the review you write caries great weight in the publishing realm as well. It can quite literally make or break a book.

So, here I am, groveling at your feet.

If you have read one (or more) of my books, would you do me the greatest of honors and leave a review?

About the Author

Katie Salidas is a best-selling author known for her unique genre-bending style.

Host of the Indie Youtube Talkshow, Spilling Ink, nerd, Doctor Who fangirl, Las Vegas Native, and SuperMom to three awesome kids, Katie gives new meaning to the term sleep-deprived.

Since 2010 she's penned four bestselling book series: the Immortalis, Olde Town Pack, Little Werewolf, and the RONE award-winning Chronicles of the Uprising. And as her not-so-secret alter ego, Rozlyn Sparks, she is a USA Today bestselling author of romance with a naughty side.

Facebook
http://www.facebook.com/pages/Katie-Salidas-Author/214780936916

Web
http://www.katiesalidas.com/

Twitter
http://twitter.com/QuixoticKatie

Email
KatieSalidas@gmail.com

SpillingInk
https://www.youtube.com/c/spillinginkshow

Join the Paranormal Posse
Connect directly with Katie and get exclusives and updates.
https://www.facebook.com/groups/ParanormalPosse/